SEABISCUIT

TOBEY MAGUIRE AS RED POLLARD.

TOBEY MAGUIRE AS RED POLLARD.

CHARLES HOWARD (JEFF BRIDGES) AND MARCELA HOWARD (ELIZABETH BANKS) ADMIRE THEIR HORSE, SEABISCUIT.

CHRIS COOPER AS TOM SMITH.

ELIZABETH BANKS AS MARCELA HOWARD.

WILLIAM H. MACY AS RACETRACK REPORTER TICK-TOCK McGLAUGHLIN.

JOCKEY AND HORSE—RED POLLARD (TOBEY MAGUIRE) AND SEABISCUIT—
IN THE STARTING GATE.

RED POLLARD (TOBEY MAGUIRE), TOM SMITH (CHRIS COOPER), MARCELA HOWARD (ELIZABETH BANKS), AND CHARLES HOWARD (JEFF BRIDGES) IN A PRERACE DISCUSSION.

ENTREPRENEUR CHARLES HOWARD (JEFF BRIDGES) ANSWERS QUESTIONS FROM THE PRESS.

RED POLLARD (TOBEY MAGUIRE), TOM SMITH (CHRIS COOPER), AND
CHARLES HOWARD (JEFF BRIDGES) DISCUSS SEABISCUIT.

CHARLES HOWARD (JEFF BRIDGES) POSES BEFORE THE PRESS WITH SEABISCUIT.

MARCELA HOWARD (ELIZABETH BANKS), CHARLES HOWARD (JEFF BRIDGES),
AND RED POLLARD (TOBEY MAGUIRE) GREET ALBUQUERQUE CROWDS ON
A CROSS-COUNTRY, WHISTLE-STOP TOUR.

RED POLLARD (TOBEY MAGUIRE) AND SEABISCUIT IN TRAINING.

CHRIS COOPER AS TOM SMITH.

A RECOVERING RED POLLARD (TOBEY MAGUIRE) COACHES JOCKEY GEORGE "THE ICEMAN" WOOLF (GARY STEVENS) FROM HIS HOSPITAL BED.

CHARLES HOWARD (JEFF BRIDGES) AND RED POLLARD (TOBEY MAGUIRE)
DISCUSS SEABISCUIT'S REHABILITATION.

RED POLLARD (TOBEY MAGUIRE) AND TOM SMITH (CHRIS COOPER)
DISCUSS SEABISCUIT'S REHABILITATION.

RED POLLARD (TOBEY MAGUIRE) ASTRIDE SEABISCUIT.

SEABISCUIT AND JOCKEY GEORGE "THE ICEMAN" WOOLF (GARY STEVENS) TAKE ON WAR ADMIRAL IN THE MATCH RACE.

SEABISCUIT AND JOCKEY GEORGE "THE ICEMAN" WOOLF
(GARY STEVENS) TAKE THE LEAD IN THE MATCH RACE AGAINST WAR ADMIRAL.

SEABISCUIT AND JOCKEY GEORGE "THE ICEMAN" WOOLF (GARY STEVENS) HEAD
TOWARD THE FINISH LINE IN THE MATCH RACE AGAINST WAR ADMIRAL.

A VICTORIOUS GEORGE "THE ICEMAN" WOOLF (GARY STEVENS) RIDES SEABISCUIT TO THE WINNER'S CIRCLE.

WRITER/DIRECTOR/PRODUCER GARY ROSS FILMS *SEABISCUIT.*

WRITER/DIRECTOR/PRODUCER GARY ROSS (LEFT) AND PRODUCER FRANK MARSHALL ON THE SET.

WRITER/DIRECTOR/PRODUCER GARY ROSS (LEFT) AND PRODUCER KATHLEEN KENNEDY ON THE SET.

WRITER/DIRECTOR/PRODUCER GARY ROSS WITH TOBEY MAGUIRE AS RED POLLARD.

WRITER/DIRECTOR/PRODUCER GARY ROSS.

WRITER/DIRECTOR/PRODUCER GARY ROSS ON THE *SEABISCUIT* SET.

RED POLLARD (TOBEY MAGUIRE) ASTRIDE SEABISCUIT.

RED POLLARD (TOBEY MAGUIRE) URGES SEABISCUIT ON.

SEABISCUIT

THE SCREENPLAY

PHOTO BY JEFF BRIDGES

PHOTO BY JEFF BRIDGES

SEABISCUIT

THE SCREENPLAY

SCREENPLAY BY

GARY ROSS

BASED ON THE BOOK BY

LAURA HILLENBRAND

BALLANTINE BOOKS
NEW YORK

CONTENTS

FOREWORD

BY LAURA HILLENBRAND

IT BEGAN ON A MORNING IN AUGUST OF 1998. I was at my
mother's house, where I was dogsitting her manic Dalmatian, Newton.
That morning I was walking in big, nervous loops around my mother's lawn while Newton bounced along behind me. The day before,
Random House had signed me on to do a book on the great Depression-
era racehorse Seabiscuit, and my initial euphoria had given way to the real-
ization that now I had to write the thing. I was in something of a panic.

Inside, the phone rang, and I trotted in to pick it up. The caller asked
for me, then introduced himself. He was a prominent movie producer,
and he said he wanted to make my book into a film. I was a little star-
struck and more than a little confused. I had told virtually no one where I
was, and had no idea how he had found my mother's number. And I
couldn't understand how he knew about a book that I hadn't even started
writing. Then he said something about hoping to beat out a host of other
producers who also wanted to acquire the film rights. He seemed to
assume that I knew what he was talking about. Bewildered, I referred him
to my agent, then called her myself to see what was going on.

My agent told me that my book proposal had been making an interesting journey. After I had submitted it to publishers, a movie scout had
come across it and faxed it to someone in Hollywood. Literally overnight,
it had made its way all over California, and my agent had spent the day
fielding calls from filmmakers interested in making a movie out of it.
Tomorrow you're going to need to talk to all these people, she said, to
decide who you want to make the film.

SEABISCUIT

THE SCREENPLAY

1 FADE IN: ON A MODEL T.

Not so much a car as a symbol. Over the frozen, grainy, black and white image, we HEAR the one voice that has become our history, and will serve as our NARRATOR: Author David McCullough.

> MCCULLOUGH
> They called it the car for Everyman. Ford himself called it a car for the "great multitude." It was functional and simple like your sewing machine or your cast iron stove. You could learn to drive it in less than a day and you could get any color you wanted so long as it was black.

2 PHOTOGRAPHS. AUTOPLANT.

The workers are dwarfed by the size of it. Same men doing the same job stretching out to infinity like a huge hall of mirrors.

> MCCULLOUGH
> When Ford first conceived the Model T it took thirteen hours to assemble. Within five years he was turning out a vehicle every ninety seconds. For the first time in history, a worker didn't have to go to the parts — the parts came to him. Instead of building the whole car, he only had to build the bumper...or the gearshift...or the door handle.

3 EXT. NEW YORK STREETS.

Choked with vehicles. There are trolley cars narrowly missing horse carts. Steam shovels dig new holes to anchor huge new buildings.

>   MCCULLOUGH
> Of course the real invention wasn't the car
> — it was the assembly line that built it.
> Pretty soon, other businesses had borrowed
> the same techniques: seamstresses became
> button sewers...furniture makers became knob
> turners....
>
>   (beat)
> It was the beginning and the end of imagina-
> tion all at the same time.

4 INT. BICYCLE FACTORY. DAY.

It is loud...oppressive. A constant clanging of metal
on metal.... A different "bicycle mechanic," CHARLES
HOWARD sits staring at his workbench. He gazes off at
a high transom window. It's the only shaft of light.

>   VOICE
> Charles, I'm talking to you.

>   HOWARD
> Hunh?

WIDER.

Howard's immediate supervisor has leaned a huge stack
of bicycle wheels next to his workbench.

>   FOREMAN
> They need spokes the same as the others.

Howard takes the broken wheel — stares at it...

>   HOWARD
> You know, they ought to make better spokes.

>   FOREMAN
> Yeah? Then what would you do?

He turns to leave as Howard thinks seriously about the
question. His gaze drifts off all over again...PUSH IN
SLOWLY ON HIS FACE as he dreams about...

5 THE WEST.

Huge. Vast. Endless. It is SOUTHERN WYOMING and the
Grand Teton Mountains lift up into a screaming blue
sky. The whole thing is so massive it almost seems
like a still frame, but slowly, out of one corner, a
small figure begins to emerge:

A horse and rider. It gets steadily larger, filling
in the detail: Stetson hat...Western saddle...bandana
around the neck...It is the outline of a Cowboy.

TOM SMITH is a part of the range that he rides on:
Weathered. Dusty. Solid. Granite. He canters toward
THE CAMERA EVENTUALLY FILLING THE FRAME IN A CLOSE
UP, coming to a halt at the top of a ridge. Smith
pauses, gazes out over his prairie, then makes a little clucking sound and the horse takes off again. As
he rides away, The CAMERA PANS 180 degrees to reveal:

...A LUSH GREEN VALLEY even more majestic in the
other direction. The West is endless and Smith
recedes into it...

                                       SMASH CUT TO:

6 STALLIONS...

...running free over the open range. They dart left
and right as the CAMERA chases them on a wild zigzag
through the expanse of land. It's an awesome display
of power.

Slowly...a cowboy enters the BOTTOM OF THE FRAME, a
lasso twirling over his head. Smith follows the pack
as it cuts left, then right, the huge rope twirling
the entire time. He sweeps it once, twice, three
times — then finally lets it go, flinging it toward
the wild horses in front of him...

                                             CUT TO:

7-8 OMITTED

9 STILLNESS.

Seven horses are tied up outside a livery stable
while Smith stands face to face with the owner. The
man wears a blacksmith's apron.

                         MAN
          Forty for all of 'em...

                         SMITH
            (shakes his head)
          That one's mine.

                              MAN
          Can you fix it?

Howard looks at the vehicle. Then an empty street.

                              HOWARD
          Uh...Sure.

                                            CUT TO:

16 INT. BICYCLE SHOP. NIGHT.

The car is disassembled all over the floor. There are
literally parts everywhere. Fenders. Pistons. The
steering wheel. Howard looks at the whole mess a little perplexed — like someone who's wandered into the
woods and can't remember how he got there. He picks
up the crankshaft and stares at it, then he glances
over at the universal joint and fits the two together...

17 THE SAME LOCATION. THE FOLLOWING DAY.

The car has been perfectly reassembled. Howard stands
beside the owner.

                              HOWARD
          This is an amazing machine! It's got a two
          stroke boiler system heated by this huge
          fire grate. I mean it's basically a portable
          locomotive...

The man nods, vaguely interested. He just wants it to
work.

                              HOWARD
          Anyway, I improved it a little bit. It
          wasn't your boiler that was blowing, it was
          the bleed valve. So, with the increased
          pressure you could get up to forty miles an
          hour.

                              MAN
          ...Really?

                              HOWARD
          Oh yeah. And if you superheat the excess, I
          could see you reaching...

**18 SAME LOCATION. NOW AN AUTO SHOWROOM. (TWO YEARS
LATER)**

                              HOWARD
          ...fifty maybe sixty miles an hour.

The bicycles have all been replaced by a windowful of Buicks.A huge sign hangs near the back of the room: "TRADE IN YOUR HORSE!" Howard is face to face with a customer.

> CUSTOMER
> Is that right?

> HOWARD
> Easily. And here's the thing of it, Mr. Coughlin. You don't feed it. You don't stable it. And unless you hit a lamppost, the thing's not gonna get sick and die on you.
>
> (leaning closer)
>
> To tell you the truth, I wouldn't pay more than five dollars for the best horse in America.

CUT TO:

18A THE RANGE.

Tom Smith lopes a horse through manzanita and sagebrush as he heads toward the high country. The CAMERA PULLS BACK with him as he gracefully weaves up the trail toward the top of the hill. It's a familiar route and Smith has the look of a man who's completely at home. He starts cantering toward the summit, when he sees something and suddenly...STOPS.

CLOSE UP. TOM SMITH.

He stares down over the neck of his horse like he's just seen a corpse. Smith pivots out of the saddle and drops to the ground. He walks slowly around to the front of his horse clutching the reins and staring at the object the entire time. The CAMERA PULLS BACK WITH HIM TO REVEAL...

A FENCE.

Barbed wire actually: a barrier across the wilderness. Smith stares at it, perplexed.

DIFFERENT ANGLE. FENCE.

It stretches to infinity, disappearing over the crest of the hill. On the other side is a well worn dirt trail that dates back to the wagon trains. Smith reaches out and touches one of the sharp little barbs...All at once there is a SOUND.

CLOSER. SMITH.

He turns to listen, but can't quite make it out. At first it seems like an insect: a high pitched droning SOUND, like a swarm of bees. After a beat or two, it starts getting louder and he looks down the trail...

HIS POV.

A small speck is moving toward him in a cloud of dust, and soon, the image of a CAR begins to emerge. As it heads toward him, the sound of the MOTOR gets louder...louder...LOUDER...

CUT TO:

19 OMITTED

20 A ROAR.

FIFTEEN CARS race through the mud, speeding their way up the SIERRA NEVADA MOUNTAINS. The drone of the engines is almost deafening as the cars slide through the springtime slop: slamming into each other...bashing into boulders...hammering the trunks of trees....

21 SIERRA SUMMIT.

Howard (slightly older now) stands perched on the hood of a car, covered with mud: his racing goggles up on his forehead. A newspaper photographer snaps a photo while he exhorts the crowd around him. Yosemite sprawls in the background.

> HOWARD
> This is not the finish line, my friends. This is the start of the race. The _future_ is the finish line. And the new Buick White Streak is the car to take us there.

There is a CHEER from the crowd.

> HOWARD
> Four in-line cylinders. Forty two and a half horse-power. We are living in a golden age, my friends. From San Francisco Bay to Donner summit in five hours and twenty six minutes. And this is the very same car that you can buy in one of our five showrooms all across The Bay Area....

CUT TO:

22 OMITTED

23 INT. HOWARD BREAKFAST ROOM.

He sits in the kitchen of their Union Square apart-
ment. Son Frank is in a high chair. His wife, ANNIE,
reads his quote to him from the newspaper.

                    ANNIE
          "... 'The age of the automobile is here,'
          boasted Howard. 'The future has arrived.'"

Frankie knocks over his oatmeal, splattering cereal
all over himself. His mother leaps up.

                    ANNIE
          Oh, my...

                    HOWARD
          Read the part about future again.

                    ANNIE
            (lifting the baby/pointed)
          I'm kind of dealing with it right now.

                    HOWARD
          Oh. Sorry.

The baby cries and fusses as she tries to wipe him
off.

                    HOWARD
          Here, I'll take him.

He lifts the youngster.

                    HOWARD
          Are you the future?

He makes a noise in the baby's face which makes him
laugh. It's easy for him.

                    HOWARD
          Are you the future, big guy? Are you gonna
          go to the moon?

Howard tosses the baby up toward the heavens and he
shrieks with delight. It's facile but loving. Howard
tosses Frankie up again. The SQUEALS of delight TURN
INTO:

TRAIN WHEELS...

SCREECHING along a track as they grind to a halt.

24 EXT. WESTERN TRAIN STATION. DAY.

There is a huge burst of STEAM. Tom Smith climbs off
one of the rear coaches carrying his saddle. He
crosses through the outdoor station and into the main
street of the small Western town.

25 EXT. MISSOULA, MONTANA. (SAME SHOT) DAY.

Smith walks into a West that is transformed. A
streetful of motorcars belches exhaust. Overhead
electrical wires power modern horseless trolley cars.
The gas lamps have all been replaced by huge incan-
descent ones.

ON SMITH.

He looks around in a daze. Smith crosses the street
and almost gets nailed by a trolley, dropping the
saddle in the process. He goes back to retrieve it,
and is almost hit by another car speeding in the
other direction. Smith picks up the twenty pound saddle and starts lugging it across the street while
vehicles whizz by him, their car horns BLARING.

When he hits the sidewalk, Smith drops the saddle,
exhausted, then looks up at the front of a dry goods
store:

HIS POV.

A large colorful poster adorns the window:

"THE WILD WEST!"
JUST THE WAY IT REALLY WAS!
BANDITS! INDIAN SHOOT-OUTS.
TRICK RIDING AND ROPING!
TEN TON IRWIN'S WILD WEST EXTRAVAGANZA
FRI, SAT, TWO TIMES ON SUNDAY!

TIGHTER POV. (INSERT POSTER)

The scene could come right out of his memory: a classic scene of the Western frontier. There is a snow
capped peak. A moose grazing by an alpine lake. White
puffy clouds in a brilliant blue sky.

MATCH CUT TO:

26 THAT EXACT SAME IMAGE ONLY LIVE.

The water ripples slightly. There's wind in the trees...

> HOWARD (OS)
> I'll take it.

27 REVERSE ANGLE.

He stands at the crest of a hill scanning the majesty in front of him. His family, some financial advisors and a real estate entourage are all in tow. The place is called Ridgewood but Xanadu would work. Howard fills his lungs with fresh air.

> ANNIE
> Do we need all this?

> HOWARD
> Well no, Muffin. We don't need it. I mean —
> we don't need anything.

Their eyes lock for a beat. A missed connection. Howard puts his arm impulsively around Frankie — draws him closer.

> LAND BROKER
> There's also a caretaker's house, a paddock,
> a barn, and some very nice stables....

> HOWARD
> How big are the stables?

> CUT TO:

28 EXT. RIDGEWOOD STABLES. DAY.

All the horses are being led out of the stable area, as Howard's huge collection of racing cars is wheeled in.

Frankie sits in the front seat of a sleek white road-ster while his dad pushes the bumper.

INT. STABLES

Each one is rolled into its own horse stall — the front end butting out of the straw. All the bridles and other tack hang uselessly in the background....

> CUT TO:

28A A REARING STALLION.

He stands up angrily on his massive hind legs — mouth open in a scream. It's a frozen image painted on the side of a huge canvas tent. Next to it, there is a swirling inscription: "TEN TON IRWIN'S WILD WEST EXTRAVAGANZA."

MRS. POLLARD
So he should earn it.

Mr. Pollard looks over at his wife. Thinks for a beat...

CUT TO:

35 INT. POLLARD DINING ROOM. NIGHT.

It is a very ornate dining room in a very elegant
home. The lavish surroundings seem a little incongru-
ous with the circus going on at the dinner table.
Most of the children are talking at once. Mr. Pollard
has a small library of books piled up at his end of
the table. Half of them are opened. Red sits just to
the right of him in a high backed chair pushed back
toward the wall. The place is a joyous madhouse.

KIDS
(overlapping)

Give him Tennyson. Ancient Mariner.
Xanadu.... Everybody knows Xanadu, Chloe.
WHITMAN! GIVE HIM WHITMAN!

MR. POLLARD
Okay...

The kids keep talking.

MR. POLLARD
Quiet!

They settle down a little. Mr. Pollard scans the
table...

MR. POLLARD
(beat)
Dickinson.

KIDS
Ooooh....!

There are various hoots and whistles as Red gets
ready for his test. Mr. Pollard clears his throat.

MR. POLLARD
"We never know how high we are..."

RED
Oh. Wait. I know that. I know it.

MR. POLLARD
Well...

Red thinks — takes a deep breath...

                    RED
          "We never know how high we are..."

               (searches for it...)

          "...Till we are called to rise."

                    MR. POLLARD
          Good!

                    RED
          "And then if we are true to plan..." Wait a
          minute.... "And then if we are true to
          plan..."

               (gropes...)

          "...our statures touch the skies!"

                    MR. POLLARD
          Excellent!

Red suddenly goes blank.

                    RED
          Uh oh...

               (thinks)

          ...Damn.

                    MRS. POLLARD
          Johnny.

                    RED
          Sorry. Wait a sec...

They wait. His father prompts.

                    MR. POLLARD
          "The heroism..."

                    RED
          Right. Right. Um — "The heroism..."

Red stares blankly.

                    MR. POLLARD
          "The heroism we recite...
          would be a daily thing...."

He looks to his son. Nothing comes back. Mr. Pollard
continues on his own.

MR. POLLARD
"Did not ourselves, The cubits warp...
For fear to be a king."

He rises from his chair and in a deep, rich BARITONE:

MR. POLLARD
(full performance)

"For tis that moment in the glass when
friend or foe we meet...
The one a shadow of ourselves, the other
whole: complete!"

He ends with a grand flourish to the applause of all
the kids including Red. Mr. Pollard looks exultant,
literally drunk on Emerson's words. He glances down
at Red, in love with his boy and the English language. Mr. Pollard ruffles his hair.

CUT TO:

36 EXT. POLLARD ESTATE. DAY.

Red leaps over a fence on his brand new pony.

37 INT. LIVING ROOM. LOOKING OUT.

His father and mother watch from the window.

MRS. POLLARD
You should be riding it. You knew the poem.

MR. POLLARD
Yeah, but he looks so perfect out there.
Doesn't he look perfect?

MRS. POLLARD
(a concession)

Yeah...He does.

Mr. Pollard presses closer to the window.

MR. POLLARD
That's the poetry, right there Agnes.

That's the poetry.

CLOSER. RED.

He approaches the trunk of a felled tree and urges
the animal slightly. The horse canters up to it,
launches himself into the air, SAILS OVER the top of
the jump...

37A A ROAST SUCKLING PIG

LANDING in the center of a dinner table.

37B INT. RIDGEWOOD GREAT ROOM. NIGHT.

The place is immense — rustic and opulent at the same time. The CAMERA begins a long slow track around Charles Howard's dinner party while he rises for a toast at the end of the table. Everyone is dressed in dinner clothes and the warmth of the candelabras makes them glow.

> HOWARD
> Thank you. Thank you all for coming.
>
> (beat)
>
> It means so much to Annie and me...I know this isn't exactly Nob Hill and we're grate-ful to all of you for making the trek up to our little cabin in the woods.

UP ANGLE. HOWARD. (HOLDING THE EXPANSE OF THE ROOM)

Some cabin. He pauses — glances down.

> HOWARD (cont'd)
> Of course, we're grateful for a lot more than that. I came here fifteen years ago with twenty-one cents in my pocket. I know lots of us have a story like that but I just can't help thinking that if a man can start there, and end up here, where can't he go in America? Where can't he end up in this great country of ours?

This brings some applause. Howard smiles shyly...

> HOWARD (cont'd)
> So — corny as it sounds, I want to propose a toast to the future. Because out here my friends — the sky is literally the limit.

Howard hoists his glass "skyward." His guests follow suit. They hold like that for a beat...

CUT TO:

37C OMITTED

38-41 OMITTED

42 "CRASH!"

The bundle of newspapers hits the sidewalk with a thud. The headline tells it all. So does the date: Oct. 29, 1929.

> MCCULLOUGH
> There were no actual suicides that day. It was a myth that would grow over time. The real effect of Oct. 29 took a little longer to sink in than that.

43 NEWSREEL FOOTAGE. (BLACK AND WHITE) LIVE ACTION.

Huge crowds stare at the public ticker outside the New York Stock Exchange. They stand riveted like they are watching a prize fight or the aftermath of a train wreck...

> MCCULLOUGH
> By noon, all the gains of the previous year had been obliterated. By four P.M. nearly ten billion dollars of market value was gone.

44 INT. STOCK EXCHANGE.

A scene of triage.

> MCCULLOUGH
> Traders stood on the floor weeping openly together...

45 INT. (WIDE ANGLE) CATHOLIC CHURCH.

The crucifix looms in the center of frame...

> MCCULLOUGH
> Nearby Trinity Church slowly filled with dazed speculators who only a week before worshipped a very different God.

46 EXT. WALL STREET. (BLACK AND WHITE) STILL FRAME

A ghost town.

> MCCULLOUGH
> Over the next two weeks the hemorrhage continued...

47 SMALL TOWN WESTERN UNION OFFICE. (BLACK AND WHITE)

A crowd huddles around the local tickertape...

> MCCULLOUGH
> Declining prices forced margin loans to be
> called, sending the markets into further
> free fall...

48 MAIN STREET. SMALL TOWN.

Windows boarded. Streets deserted.

> MCCULLOUGH
> Before long, 25 percent of the work force
> was unemployed.

49 STILL FRAME. OPULENT HOUSE.

A family is turned out on the sidewalk by the Sheriff
and a local bank rep — their belongings literally
piled next to them in the street.

> MCCULLOUGH
> Mortgages went the way of the margin calls
> and soon people found themselves losing
> homes they had lived in for generations.

PUSH IN:

CLOSER.

The family on the sidewalk is RED POLLARD, his parents and his siblings. Mr. Pollard stands frozen
within — dazed expression on his face: his whole life
scattered across the driveway...

> MCCULLOUGH
> A great national migration ensued.

50 STILL FRAME. ROAD. (BLACK AND WHITE)

The jalopies, bursting with a lifetime of accumulated
possessions, pass each other going opposite direc-
tions. The long line of desperation is infinite — a
traffic jam of poverty.

> MCCULLOUGH
> Displaced families took to the American
> highway in the last possession that remained
> to them — their automobile.

51 CLOSER. A CAR.

It is packed with everything that should be in a
house: couches, chairs, ironing board, a sewing
machine.

MCCULLOUGH
And all at once, millions of Americans had a
new definition of "home."

52 EXT. A TREE. NIGHT.

It's an oak actually. One man lies alone in the darkness at the base of the trunk.

53 CLOSER. TOM SMITH.

He stares up at the night sky.

54 HIS POV.

There are no stars now — only blackness. Smith closes
his eyes.

CUT TO:

55 RACE HORSES.

THUNDERING by the CAMERA. The earth literally moves
as the torrent of hooves rushes by.

56 WIDER. MAKESHIFT RACETRACK.

It's cut into a farmer's hayfield. The oval is
described by a trampled area and a flimsy "rail" made
of fence posts and rope.

REVERSE ANGLE. LONG LENS.

The horses CLEAR frame to reveal RED: staring
enthralled at the spectacle in front of him. He beams
with the delight of someone who has discovered something totally new and yet stunningly familiar. He's
home. Transfixed. In love.

DISSOLVE TO:

57 EXT. MIGRANT CAMP. DUSK.

It is the rural version of a Hooverville. Dozens of
old jalopies and squalid "campsites" are scattered
through an apple orchard. Empty bushels and picking
ladders are littered across the ground. Children run
in and out of the tree trunks oblivious to the scope
of the situation: this is farm labor and it's a family business.

DIFFERENT ANGLE. POLLARD "CAMP."

They have strung up some shelter next to their car. The orange glow of a campfire cuts the blue gray haze of dusk. Mrs. Pollard stirs some kind of dinner in a large open pot: Grits? Oats? Beans?

Mr. Pollard sits on the tailgate of their car, staring blankly at the flames. Finally he hears something and glances up.

HIS POV. THROUGH THE SMOKE.

Red appears to him in the campfire, emerging from the shadow of the fruit trees. Maybe it's the smoke or the firelight, but he seems suddenly larger, like something has changed. He takes a step forward...

                    RED
      I made two dollars.

                  MR. POLLARD
      What?

DIFFERENT ANGLE.

He moves around toward his dad.

                    RED
      I made two dollars. See.

He holds out his hand. There are two "Liberty" silver dollars.

                    RED
      Here.

He hands them to his father.

                  MR. POLLARD
       (recoiling)

      No.

                    RED
      It's fine. I can make more tomorrow.

His father looks down at his own hand. Stares at the shiny silver dollars. It's a weird combination of emotions: Relief. Confusion. Amazement. Grief. He looks up:

                  MR. POLLARD
      Where'd you get this?

58 THE RACE TRACK. DAY.

The CAMERA swoops across the small crowd milling about the trampled field. It's a carnival in the darkest sense: "Race" horses are tied to various trees. Side bets are happening all over the place.

59 SHOT. MAKESHIFT CORRAL.

A long line of horses are tied to a rope strung between two trees. A bush-league "trainer" talks to Red and his family.

> TRAINER
> Yeah, your boy combed 'em out. Changed all the tack. — I didn't even need to tell him a thing.
>
> (coining a nickname)
>
> Hey "Red," where'd a young fella like you learn so much about horses?

> MRS. POLLARD
> His name is Johnny.

> RED
> (beat/smiles)
>
> ...You can call me Red.

The man smiles and ruffles his hair. Mr. Pollard takes it all in...

CUT TO:

60 THE STARTING LINE.

It's a rope actually. The various horses jostle for position, waiting for the rope to drop.

CLOSER. A JOCKEY.

He guides his horse back and forth through an expert combination of reins and feet.

SHOT. RED.

He stands across the track at the rail, eyes riveted on the jockey.

A GUNSHOT.

...the ROPE DROPS and horses are off. "Our" jockey breaks to the lead, dropping down to the inside and hunching over the withers of his horse. He stays in a perfect crouch, eyes forward on the race track.

INSERT. JOCKEY'S HANDS.

He pumps the reins expertly, "throwing" his hands away from him in a circular motion.

SHOT. RED.

He unconsciously pumps his hands in the exact same way.

DIFFERENT ANGLE OVER RED.

Far in the background, his parents are talking to the trainer. Mrs. Pollard turns partially away staring down at the ground while Red's father leans in close — talking and nodding.

SHOT. RACE TRACK.

The jockey leans into the turn.

SHOT. RED.

He does the same — weighting his inside leg and urging the horse into the stretch.

WIDER.

The horses THUNDER by. Down at the rail the NOISE is deafening. Red watches his jockey fly by in a burst of sound and color. He whirls around toward his parents with an exultant grin on his face...

CLOSER.

All at once the grin freezes.

RED'S POV. HIS MOTHER. (CLOSE UP)

She is staring at him from a few feet away. Her eyes are red. Her face is stained with tears.

WIDER.

She grabs him, suddenly, clinging on for several seconds. When she finally lets go, Red looks up to see his father standing a few feet away, clutching a pillow case with some heavy objects inside it. He hesitates...

                          RED
          What's this?

                    MR. POLLARD
          Um — everything...

               (deep breath)

          Dickens. Wordsworth...

               (forces a smile)

          There's your Arabian Nights and Moby Dick.
          Even the Milne from when you were...when you
          were...

He can't finish it. He turns his head away. The voice
that comes out is small and faint.

                    MR. POLLARD
          I'm sorry. I'm so sorry.

He looks back at Red. There are tears in his eyes
too.

                    MR. POLLARD
          Look. Mr. Blodget here has a house. A real
          house...

NEW ANGLE.

Red looks up to see the trainer that he worked for
standing a couple of feet away.

                    MR. POLLARD
          There's even a phone next door so we can
          call you every couple of weeks and let you
          know where we are...

                    RED
          No...

                    MR. POLLARD
               (reaches down. Hugs his son — a whisper)
          You'll be great at this. You've got a gift
          ...

               (convincing himself)

          We'll come back...

               (hugs him again)

          We will...We will.

Red watches as his father leans back. He looks around
the fading light of the race track/fairground. He looks
at his son for a moment as the CAMERA begins to pull
back rapidly leaving them a small part of the crowd...

61 EXT. RIDGEWOOD. DAY.

Smoke rises from the chimney. The huge log home stands out against the sky. Solid. Warm. Safe. The TITLE:

"SIX YEARS LATER"

> HOWARD (VO)
> No, Bill. I'm not gonna do it. No more lay-offs...

62 INT. HOWARD'S FOYER.

He speaks into the mouthpiece of a handcrank wall-phone.

> HOWARD
> Well it can't get any worse...Look, if it stays like this we'll just tighten our belts a little bit.
>
> (beat)
>
> We'll be fine, Bill. Really. We will.

63 INT. LIVING ROOM.

Howard's son Frankie, now fourteen, lies on the couch reading a dime novel. Howard crosses through the living room — sees him.

> HOWARD
> (a little tense)
>
> It's a glorious day outside. Why don't you go fishing or something?

> FRANKIE
> (looking up)
>
> ...I'm reading.

> HOWARD
> You can read when it's raining. C'mon. I'll teach you to drive the truck.

> FRANKIE
> You taught me to drive the truck.

> HOWARD
> (looks at the book)
>
> What is it?

                              FRANKIE
          Flash Gordon.

Howard rolls his eyes.

                              FRANKIE
          C'mon, Dad. It's about the future.

Howard can't help smiling. He crosses to the couch
and ruffles his son's hair...

64 EXT. RIDGEWOOD DRIVEWAY. LATER.

A Buick Coachman stands rumbling in the driveway
being loaded with luggage. Annie sits in the passenger's seat. Howard gives last minute instructions to
his caretaker: Sam.

                              HOWARD
          We'll be in San Francisco till Wednesday. If
          you need me call Bill at the dealership in
          Hillhurst.

                              SAM
          Will do.

                              HOWARD
          And make sure Frankie eats breakfast.

65 INT. FRANKIE'S ROOM.

He lies on his bed finishing the Flash Gordon.
Frankie HEARS a car door SLAM and goes to his window.

66 INT. FRANKIE'S POV. DRIVEWAY.

His father has just shut the trunk and is climbing in
behind the wheel. Frankie watches as the car fires
up, then disappears down the long road through the
woods...

                                        CUT TO:

67 INSERT. GARAGE AREA.

Frankie's hand reaches up and clutches a fishing pole
from the rafters of the garage...

INSERT. BACK OF TRUCK.

A tackle box and pole are tossed in the open bed of
the pickup.

68 INT. TRUCK.

The door slams — Frankie sits behind the wheel. The fourteen year old boy takes the key...fits it in the ignition...

69 WIDE SHOT. RIDGEWOOD.

Wind in the trees. A mockingbird. Suddenly, the distant SOUND of an ENGINE being fired...

CUT TO:

70 EXT. MOUNTAIN ROAD. (OVER THE FRONT TIRE OF THE TRUCK)

It meanders up the dirt road high into the Sierras. The ground is still muddy from a fresh rain and the truck slides a little: first toward the edge and then away from it.

71 INT. TRUCK.

Frankie cranes to see over the dashboard. The uphill angle doesn't make it any easier as he gives a burst of acceleration, then brake, then gas, then brake....

72 A DIFFERENT PART OF THE ROAD.

A logging truck heads inexorably in the other direction.

FRANKIE'S TRUCK.

It gives a burst of acceleration around a curve.

THE LOGGING TRUCK.

It hurtles downward toward the same bend in the road.

ON FRANKIE'S BUMPER.

The truck turns the corner. There is a sudden squealing of brakes. Frankie skids in the mud — first right then left...

He spins a hundred and eighty degrees hurtling toward the edge of the road...

73 EXTREME WIDE ANGLE. RIVER CANYON.

There is a distant sound of metal, gnashing through the pine trees. Off in one corner of the FRAME all that can be seen is a long plume of dust, heading like a weird serpent downhill...

Red steps off wearing tattered jockey silks and riding boots.

At five foot eight they're a little tight.
Nonetheless, he's been transformed — a rider now. Red
turns to a craggy looking man beside him. "DUTCH"
Doogan is somewhere between fifty and death — it's
hard to tell with all the "character" in his face.

                    DUTCH
          Still pretty tall to be a jock.

                         RED
              (a lie)
          Never been over one fifteen.

                    DUTCH
              (nods...)
          Where'd you learn to ride like that?

                         RED
              ...Home.

The old man thinks for a beat.

                    DUTCH
          Alright, here's how it works. I pay you
          twenty dollars a week for riding. You owe me
          ten for your meals, six for sleepin' in the
          stall and three for your tack fee.

                         RED
          Well, how do I pay all that back?

                    DUTCH
              ...You win.

HARD CUT TO:

85 A HORSE RACE.

Two jockeys are beating the shit out of each other at
the front of the pack. They club each other with
their whips while they head into the turn at forty
miles an hour.

OVER RED....

He's pinned in at the rail while the slugfest plays
out in front of him. It's a combination of Ben Hur and
Mad Max, as one of the jockeys grabs the other's bridle and jerks the horse's head violently backwards.

The horse props and his jockey flies over the front
literally disappearing OUT OF FRAME. Now Red is riding behind one jockey and a riderless horse.

HIS POV.

The horses have drifted wide in the melee so Red
tries to shoot through a hole at the rail. Just as he
begins to overtake the other rider he is clothes-
lined by the other jockey's whip.

BEHIND BOTH OF THEM.

Red fights him off but the other jockey has grabbed
his silks and is trying to pull him backward off the
horse. Red cracks him across his arm and the jockey
momentarily loses his grip, allowing Red to pull away.

RAKED ANGLE.

Red drives toward the finish line. The other jock
reaches out and desperately grabs a hold of his sad-
dlecloth, literally being towed behind him. Red
drives his horse who is starting to veer wide under
the weight of two jockeys and another animal. Just as
they approach the wire...

A THIRD HORSE.

Shoots past both of them to win along the rail. Its
jockey leaps up in the irons thrusting his fist in
victory. Red watches stunned as he pulls away from
them, galloping his horse out after the wire....

                                              CUT TO:

86 AN EMPTY STALL...

                    DUTCH'S VOICE (OS)
          A nose! You lose that race a nose!

Red is violently hurled against the back wall.

REVERSE ANGLE. STALL DOOR.

Dutch stands there, blocking the light.

                         DUTCH
          You lose that race a nose, you better fall
          off tryin'!

               (he flings a shovel toward Red)
          Here. Muck those stalls.

DOWN ANGLE. RED.

The shovel hits next to him on the wall. The CAMERA beings to push in slowly on Red in the far corner of the stall. As it does, the HEAVY SOUND of steel wheels against a train-track begins to fill the scene. The image begins to sway slightly as...

86A THE FACES OF FIFTEEN MEN

appear ghostlike in a DISSOLVE. They line the walls of a BOXCAR — staring broken, dazed, straight ahead. Tom Smith sits in the corner (where Red used to be) looking at the blank space just in front of him (a small pocket of privacy). The CAMERA pushes in tighter.

CUT TO:

87-92 OMITTED

93 THE EXACT SAME EXPRESSION.

This time on Charles Howard. He sits all alone in the palatial LIVING ROOM of RIDGEWOOD — a fire roaring somewhere behind him. Howard shifts his gaze two degrees. Fixes on some new point in the distance.

JUMP CUT TO:

93A A NEW CHAIR.

New position — same old stare. It's daylight now. He's gazing out the window, at...

ANNIE

Scrubbing the porch in the fading light. She has a bucket. A mop. A scrub brush. Annie furiously works the suds into a varnish trying to scrub out the past.

> HOWARD (O.S.)
> Come inside.

(A jump cut) He's standing near the door to the porch.

> ANNIE
> (barely looks)
> I'm not done.

                         HOWARD
          It's cold.

                         ANNIE
          I'm fine.

CLOSER

She brushes away a loose strand of hair and goes back
to scrubbing...harder...

                         HOWARD
          Sam can do that.

                         ANNIE
              (sharp)
          I don't want Sam to do it. I want to do it...

Her voice wavers. She stops herself. Scrubs some
more.

MOS. THROUGH THE WINDOW...

He moves over to her. Touches her shoulders. She
flinches...nearly jumps...

                                        CUT TO:

94 INT. FRANKIE'S ROOM

Howard stands near the window by the bed. He holds
one of Frankie's books in his hand.

INSERT. BOOK.

It's Flash Gordon. Used to be about the future. He
glances out the same window that Frankie did.

HIS POV

The same car is parked in the same driveway...The
same suitcases are being loaded.

WIDE ANGLE. BEHIND THE CAR

This time it's Annie who's leaving. She climbs into
the back seat of the car and the door slams. The
Buick Coachman fires up and starts down the long
gravel driveway that leads away from the ranch...

INT. ROOM

Howard's gaze shifts back toward the book. Cradles it
in his hands.

INSERT. FLASH GORDON

The illustration is brave and childlike all at the same time. Flash fights the demons of Mongol with no regard for his own personal safety...

>   VOICE (OS)
> What are you reading?

95 OMITTED

95A INT. HORSE STALL. NIGHT.

Red sleeps in a bed of rough straw next to one of the other jocks. The kid (TEDDY) is no more than thirteen years old.

He hasn't shaved yet — the voice is still high. Red has the pillowcase of books next to him. He reads by a single candle.

>   TEDDY
> What is it?

>   RED
> Just a story.

>   TEDDY
> Where'd you get it?

>   RED
>   (beat)
> My Dad gave it to me.

CLOSER

The cover of the book is strange and exotic — a child's wonderland. ARABIAN NIGHTS is written in swirling script next to a puff of blue smoke with a genie in the middle. Teddy studies the book.

>   TEDDY
> What's it about?

>   RED
> Arabian nights.

Red turns and looks at him. The boy clutches the corners of his blanket like he might be a lot younger.

>   RED (cont'd)
> It's about this boy. Aladdin.

Teddy looks blankly at him.

                    TEDDY
          So what happens?

                    RED
          Well, he's sort of this wild kid. His par-
          ents are dead and he lives in the
          streets...you know...any way he can.

He pauses. The metaphor hits him.

                    TEDDY
          Can you read it?

                    RED
          What?

                    TEDDY
          Can you read it to me?

                    RED
          Uh ...Sure. I guess.

Red pulls the candle closer and looks over the book.
Teddy curls up under his blanket to listen.

                    RED (cont'd)
               (reading)
          "...So the genie granted Aladdin the sum of
          three wishes..."

                    TEDDY
          Wishes?

                    RED
          Yeah.

                    TEDDY
          You mean, anything he wants?

                    RED
          Yeah, you know — they're wishes.

Teddy curls up a little tighter. Red keeps
reading.

                    RED (cont'd)
          "... So the first thing Aladdin imagined was
          a great night garden. In his mind, he saw
          trees laden with fruit and a huge table
          filled with honey cakes and figs and apri-
          cots and..."

          Stop it.

WIDER. (WE'RE SOMEPLACE ELSE...)

He lies on the floor of a bus depot or a train station — the pillow case from his father spilled open
beside him. Red squints at the page in the foreground, struggling to bring it into focus with his
one good eye. The CAMERA moves around to the front of
his face revealing both of them: one ravaged, the
other untouched, almost like he's two different people.

Red reaches forward and turns the page as...

97 A HUGE CHEER

...goes up from another crowd — this one his harsh,
white daylight. They leer at some action playing out
in front of them in the center of the "ring."

REVERSE ANGLE. A COCK FIGHT.

Two game birds savage each other while the crowd
screams themselves hoarse.

> "TIJUANA, MEXICO...
> 1933"

The CAMERA booms up from the cock fight and begins to
move over the crowd and into the Avenida Revolucion.
A dog runs by in the foreground. A liquor cart passes
the other way...

> MCCULLOUGH
> At a time when the world really needed a
> drink, you couldn't get one in the United
> States of America.

The CAMERA moves down the block with the liquor cart,
passing by an exploding string of firecrackers. It
tilts up to reveal the rest of the block. Quickie
divorces. Pawn shops. "American" bars...

> MCCULLOUGH (cont'd)
> Liquor was illegal, diversions were scarce
> and there's just so much a human being can
> do without...

It CROSSES the street toward a small crowd gathered
around a contortionist. Next to it, some tourists are
being photographed with a "zebra" (actually a burro
painted with black and white stripes).

> MCCULLOUGH (cont'd)
> ...soon the border town was born, providing everything to the South that their neighbor to the North would not.

HARD CUT TO:

97A EXT. MOLINA ROJO. DAY.

It's the Baja version of the Moulin Rouge (there's a red windmill but it's pretty small by Montmartre standards). Even in the daylight, the flickering neon beckons men and boys down a long road where the women will handle everything professionally. Many of them hang out the windows in a personal piece of advertisement.

> MCCULLOUGH
> You could find food, "companionship," decent gin...And, at a time when gambling was outlawed as well...

REVERSE ANGLE. PAST THE WINDMILL FROM THE ROOF.

The race track lies in the background. The CAMERA pushes past the blades of the windmill toward the grandstand of Aqua Caliente below.

> MCCULLOUGH (cont'd)
> ...a chance to turn back luck into good.

THERE'S A LOUD BELL AND...

98 OMITTED

99 A VINTAGE STARTING GATE

bursts open as an explosion of color fills the screen.

WITH THE HORSES (LONG LENS)...

They thunder toward us. The CAMERA TRIES TO RETREAT as the wall of gleaming silks GROWS BIGGER AND BIGGER IN THE FRAME.

It is a riot of color against the green grass of the turf course: chartreuse, hot pink, bright yellow, orange....

100 EXT. AGUA CALIENTE GRANDSTAND. DAY.

This is the big time — the Grand Dame of 30's racing. A thousand binoculars lower simultaneously as the horses fly by the finish line. Behind one of them is...

CHARLES HOWARD.

He continues to stare blankly ahead as if the race is still going on. It's more of a distraction to him than a sporting event. Howard's eyes focus on middle space, where his grief seems to be.

101 DIFFERENT ANGLE. GRANDSTAND BOX. A BEAUTIFUL YOUNG WOMAN.

MARCELA ZABALA is staring at him from several boxes away.

She has jet black hair and porcelain skin that shines...like a piano. Marcela seems drawn to his stillness. She lowers her binoculars...

>   MARCELA
>   Who's that?

HER POV

Howard is surrounded by wealth and gaiety: Walter Hinkle. Alberto Giannini. Charles Strubb. They're locked in a boy's club. He's momentarily distracted by something else.

>   WALTER
>   (answering Howard)
>
>   Oh. That's George Woolf — greatest jockey in
>   the world.

HIS POV.

A short, handsome man is climbing out of a white Cord Roadster.

He wears a white buckskin jacket with five inch fringe. Woolf has on a white Stetson and gleaming silver bolo.

CLOSER...

The sun shines all over George Woolf. He has a different glow than anyone else in the vicinity. His eyes gleam. His hat gleams. His teeth gleam. He surveys his racetrack with the confidence of a man who was born to win...

FULL SHOT. HOWARD.

He glances down. Used to have it. Lost it. Envy? Not really. Just....

FULL SHOT. MARCELA.

She looks right at him. Feeling it with him for a beat. Feeling something new and strange for a man who seems to be feeling so much...

> MARCELA
> That's Charles Howard?

> FRIEND
> Yeah.

> MARCELA
> (beat)
> I thought he came down here for...

> FRIEND
> A quickie divorce.

She looks at her friend then back at Howard. All empathy:

> MARCELA
> There's nothing quick about that.

The race becomes "OFFICIAL" as a ROAR goes up from the crowd.

                                              CUT TO:

102 A BLANK WALL.

And the offstage sound of a man VOMITING. RED'S HEAD lurches up into THE FRAME: a tight CLOSE UP. He is drawn and ashen. There is sweat on his forehead. The scar has healed but it's still visible above his right eye. He opens his mouth, sticks his finger in it and lurches OUT OF FRAME...

                                              CUT TO:

103 A SCALE.

Red's face is reflected in the glass as the large dial spins around to a hundred and fourteen pounds...

104 INT. JOCK'S ROOM. LATER.

It is part locker room, part club house — the only home they know. Gathered around a series of benches is a group of jockeys in various states of dress.

Colored silks and tack hang all over the room: saddles, whips, boots, plastic madonnas, girly-pinups and stirrups. Red holds court in the middle of the group, painting the air with a hand, as he spins a yarn for the younger jockeys.

>   RED
>   It was in the palace of the great Sultan...

>   YOUNG JOCKEY
>   Sultan of where?

>   RED
>   Um — Sultan of The A-rabie.

They nod...

CLOSER

He looks older now. Seasoned. Thinner. A veteran. Red leans forward as if he is clueing them in on a closely held secret.

>   RED
>   I had been living there for almost a year —
>   racing his Arabians across the desert and
>   finishing my personal history of the region
>   by night.

They nod again — impressed.

>   RED
>   Then one day the Sultan summoned me into his
>   throne room.

Red pauses for effect. They lean forward a little.

>   RED
>   He looked at me and said...

>   WOOLF (OS)
>   (finishing the line)

>   "John Pollard: You are my greatest jockey.
>   It is you who will ride in my hundred mile
>   race from Kusmat to Tripoli."

WIDER.

Woolf breezes into the jock's room still wearing his gleaming white buckskin.

                              RED
                    (beat/chilly)
          Two hundred mile.

                              WOOLF
          Oh. Right. Two hundred mile. 'Scuse me Sa-
          hib.

     Red glares. The other jocks crack up...

                                             CUT TO:

     105 POST PARADE. AGUA CALIENTE RACE TRACK.

     Red and George ride side by side on their way to the
     gate.

                              RED
          You didn't need to wreck it Georgie.

                              WOOLF
          Ya know, when you started tellin' that
          story, it was only fifty miles.

                              RED
          Yeah, well...Everything gets longer in the
          retelling...

                    (glances to his left)
          Just ask Wanda.

     DIFFERENT ANGLE.

     Red motions TOWARD A SMALL HILL that rises behind the
     track.

     THE MOLINA ROJO sits on top with its windmill turn-
     ing.

                              WOOLF
                    (glances uphill/smiles)
          You leave Wanda out of this.

                              RED
                    (quoting Omar Khayyam, re: Wanda)
          "Myself when young, did eagerly
          frequent...Both saint and whore and heard no
          agreement..."

> WOOLF
> Ya know Red, if you rode a little more and
> talked a little less you might start winnin'
> some races.

Friendly but it stings.

> RED
> I got two bucks says I beat you in this one.

> WOOLF
> Make it five.

A BELL:

106 STARTING GATE.

The horses explode.

MOVING WITH THEM...THE BACK OF THE PACK.

Red and George continue their conversation in the
middle of the race. They ride side by side at the
back of the pack — dirt flies in their faces.

> RED
> Gimme odds. You're the favorite.

The horses bump a little.

> WOOLF
> Morning line.

> RED
> Forget it. Two to one.

> WOOLF
> Done.

They move closer to each other at the rail. Both men
lean in as they enter the turn. They're still at the
back of the pack, but it's drawing tighter.

> WOOLF
> You got a speed horse Johnny. Why're you
> sittin' back here with me?

> RED
> I like the conversation. And he's not a
> speed horse — don't try to hook me.
>
> (beat)
>
> You going tonight?

WOOLF

Naw. You?

RED

Naw.

WOOLF

So, what time?

RED
(smiles)

I don't know. Eight?

WOOLF

Okey-doke. Ooops, there's my hole Johnny.
Gotta fly.

BEHIND THEM.

Sure enough a hole has opened in front of them and
Woolf shoots through it with perfect speed and dex-
terity. As soon as he is through it seals up in front
of Red like a secret passage cut in the rock.

RED

God dammit.

He presses his horse but there's nowhere to go. Red
pulls to the outside and starts to lumber slowly out
of frame...

AS HE DOES...

The horses clear FRAME but the CAMERA KEEPS GOING. IT
DRIFTS ALL THE WAY ACROSS THE TRACK, OVER THE HEDGE
AT THE FAR RAIL, AND FINALLY COMES TO REST IN THE
BARN AREA, where four blacksmiths are shoeing horses.
One of them is...

107 TOM SMITH.

He BANGS with the same monotonous drone of the other
blacksmiths. Tom picks up the horse's hoof and examines it for a moment. He bends back the foreleg. The
horse jerks.

VOICE (OS)

What the hell are you doing?

WIDER

The trainer he works for is standing over him.

                              SMITH
              Oh.... He's got a lame foreleg.

                             TRAINER
              I don't care. Just shoe the horse.

                              SMITH
                   (taking a chance)

              Look — if you let me fix him, he'll give you
              more than six furlongs. This horse'll take
              you 'round two turns...

                             TRAINER
              Did I ask you what you think? Just shoe the
              goddamn horse!

He throws a horseshoe over toward Smith and glares at
him. The older man hesitates for a beat, then picks
it up...

                                            CUT TO:

108 EXT. "THE HILL." NIGHT.

A jockey limps up the long hill that leads to the
Molina Rojo.

The huge WINDMILL calls the riders like a siren song.
Blaring MEXICAN HORNS play over...

109 INT. MOLINA ROJO. NIGHT.

It's somewhere between a fiesta and a whorehouse.
Little jockeys dance with big hookers hitting them
somewhere in the middle of their chests. The place is
decorated with horse paraphernalia, particularly whips
and stirrups.

ANGLE. BAR AREA.

A huge woman puts a shot glass of tequila between her
tits and pushes her arms together, securing it in her
cleavage. Then she picks up one of the little jockeys
and turns him upside down, so his mouth is on the
glass and his feet are straight up in the air. All of
his comrades pound the bar as she suddenly bends
over, dumping the contents of the glass in his mouth
and landing him perfectly back on his feet. It's a
pretty impressive sight.

OTHER END OF THE BAR.

Red is all booze, no show. He slams back a shot of tequila and shudders for a beat.

CLOSER...

He's already pretty drunk. The Irish complexion has gone bright red and his eyes are starting to droop. Red picks up the glass and looks at it...

110 FLASHBACK. RACE TRACK.

He jostles side by side with George Woolf.

>   WOOLF
>   Oops — there's my hole Johnny. Gotta fly.

111 LIVE ACTION.

Red bangs down a new shot as his trainer's VOICE PLAYS OVER:

>   TRAINER'S VOICE (VO)
>   How the hell do you miss a hole like that.
>   Are you blind!

He looks, bemused at the tequila.

>   CUT TO:

112 INT. UPSTAIRS LATER.

The camera pushes up the long corridor where the women do their business. Half dressed jockeys (on the backs of half-dressed women) race down the hallway: disappearing "around the turn."

As the CAMERA PUSHES UP THE HALLWAY, Red's drunken VOICE gets progressively louder.

>   RED
>   There once was a princess from Siam.
>   Who was sitting here, sort of like I am.
>
>   I wined her and dined her,
>
>   and then I reclined her...
>
>   (beat)
>
>   Oh shit...what rhymes with Siam?

113 INT. WHORE'S ROOM.

Red lies back against the wall while the woman sits beside him on the bed.

                              WOMAN
            Tha's great! You make that up?

                              RED
            Pretty obvious, hunh.

                              WOMAN
            Tha's beautiful.

                              RED
                (drunk)
            ...You're beautiful.

                              WOMAN
            Oh — you don' have to say that. You pay me.

Red smiles. Downs the end of his last shot....

                              WOMAN
            You a lot bigger than the other jocks.

                              RED
                (winces)
            I know.

                              WOMAN
            No — tha's good.

                              RED
            In here, that's good.

Pause.

                              WOMAN
            So — you wanna...You know — get going?

Red pauses...thinks about it. The room swims a little.

                              RED
            Sure. Why not.

REVERSE ANGLE. OVER HER TO RED.

The woman stands up and faces Red lying on the bed.
From behind her, we see him lying back against the
pillow, gazing up at her. The woman reaches up and
pulls down the straps of her slip, letting it fall to
the floor. She stands topless in front of Red, her
naked back in the FOREGROUND of the FRAME.

TIGHTER.

Red looks at her with a sad tinge of irony. Instead
of lust there's something else...

HIS POV. NO WOMAN.

Instead of seeing her naked body, HALF THE FRAME IS COMPLETELY DARK. On the left side there is a lamp, the torn screen of the window and some peeling wallpaper. On the right side it is black.

114 FLASHBACK. TRAINER.

> TRAINER
> "How do you miss a hole like that?"

115 FLASHBACK. RACE.

George Woolf shoots through the hole that Red didn't see.

116 FLASHBACK. BOXING MATCH.

He is pummeled in his right eye. The socket has swollen shut.

117 LIVE ACTION. RED'S POV.

The image "pans" right to reveal the woman, now standing in the "good" side of the frame. Red is blind in his right eye.

OVER HER TO HIM.

> WOMAN
> You okay, angel?

> RED
> ...Yeah.

He touches the scar on the side of his face — runs his finger along the line where the cut used to be....

                                        CUT TO:

118 BLOOD.

Oozing from the back of a bull as brightly colored darts dangle from his skin.

WIDE ANGLE. BULLFIGHT.

It's the full spectacle: A jammed bullring...A hooting and jeering crowd...The matador makes a particularly dangerous cape pass...OLE!

ANGLE. CHARLES HOWARD.

He sits with Strubb and Giannini glancing down.
Howard scans the crowd, the floor, the sky, his
friends — anything not to look at the pageant in
front of him. Howard glances up.

ANGLE. BULLRING.

A "bandillero" approaches the bull with two more
darts, but these have been broken in half to make the
act more dangerous.

He runs toward the animal...

                                        CUT TO:

119 A CHILD. (LONG LENS) IN A VACANT LOT.

He kicks a soccer ball through a makeshift goal and
thrusts his hands in the air.

120 REVERSE ANGLE. EXT. BULLRING.

Howard stands watching him in the long arcade of the
bullring that faces out over Tijuana. With the bullfight on the other side of the thick stucco walls,
the cheers seem kind of muted: Ole...Ole...It sounds
like the ocean.

CLOSER.

He lights a cigarette. Howard takes a long drag and
leans against one of the arches and exhales slowly.
There is a VOICE next to him...

                    MARCELA (OS)
            (flawless American accent)
        You don't want to watch?

WIDER.

Marcela is standing beside him. She's even more beautiful than she was at the racetrack. The late afternoon sun makes her glow.

                    HOWARD
        No...Not really.

                    MARCELA
        I don't either.

121 She stares out over the city. Two boys kick their
deflated soccer ball back and forth across the dirt. A
man tinkers with his engine beneath the hood of a car.

                    MARCELA
          (shrugs)

     We can watch this instead.

She leans forward against the rail. The Spanish from
the boys mixes with their bursts of occasional laughter. The sun is going down.

                    MARCELA
     So what? They brought you down here to make
     you feel better? Is that it?

                    HOWARD
Sort of.

                    MARCELA
          (shakes her head)

     Those men. They think everything is fixed
     with a party.

Howard turns and looks at her

                    HOWARD
     Who are you?

                    MARCELA
          (smiles)

     Oh. I'm your second cousin.

          (extends her hand)

     Mucho Gusto.

She looks him in the eye. It's charged. Howard takes
her hand and shakes it.

                    MARCELA
     Isabella's my sister.

He just stares.

                    MARCELA
     You know — she's married to...

                    HOWARD
     No, no...I know.

Ole...Ole...

                    MARCELA
          So...
               (hesitates/means it)
          ...do you feel better?

                    HOWARD
          (beat)
     No. Not really.

                    MARCELA
     How could you?

          (all honesty/gentle)
     I mean, something like that. You can't stop
     feeling it, can you? I guess you just try to
     feel something else too.

CLOSER.

There's compassion in her voice. Empathy and kindness
but no fear. No fear to talk about it. He's been aching
to talk about it...A HUGE ROAR goes up from the crowd.

                    HOWARD
          Listen...
He stops himself.

                    MARCELA
     What?

          (pause...)
     Oh. You're right.

                    HOWARD
     What?

                    MARCELA
     No. You're right. Listen.

CLOSER

Howard cocks his head. Through the noise from the
crowd there is the distant RINGING OF CHURCH BELLS.
Marcela smiles...

                              CUT TO:

123 EXT. LA PATERA RANCHO. MORNING. BELLS are PEALING
in the cupola of the Rancho's private chapel.They
swing almost 360 degrees, exuberantly celebrating...

EASTER

_____

A long procession of Mexican women winds its way up the dirt road that leads to the chapel. The hymns are in Spanish; the women are dressed in white. It's a festival of rebirth.

124 SHOT. CORRAL.

This is a massive "land-grant" rancho and the barns and corrals are extensive. Marcela sits on horseback, graceful, comfortable in a gaucho jacket and flat-brimmed hat. She holds the lead rope of another horse, offering it to Howard.

> HOWARD
> Been twenty years since I've been on a horse...

> MARCELA
> He's not going to bite.

The horse tries to bite him.

> MARCELA
> Twice.

They both laugh. Howard looks at the horse.

> MARCELA (cont'd)
> (just a dash of innuendo)

> Don't worry. It's the kind of thing that comes right back to you.

Now he's looking at her. Howard takes the lead rope and swings himself high into the saddle...

> CUT TO:

125 A HILLSIDE. (LA PATERA RANCHO)

They ride across a high plane that overlooks the sea. There's no trail to speak of — just a wide open hill-side with scrub and chaparral. All at once, Marcela kicks her horse and starts up a long dirt road that heads toward a crest in the hill. Howard turns with her as the horses start to canter.

CLOSER.

He catches up with her and the speed increases slightly. As they head uphill, they begin to drive one another faster and faster...

First she takes the lead...Then him...Then her...Then him.

They both urge their horses as the caution leaves and a full gallop takes over. Pretty soon they are running together — the horses laboring, as they press harder and harder toward the top of the hill. It's more than a metaphor. By the time they get near the crest they are almost out of control and the animals fly toward the ridge, becoming suddenly airborne.

OTHER SIDE OF THE RIDGE.

They sail over the top of it...together. Charles and Marcela land simultaneously and begin to hurtle downhill toward the rich grassy plane that spreads out before them. They try to slow their horses, but they are literally out of control flying forty miles an hour toward the field at the bottom.

MOVING WITH THEM...

When they do start to slow it's a gradual thing: first one, then the other, then finally together...They come to a stop near the bottom and gather themselves before they turn and look at each other: both of them still breathing hard...

                                        CUT TO:

126 THE SAME CHURCH.

...only now there are WEDDING BELLS...

"SIX MONTHS LATER..."

Charles and Marcela emerge from the chapel to a hail of rice. He wears a morning suit. She has a white dress and veil.

FLASHBULBS.

They smile and pose. The CAMERA SWINGS with them as they head down the small hill toward a waiting horse cart. It's decorated in white ribbons. The wheels are white. The flowers are white. Even the horse pulling it is a beautiful white stallion. Charles and Marcela climb in and wave...

                                        CUT TO:

127 ANOTHER WHITE STALLION

Being slammed down into the dirt. His head is held by three pairs of hands. A rifle enters the frame.

CLOSER.

The horse is still thrashing around so the rifle tries to move with it — the barrel of the gun trying to steady itself on the center of the horse's head. All at once a VOICE splits the scene.

> SMITH (OS)
> I'll take him.

127A EXT. BARN AREA. (BACKSTRETCH) DAY.

Five men turn to see Tom Smith standing at the gate to the corral.

> TRAINER
> Get the hell out of here.

> SMITH
> I said, I'll take him. If yer gonna shoot him anyway, I'll save ya the bullet.

> TRAINER
> He's got a fractured foot.

> SMITH
> I'll take him anyway. They look at each other. This guy is nuts. The trainer shakes his head.

> TRAINER
> Fine.

He pulls back the gun and slowly the grooms begin to let go. The stallion stumbles to his feet, lifting the right foreleg. He's a huge horse with a big flowing mane. Even wounded the sight is majestic.

SHOT. SMITH.

He moves forward with a gentle shshhing sound. Smith takes the rope and leads him, limping away: back from the dead...

> CUT TO:

128 THE STARTING GATE.

Bursting open as twelve horses GALLOP toward camera. They fly down the chute of the turf course receding in an instant.

                         WALTER (VO)
             You want to win, or just own 'em.

129 EXT. TIJUANA BAZAAR. DAY.

The whole gang is there. Giannini. Walter. Strubb.
Howard.

Now, Marcela. The grandstand rises in the background.
It's dusk and the track has started to empty.

                         HOWARD
                 (beat/an old feeling)

             I want to win.

                         WALTER
             Well, you're gonna need a trainer before you
             buy horses.

                         GIANNINI
                 (thick Italian)

             Need two trainers. So you can fire one.

Everyone laughs.

                                            CUT TO:

130 EXT. BACKSTRETCH. DAY.

Charles walks with the entire group through the barn
area.

                         WALTER
             This is Randy Thatcher's barn. He trains
             about fifty, sixty ponies. Good fella too.
             Real horse person.

                         GIANNINI
             Real horse-shitter....

                         STRUBB
             Maybe you want a smaller barn. Somebody
             who's gonna take the time...

                         HOWARD
                 (points)

             Who's that?

HIS POV. BEYOND THE BACKSTRETCH.

A man stands way off in the distance among the scrub
and chaparral. Next to him, a large white stallion is
tied to the limb of a yucca tree. The head of the

animal looms above the brush like the prow of a ship. He stands motionless with his face in the wind.

> WALTER
> Oh that guy's a crackpot. Lives alone out there in the bushes.

> HOWARD
> What does he do?

> WALTER
> I don't know. Used to be a trainer...Or a farrier. Now he just takes care of that horse.

HOWARD'S POV. TOM SMITH.

He stands all alone against open scrub of Baja — a lost image of the West. Smith makes a motion with his hand and the lame horse starts to limp toward him.

> CUT TO:

131 A CAMPFIRE.

There's a long plume of red sparks as a hand adjusts some hobo stew.

WIDER.

Smith sits by the fire with the white stallion behind him. He warms his hands for a beat, then hears something and looks up.

REVERSE ANGLE.

A man in a business suit is emerging out of the darkness.

Howard steps into the ring of light.

> SMITH
> Howdy.

> HOWARD
> Hello.

He looks at Smith for a beat...a little awkwardly.

> SMITH
> Ya hungry.

> HOWARD
> Oh — no.... Thanks.

                         SMITH
          It's okay if you are. There's plenty.

                         HOWARD
               (smiles)
          I'm fine.

               (extends his hand)
          Charles Howard.

                         SMITH
          Tom Smith.

They shake. Howard looks over at the stallion. His
right foreleg is wrapped in muslin with "twigs"
sticking out of the top.

                         HOWARD
          What's in the bandage.

                         SMITH
          Oh that's hawthorne root. Increases circula-
          tion.

                         HOWARD
          What's wrong with him?

                         SMITH
          Ligament.

                         HOWARD
          Will he get better?

                         SMITH
          Already is a little.

Howard examines the horse — looks for a sign of the
healing.

                         HOWARD
          ...Will he race?

                         SMITH
          Oh no. Not that one.

                         HOWARD
          So, why are you fixing him?

SHOT. CHARLES HOWARD.

It's more than just a question. He has a burning need
to know.

_____

                    SMITH
          'Cause I can.

ON SMITH.

                    SMITH
          Every horse is good for somethin'. He could
          be a cart horse or a lead pony.

          He's still nice to look at.

          (beat)

          You don't throw a whole life away just cause
          it's banged up a little.

SHOT. HOWARD.

He hesitates...

                    HOWARD
          Is that coffee?

                    SMITH
          Yeah. It's bad though.

                    HOWARD
          You always tell the truth.

                    SMITH
          Try to.

Howard just looks at him for a beat.

                                             CUT TO:

132 WHAM!

A left hook catches Red squarely in the jaw. It staggers him backwards.

EXT. AVENIDA REVOLUCION. DUSK.

He's boxing again. The lip is puffy. The eye is
swollen shut. A makeshift ring has been erected outside a small saloon. SHOUTS and CHEERING pierce the
night in Spanish.

WHAM!

He gets spun around into the arms of spectators
pressed against the ropes. The crowd screams. Red
fights to clear his head. Wham, wham.... WHAM!

                                             CUT TO:

133 BLACK.

There is silence.... Then a gentle slapping sound.

SHOT. RED.

A hand is slapping his face. The fight is over and he's still getting hit.

REVERSE ANGLE.

Red opens his eyes to see George Woolf. The other jockey crouches over him.

> GEORGE
> C'mon Buddy. Wake up.

WIDER.

Red lies against the side of a building on the Avenida. The crowd is gone — the street is empty except for some trash.

Woolf kneels beside Red in a pool of cheap neon.

> RED
> (beat)
> Did I lose?

> GEORGE
> Oh, no. You clobbered him.

Red winces — the eye looks bad. He tries to get up — stumbles.

> GEORGE
> Easy.

> RED
> I'm fine.

DIFFERENT ANGLE.

He fights his way to his feet. Red starts to weave down the Avenida...

> GEORGE
> C'mon. Lemme buy you some turtle soup.

> RED
> I'm fine Georgie! Why don't you just go win a race or something?

He stumbles into a post — worst moment of all

                         RED
        ...Damn!

                       GEORGE
        Look, why don't we go to Sloan's and...

                         RED
        I don't need your help, George. And I sure
        as shit don't need your charity.

He says it like a dirty word — stumbles backwards out
of the light.

                         RED
        Just leave me alone, alright.

MOVING WITH HIM.

Red staggers out of the neon flicker, into near darkness at the end of the block. He presses his palm
against the bad eye, turning his back to hide it from
Woolf. After a beat, Red reaches into the pocket of
his trunks — pulls out a couple of coins. Looks at
them. Stuffs them back inside.

                      MCCULLOUGH
        They called them forgotten men, but it was
        really a misnomer. They were wanderers. Men
        who left a shattered life in search of some-
        thing new...

Red wanders totally out of the light, receding into
BLACK.

                                            CUT TO:

134 BLINDING WHITE LIGHT.... EXT. ST. LOUIS STREET. DAY.

He carries all that he owns. The street is lined with
victims of the era staring straight ahead: Blank.
Idle. Frustrated. Broken.

                      MCCULLOUGH
        Men who left something new, desperately in
        search of something old...

135 EXT. PARK BENCH. CHICAGO. DUSK.

Red still reads. The pillow case sits beside him open
on the bench while he forces himself through a volume
of Emerson, in the fading light.

                    MCCULLOUGH
          Simple things were suddenly precious. Food.
          Shelter. Clothing. Water....

**136 BLACK AND WHITE PHOTO. A BREADLINE (PITTS-
BURGH)...**

It's huge. The CAMERA PANS across the still photograph until it reaches the end of the block. IT SUD-
DENLY ERUPTS INTO FULL COLOR, as Red walks by, refus-
ing to join.

                    MCCULLOUGH
          All at once, staying alive took the place of
          living.

137 INT. BOXING RING. A SALOON. NIGHT.

He's fighting again. Red falls forward into a clinch.
The clinch becomes...

**138 A MARATHON DANCE.... Red pulls a nearly comatose
woman across the floor.**

                    MCCULLOUGH
          In the depths of their despair, the slight-
          est diversion was embraced...Prohibition was
          repealed, movie attendance set records and
          even gambling was legalized, as horse racing
          returned to American soil for the first time
          in fourteen years.

139 OMITTED

140 EXT. SARATOGA RACE TRACK. DAY.

It is the grand dame of race tracks. Looming spires.
Gabled roofs. It looks like a cross between someone's
mansion and a baseball stadium. The place is almost
empty as a scattered crowd watches the early morning
workouts.

141 ANGLE. CLUBHOUSE BOXES.

Howard sits in his box with Marcela and the newly
hired Tom Smith. The workouts play out in front of
them. Howard sports a snappy new suit. Smith wears
his usual Stetson hat.

                    SMITH
          It ain't just the speed — it's the heart.
          You want something that's not afraid to

compete — something that's not gonna quit on
ya. Half o' these horses are just show
ponies. You want a horse that's not gonna
run from a fight.

                    HOWARD
          And how do you find that?

142 EXT. BACKSTRETCH.

Red stands outside one of the barns, shoving an old
Racing Form at a local trainer.

                    RED
          Look — I won the Robles Handicap...I was
          second at the Tijuana Derby. I won the
          Manzanita Oaks. You know that used to be a
          stakes race...

                    TRAINER
          I know — well, look...we'll call you.

                    RED
          I woulda won T.J. but the piece of shit
          lugged out on me.

                    TRAINER
          Sounds great. We'll let you know.

Red looks him in the eye — deep breath...

                    RED
          Look...
             (sighs)

                    RED (cont'd)
          I can even work 'em out in the morning
          or...hot-walk 'em if you need me to.

                    TRAINER
             (beat)
          Really? You'll hot-walk 'em?

                                        CUT TO:

142A DUSK.

Red is "hot-walking." He leads the horse round and
round in a concentric circle while the animal is
hitched to a large carousel, much like a drying rack
for clothes...

RED

    ...Goddamn sack o' crap old plater. Prob'ly the fastest you're gonna run in your stupid life, you piece o' shit old glue-pot....

REVERSE ANGLE. TOP OF THE SHED ROWS.

Tom Smith is headed the other direction, carrying some tack. He hears the cursing and stops for a beat.

HIS POV.

Tom looks at this strange hot-walker berating the horse as he leads him in a circle. Red literally talks a mile a minute, growing in intensity with each new revolution.

ANGLE. RED.

He looks up and stops. Their eyes catch for a beat. Red stares at him then glances down as he continues to walk the horse.

SHOT. SMITH.

He takes it in for a beat then heads down the shed rows...

                                CUT TO:

143 EXT. RACETRACK "THE GAP." DAWN.

It is early morning workouts and the horses are being led through the mist. The Gap is the local market-place of a racetrack: the area at the top of the stretch, between the track and the barns, where jock-eys, trainers, clockers and agents congregate at first light.

UP-ANGLE. HORSES.

Emerging through the mist they look otherworldy — huge looming creatures like Cortez might have seen them. Every now and then a lone horse THUNDERS around the turn finishing his workout. The clockers and trainers nod and take note.

ANGLE. TOM SMITH.

He stands by the rail without a watch. Everyone else stares down at the fractions — measuring the horses by fifths of a second. Smith looks at their feet, their rumps, their withers, their eyes. He takes a glance at each horse as it goes by him on its way to the morning workout. All at once Smith freezes.

CLOSER. (OVERCRANKED)

Smith literally seems to lift up. His posture changes. His eyes widen. Smith recoils in some instantaneous reaction, as instinctive as any of the animals he's looking at. He's seen it.

HIS POV.

A smallish bay colt is walking toward him through the mist. All four feet are bandaged. The gait is uneven. The head bobs up and down. Still the animal seems to have a power — an intensity about him oblivious to any injury. He lifts his head and looks Smith right in the eye.

> MCCULLOUGH
> The first time he saw Seabiscuit, the colt was walking through the fog at five in the morning. Smith would say later that the horse looked right through him: as if to say "What the hell are you looking at? Who do you think you are?"

Seabiscuit jerks away from his lead rider and moves toward Smith. They stand face to face at the rail.

> MCCULLOUGH
> He was a small horse. Barely fifteen hands. He was hurting too. There was a limp in his walk — a wheezing when he breathed...Smith didn't pay attention to that. He was looking the horse in the eye.

Seabiscuit stares at him for a beat, then decides he's had enough. He wheels away from Smith on his own time, and heads off into the fog.

AS HE WALKS AWAY....

> MCCULLOUGH
> Everything was wrong with him. He was too short. His legs were stubby. His knees couldn't straighten, leaving him in a perpetual semi-crouch. The horse had all the aerodynamic construction of cinderblock and had at various times in his life been compared to a duck, a frog, and a milk wagon.

                              SMITH
                    (half whisper)
          Hot damn.

Seabiscuit disappears into the fog just as Red
Pollard emerges on foot, walking a horse in the other
direction.

                          MCCULLOUGH
               He was a very unlikely champion. He came
               from good breeding but you would never real-
               ly know it....

144 INT. FOALING STALL. FLASHBACK.

A newborn colt is pulled from its mother as she lies
prone in the straw. His fur is wet...He's fresh to
the world.

                            GROOM
               Puny little runt.

                          MCCULLOUGH
               He was the son of Hard Tack, sired by the
               mighty horse Man O' War, but the breeding did
               little to impress anyone at Claiborne farms.

145 EXT. PADDOCK...

Several men watch the new foal running in the open
pasture with its mother.

                        FARM MANAGER
                    (dispassionately)
          Get rid of him.

146 SHOT. RAIL FENCE.

The brood mare (Seabiscuit's mother) WHINNIES/SCREAMS
while the CAMERA whip-pans to Seabiscuit, being led
into a horse trailer.

                          MCCULLOUGH
               At six months he was shipped off to train
               with the legendary trainer Sunny Fitzsimmons
               who developed a similar opinion of the colt.

147 EXT. FITZSIMMONS' STABLE.

Fitzsimmons, crippled and bent with a back disorder,
examines the yearling as he is led into a stall.

_____

> FITZSIMMONS
> Is that a race horse or a lead pony?

148 EXT. FITZSIMMONS' PADDOCK.

Seabiscuit rolls playfully in the grass.

> MCCULLOUGH
> The judgement wasn't helped by his gentle
> nature. Where his sire had been a fierce,
> almost violent competitor, Seabiscuit took to
> sleeping for huge chunks of the day and
> enjoyed lolling for hours under the boughs
> of the juniper trees.

He rolls over in the grass.

149 INT. STALLS.

> MCCULLOUGH
> His other great talent was eating. Though
> half the size of other colts, Seabiscuit
> could frequently eat twice as much.

A groom looks at an empty feed bucket in disbelief.

150 EXT. PADDOCK...

Fitzsimmons watches while Seabiscuit grazes like a
cow. The other horses are running in the field. He's
having an afternoon snack.

> MCCULLOUGH
> Fitzsimmons decided the horse was lazy and
> felt sure he could train the obstinance out
> of him.

151 EXT. TRAINING TRACK.

Seabiscuit stands saddled with an exercise rider
along the rail.

> FITZSIMMONS
> (handing him a whip)

> I want you to hit him as many times as you
> can over a quarter of a mile.

LONG LENS. WORKOUT.

The rider does just that...literally beats the horse
down the stretch as Seabiscuit runs toward the wire.

> MCCULLOUGH
>
> When he didn't improve, they decided the
> colt was incorrigible.

152 OMITTED

153 ANGLE. TOP OF THE CHUTE.

Seabiscuit is held in position next to a much larger
horse.

> MCCULLOUGH
>
> They made him a training partner to "better"
> horses, forcing him to lose head to head
> duels to boost the confidence of the other
> animal....

SHOT. MIDWORKOUT.

The exercise rider pulls back on Seabiscuit's reins
letting the larger horse take the lead.

> MCCULLOUGH
>
> When they finally did race him, he did just
> what they had trained him to do...He lost.

154 EXT. COUNTRY FAIRGROUNDS. (RAIN)

SEABISCUIT LOSES by twelve lengths in the driving rain.

> MCCULLOUGH
>
> By the time he was a three year old,
> Seabiscuit was running in two cheap claiming
> races a week. Soon he grew as bitter and
> angry as his sire Hard Tack had been....

155 OMITTED

156 INT. STALL.

It's a prison riot. Seabiscuit kicks the door, rears
back against the far wall. Thrashes around with a
feed bucket in his mouth.

> MCCULLOUGH
>
> He was sold for the rock bottom price of two
> thousand dollars.

157 EXT. STALL

It takes three grooms to move him out. They have a
twitch on his lip and restraints on his back legs.
Nobody goes near there.

> MCCULLOUGH
> And of course it all made sense...

158 OMITTED

159 SHOT. WINNER'S CIRCLE.

A JET BLACK HORSE stands proudly for a photograph.

> MCCULLOUGH
> Champions were large. They were sleek. They were without imperfection...

SEABISCUIT is led behind him, pulling and jerking, toward the barns...

> MCCULLOUGH
> This horse ran as they had always expected him to.

160 INT. STALL.

He rears up on his back legs and literally pounds away at the wooden slats. The rage is overwhelming. Seabiscuit grabs a feed bucket in his teeth and swings it violently.

REVERSE ANGLE.

Charles, Marcela and Tom Smith stand at the door to the stall watching the spectacle. The place is half wrecked.

> HOWARD
> And what exactly is it you like?

Seabiscuit rears up — kicks the back wall.

> SMITH
> Got spirit.

> MARCELA
> I'll say.

There is a long, screaming WHINNY. They all look at him.

> HOWARD
> Can he be ridden?

> SMITH
> Sure.

CRASH...

SMITH

Eventually.

161 EXT. BACKSTRETCH LATER.

Four grooms are wrestling Seabiscuit to a standstill.
A racing saddle is on his back. A jockey swaggers
toward him.

SMITH

Listen, he can be a little touchy...

JOCKEY

Yeah, yeah...I get it.

SMITH

No — honestly...

He strides up to the horse and reaches right for the
saddle. Seabiscuit whirls on him and tries to stomp
him to death.

JOCKEY

Jesus Christ!

He turns and tries to get out of the way, but
Seabiscuit grabs a mouthful of shirt and rips the
silks off his back.

JOCKEY

Ahhh!

He turns and runs down the backstretch missing half
his clothes. The grooms wrestle Seabiscuit to a
standstill while he flails around with the jockey's
silks in his mouth.

ON SMITH. (HAND HELD)

He rolls his eyes and starts walking away. The CAMERA
FOLLOWS him as he heads to the top of the shed rows
muttering. Smith turns the corner and is about to
head away from the barns when he sees something and
suddenly stops.

HIS POV.

Red Pollard is engaged in a fistfight with four stable hands. His hands are cocked, his feet planted
wide as he screams a challenge to the other men.

                         RED
          C'mon! Right now! I'm not afraid o' you.
          I'll take all you sons o' bitches.

ANGLE. SMITH.

He looks at Red fighting with four grooms...Then he
turns and looks back at Seabiscuit, fighting with
four grooms of his own. Smith pauses and thinks for a
beat...

                                         CUT TO:

162 THE STABLE DOOR.

Red stands in the blinding light staring inside the
stall.

There is a SCREAM/WHINNY and the sound of kicking.

WIDER. OUTSIDE THE STALL DOOR.

Smith watches from a couple of feet away. All at once
Red reaches down and unlatches the bottom half of the
door. Smith makes a slight motion forward but stops
himself...

163 INT. STALL.

Seabiscuit is frothing at Red from the other side of
the room. He has ripped up the place...Destroyed a
feed bag...Punched several holes in the wooden slats.
He presses himself against the far corner, snorting
and breathing hard, a weird posture for a horse.

                         RED
          It's okay, Pops.

REVERSE ANGLE.

Seabiscuit WHINNIES and kicks the wood. Red moves
forward slowly.

                         RED
             (softly)

          It's okay Pops. I'm not afraid o' you. I
          know what you're all about.

The horse snorts louder...backs up against the wall
and kicks it hard. Red pauses, just looks at him.

                         RED
          Sure. I know.

They stare at each other like that for a beat when Red reaches into his pocket and takes out an old apple. It's wrapped in a handkerchief, turning brown...

> RED (cont'd)
> Here ya go.

He extends the apple and Seabiscuit looks at him: a Mexican standoff. After a beat, he takes a step forward.

CLOSER.

For an instant, it seems as if he's going to bite the apple but he doesn't. Seabiscuit just reaches forward with his long brown muzzle and smells Red's hand. Then he turns away, and leaves the apple behind.

CLOSE UP. RED.

He stares at his own match and smiles slightly.

> CUT TO:

164 BLUE SKY.

Red springs into it wearing bright yellow jockey silks. He lands in the saddle of...

SEABISCUIT standing on the edge of the Saratoga TRAINING TRACK being held by a SINGLE groom.

WIDER.

Charles and Marcela watch from the side of the track in disbelief. Smith stands at the bridle of the horse.

> SMITH
> (introductions)
> Red Pollard — Mr. and Mrs. Howard.

Howard moves cautiously toward the horse.

> HOWARD
> (shakes quickly)
> Yeah...Hi. How do you do.

> RED
> Pleasure.

Howard clears away, quickly.

                         SMITH
          Why don't you just breeze him around one
          turn. Give the folks a look.

                         RED
          Great.

              (beat)

          Does he breeze?

                         SMITH
          We'll find out.

                                              CUT TO:

165 THE TRACK.

Seabiscuit is all over the place. He lugs. He props.
He runs wide in the turn. He flings his head around
wildly as he veers out from the rail, coming into the
stretch. It's a wrestling match between him and Red
as he fights to gain control of the horse...

166 EXT. STANDS. LATER...

Smith sits with Howard and Marcela in their box.

                         MARCELA
          Seems pretty fast.

                         SMITH
          Yeah — in every direction.

Howard picks up his binoculars — looks toward the
track...

                         SMITH (cont'd)
          Look...There's horses with better breedin'.
          And there's faster horses. And there's defi-
          nitely bigger horses. Hell, he's so beat up
          it's hard to tell what he's like, but...

167 HOWARD'S POV.

Instead of looking at Seabiscuit he is staring at
Red. The jockey sits tall in the saddle — knees to
his chest — almost too tall to be a race rider...

                         SMITH
          I just can't help feelin' they got him so
          screwed up runnin' in a circle, he's forgot-
          ten what he was born to do.

Howard lowers the glasses — hears him.

> SMITH (cont'd)
> He just needs to learn how to be a horse
> again.

> HOWARD
> Well how do you do that?

CUT TO:

168 OMITTED

169 COUNTRY ROAD. UPSTATE NEW YORK.

Fall has exploded in a riot of color. Red sits atop
Seabiscuit at the head of a long dirt road. Off into
the distance, FARMLAND stretches and rolls like the
ocean. It's an odd sight: A race horse and a jockey
in the middle of a country road — like a long race to
nowhere. Smith holds onto the bridle.

> RED
> How far do you want me to take him?

> SMITH
> Till he stops.

RED'S POV.

The road seems endless.

> RED
> That seems like a pretty good ride.

> SMITH
> Hope so.

WIDER.

Red looks at him. Smith smiles, then CLUCKS and SLAPS
the horse on the rump, lurching Seabiscuit into action.
The animal bolts forward as Red hangs on to the mane...

MOVING WITH THEM.

Within three strides they've reached a full gallop.
Red settles over the withers as the two of them begin
to fly through a quarter mile of countryside. The
autumn leaves whizz by in a blur as Seabiscuit's
hooves POUND over the hard packed road.

ON RED.

He settles down in the saddle a little bit. A familiar smile crosses his face. Red flattens his back and
actually seems to take a deep breath, as they bank
around a gentle turn, hugging tight to the white rail
fence.

                    RED
          C'mon Pops. Lemme see what you got.

Red clicks twice and urges with his hands. All at
once Seabiscuit accelerates, lengthening his stride
and devouring huge sections of country road. Red
balances himself and leans forward a little more.
This horse has power.

                    RED
          Whoa...

AERIAL. MOVING WITH THEM...

He's tight to the withers now, pressed up against the
horse's neck. Red flings his hands away from him,
syncopating to Seabiscuit's stride. They eat up huge
chunks of road together, sailing over fifteen feet in
a single stride. They fly past millpond...Thunder
over a wooden bridge...Swoop down into a small dip in
the road and come exploding out of the other side.
The colors on the fall trees whizz together around
them like a crazy piece of spin-art. This is a horse
race in heaven.

SHOT. MARCELA, HOWARD, AND TOM SMITH.

They stand silently by their car at the head of the
country road. Howard glances down at his watch.

                    MARCELA
          Well, at least he wasn't expensive.

                    HOWARD
          No. That's true.

RESUME — AERIAL SHOT. COUNTRY ROAD.

RED IS LAUGHING now. They are flying through the
countryside at almost fifty miles an hour — the reins
loose in his fingers. His arms are pumping back and
forth like he's trying to grab the road in front of
him.

                    RED
          God-DAMMIT you are an amazing animal!

They fly through a covered bridge and burst out on the other side. Red lets out a WAR WHOOP as a flock of birds erupts in front of them. He's alive again. They both are.

> RED
> C'mon, Buddy. Don't stop. Don't ever stop!

They bank hard around a bend in the road as the CAMERA BEGINS TO LOOSEN SLIGHTLY. Man and animal fly through the countryside together — conquering it — literally consuming it. THE CAMERA PULLS BACK WIDER, as they THUNDER into the distance leaving a huge cloud of dust in their wake. Seabiscuit and Red bank to the right, drive up a small rise in the road, and disappear on the other side as we....

> DISSOLVE TO:

170 A TRAIN...

Flying through the countryside at DUSK. It's an image from childhood memory. Dining car. Baggage car. Sleeper car. Club Car. And at the back, a private coach.

171 OMITTED

172 EXT. OUTSIDE THE CAR....

Red shivers, smokes a cigarette, hunching against the cold. He paces to the extent that one can between the cars. The door opens behind him.

DIFFERENT ANGLE.

Marcela sticks her head out. She seems to be freezing.

> MARCELA
> You know you can come inside.

> RED
> Oh no. I'm fine out here.

> MARCELA
> Yeah, you look it.

Red has tossed the cigarette. He's blowing on his hands.

> RED
> (beat)
> Really. I'm fine.

Marcela hesitates but he isn't moving. Finally, she nods, then turns and heads inside. Red watches her recede into the warmth of the car as the CAMERA pushes past him onto the door...

                                              CUT TO:

173 ANOTHER DOOR...

Opening in front of us. The GREAT ROOM at Ridgewood spreads out before the CAMERA. A fire is roaring. It's warm and solid. Red walks into THE SHOT, looking up at the opulence of the huge log home. He's seen it before but it's been a long time. Red carries his pillow case and his tack: a beat-up saddle...a pair of old boots...

JUMP TO:

174 INT. RIDGEWOOD DINING ROOM.

They sit at a long wooden table. Howard, Marcela, Smith, and Red. It's raining outside. There's a warm bowl of soup.

CLOSER. RED.

The smells waft up at him — almost intoxicating. Red glances down at it. Pulls himself out of the moment.

                          HOWARD
              It's okay.

WIDER.

Red looks up. Howard is staring at him from the end of the table.

                           RED
               I'm not really that hungry.

                          HOWARD
                Sure you're not.

                           RED
               It's just...a lot of food.

SHOT. HOWARD.

He nods...

                          HOWARD
                     (gently)
               It's okay. I'd rather have you strong than thin.

                                                              79

Red looks at him startled. Howard gets it — gets all of it.

Smith seems startled too — this guy knows more about racing than he thought. Red hesitates, then reaches for his spoon. Slowly, he dips it in the soup.

CLOSER...RED.

He lifts it up — the steam rises. When he does taste it, it's slow and deliberate, almost ritualistic, like he wants it to last forever...

>   MCCULLOUGH
>   They called it relief but it was a lot more
>   than that.

175 FULL SHOT. AN NRA BANNER.

The National Recovery Act. There is a huge black eagle: the symbol of recovery. The slogan is inscribed in 30's script: "A New Deal for American Families"

176 BLACK AND WHITE NEWSREEL. RELIEF OFFICE.

Families line up, waiting to receive assistance.

>   MCCULLOUGH
>   It had dozens of names: NRA, WPA, CCC, PWA,
>   but it really came down to just one thing...

NEWSREEL. FDR.

He waves with patrician smile and cigarette holder.

>   MCCULLOUGH
>   For the first time, in a long time, someone
>   cared...

177 SHOT. RIDGEWOOD. DUSK.

The mountains loom in the distance. Smoke pours out of the chimney.

>   MCCULLOUGH
>   For the first time in a long time, you were
>   no longer alone....

178 INT. RIDGEWOOD. SECOND FLOOR LANDING.

Howard reaches the top of the stairs and looks down the hall.

HIS POV.

A slit of light is coming from a room at the end.

SHOT. HOWARD.

He hesitates then heads softly toward it...

CUT TO:

179 INSERT. GARAGE DOOR.

A key opens the old padlock.

180 SHOT. GARAGE AREA.

Howard's old race cars are wheeled out into the fading light. It's been a while and they seem like relics.

181 INT. GARAGE.

The doors to the stalls are thrown open. Smith watches as a couple of grooms bring in bales of straw...

182 EXT. GARAGE AREA.

Seabiscuit is led into his new home, now fully restored to a stable. The cars are out. The horse has returned....

183 INT. FRANKIE'S ROOM.

Howard stands at the entrance, staring. A soft light is coming from the corner.

REVERSE ANGLE.

It's still empty. The bed is made. The copy of Flash Gordon lies untouched beside the pillow. Howard crosses over and picks up the book again. He glances out of Frankie's window.

183A HIS POV.

It's blue outside. A dim light is coming from the barn.

183B INT. EMPTY HORSE STALL.

Red reads by a single flashlight. He lies in the straw with a jacket pulled up over him. Red still squints with his one good eye. He reaches out...turns the page, as...

184 SMITH rolls over to face the sky. A saddle blanket is folded under his head as a pillow. He stares straight ahead.

HIS POV. THE SKY.

The stars are back. Millions of them. They swirl and dance...sing at him in full CGI splendor.

ON SMITH.

There's the sound of A WHINNY.... A KICK....

CUT TO:

185 EXT. STABLE (GARAGE) AREA. THE NEXT MORNING.

He's RAMPAGING again. Smith stands outside the stable, just listening...

186 LATER...

Smith carries a small goat from the barnyard. Howard steps into the shot.

> HOWARD
> ...Goat racing?

> SMITH
> Oh, no. Just tryin' to calm him down a lit-
> tle. The smart ones hate bein' alone all the
> time.

Seabiscuit SCREAMS/KICKS inside the building...

> SMITH
> Sometimes another animal just soothes 'em a
> bit.

Howard nods as Smith starts into the stables....

CUT TO:

187 THE GOAT. MOMENTS LATER....

As it comes FLYING OUT OF THE STALL WINDOW. It gets flung a good fifteen feet through the air, landing on the grass. The goat springs BLEATING to its feet, and takes off toward the barnyard.

SHOT. SMITH.

He watches the tiny animal run for its life.

CUT TO:

188 THE CORRAL.

Smith leads a HUGE yellow plow horse up the path toward the stables. At 4000 pounds, it is the size of a Clydesdale, the width of a car. Try flinging this thing.

189 INT. STALL.

Seabiscuit looks up. He backs up against the far wall as the huge plow horse lumbers in and plops down in the straw, eating its bed.

190 EXT. STABLE LATER.

Marcela walks by. Smith leans against the wall, whittling.

IT'S QUIET INSIDE.

> MARCELA
> What'd you do?

Smith motions for her to "take a look." Marcela peeks through a window.

HER POV.

Seabiscuit is sleeping in the straw side by side with Pumpkin.

Next to them are a dog and three rabbits....

CUT TO:

191 INT. WILLETS PRESBYTERIAN CHURCH (HOWARD FAMILY PEW).

It looks a lot like the stall. Howard sits next to his thirty year old wife, a sixty year old cowboy, a five foot seven jockey, and SAM, his African American stablehand.

192 EXT. TANFORAN RACE TRACK. DAY.

The place is closed except for some workouts...Several horses are breezing at various locations around the track.

193 "THREE WEEKS LATER..."

FULL SHOT. VIEWING STAND.

Smith stands down by the rail giving Red some last minute instructions. Howard and Marcela watch nervously from the stand behind them.

> SMITH
> Okay. Don't break him or anything but we
> gotta see what he's got. Take him to the
> five and a half pole and turn him loose.

                         RED
          Turn him loose?

                       SMITH
          Yeah son. He's a race horse.

Red nods in anticipation and starts to jog the
Biscuit down the track. The jog turns into a...

                                      CUT TO:

GALLOP.

Red reaches the five and a half pole then clucks to
start the workout. The Biscuit bolts into a run, legs
flailing in every direction.

ANGLE STAND.

Smith clicks his stopwatch and stares through his
binoculars. After a moment or two he winces...

                       MARCELA
          How's he look?

                       SMITH
          Asleep.

SHOT. RED.

He's driving the Biscuit with his hands, trying to
coax a little more out of him. The horse lugs wide
into the lane and seems to be laboring down the backstretch.

                         RED
          C'mon Pops. I know you got more than this.

Red flashes the stick in front of his eye but the
horse only seems to snort. He tries driving harder
with his hands.

ANGLE. SMITH.

He lowers his binoculars and turns away in disgust.
Smith gazes up into a nearby pine tree.

SHOT. RED AND THE BISCUIT.

He drives hard in Seabiscuit's withers almost begging
the animal to perform.

                      RED (cont'd)
          C'mon Pops. Give it to me...

_____

OVER THEM — TO THE FAR TURN...

They labor out of the backstretch, when all at once, another horse comes into view. He's breezing at a pretty good clip somewhere near the quarter pole.

CLOSE UP. SEABISCUIT.

He sees the other animal then yanks at the bit and pins back his ears. Seabiscuit explodes in a sudden display of raw power.

                    RED (cont'd)
          Jesus Christ.

ANGLE. VIEWING STAND.

Marcela and Howard are watching through their binoculars.

                    MARCELA
          Oh my gosh.

Smith glances back from his pine tree. Suddenly lifts up his glasses.

ANGLE. SEABISCUIT.

He has taken a bead on the other horse and is gaining ground at a rate of two to one. The Biscuit banks hard through the turn and starts to devour the race track in front of him. The other horse is moving pretty well but the Biscuit digs deep and literally crushes his opponent. By the time they hit the home stretch, they are even and half a furlong later Seabiscuit is three lengths in front. Red hangs on like he's riding an errant missile as they hurtle toward the finish line behind a cloud of dust.

ANGLE. SMITH.

He turns to Howard and Marcela.

                    SMITH
          Sometimes they just hanker fer a little com-
          petition.

Howard nods and looks down the stretch.

                                        CUT TO:

194-201 OMITTED

202 OMITTED

Seabiscuit is eyeing the gray already — chewing the bit and starting to breathe harder. The other horse starts to make his way out of the paddock and Smith has to hold him back by the bridle.

                                          CUT TO:

207B THE POST PARADE.

Red walks in the back of the pack eyeing the gray ahead of him. After a little while the horse starts to jog and Red follows suit, bringing Seabiscuit to a gentle lope...

207C FULL SHOT. STARTING GATE.

The gray is loaded in directly toward the camera. The CAMERA SUDDENLY RACKS to Red and Seabiscuit directly behind him.

OVER RED...

He watches the other horse load in. The starters drag him toward the gate. Shut the rear gate behind him.

RAKED. THE STARTING GATE.

Red is just being loaded in when he hears a familiar voice beside him.

                    WOOLF
          Hey Red. Kinda little ain't he?

He turns to see Woolf grinning at him from a couple of stalls away.

                    RED
          (smiles)
        He's gonna look a lot smaller in a second.

                    WOOLF
          I got five bucks says he don't.

                    RED
        Done.

He yanks down his goggles and looks straight ahead. They settle over the saddle. The flag is up...

207D FULL SHOT. STARTING GATE.

They burst INTO FRAME at the SOUND OF THE BELL. Nine horses fly through at once.

OVER RED...IN THE RACE.

He settles in behind the gray, stalking him from two
lengths back. Red sits just outside of the horse's right
flank, maintaining an even distance the entire time.

CLOSE UP. RED.

His eyes are focused on the other jockey, waiting for
the slightest move, the subtlest twitch. Red watches
his hold on the reins, poised to move whenever he
does.

WIDER. BEHIND RED...

The two horses run smoothly — evenly, like planets
locked in an alignment. Red sits motionless on top of
Seabiscuit when all at once a chestnut colt bolts
through on the rail and cuts right in front of Red,
almost ramming Seabiscuit in the process. Red checks
sharply to keep from clipping heels as the other
horse takes off down the track.

ON RED...

                    RED
          You son of a bitch!

REVERSE ANGLE. BEHIND SEABISCUIT.

Red flings the reins and takes off after the horse
that almost fouled him, cursing the entire time. The
two horses fly through the pack together leaving the
gray in their wake. It looks a little like a car
chase.

                    RED
          Piece of shit bastard.

CLOSE UP. SEABISCUIT.

He locks in on his brand new adversary giving a massive charge. Pretty soon both horses are eight
lengths in front of the pack locked in a blazing
speed duel.

207E ANGLE SMITH.

He stands at the top of an aisle in the grandstand
next to some ushers.

                    SMITH
          What the hell is he doing?

207F WIDE SHOT. THE HORSE RACE.

It can't be contained all in one frame. Red and the
other horse are entering the turns and the CAMERA has
to PAN twelve lengths back to the rest of the pack.
They're burning out the engine.

UP ANGLE. RED AND OTHER HORSE.

He catches up to him in the turn and leans on him
toward the inside.

                    RED
          (screams over the noise)
     There! You like getting shut off at the
     rail!

                    OTHER JOCKEY
          (screaming back)
     Get offa me!

                    RED
     Sack of shit...

LONG LENS. TOP OF THE STRETCH.

The two horses fly out the turn together oblivious to
the cavalry charge that has mounted behind them. No
sooner have they cleared frame than a wall of horses
appears behind them led of course by the gray.
Seabiscuit and the other horse begin to tire in the
stretch as the pack pours on a huge burst of strength.

SHOT. SMITH.

He looks down at the ground, shaking his head.

SHOT. RED.

He tries to drive Seabiscuit but it's no use. First
he gets passed by the gray then a couple of roans.
Then a chestnut colt. Then a black...

207G ANGLE. THE HOWARDS' BOX.

They lower their binoculars and look in pain toward
the finish line.

207H THEIR POV. THE FINISH.

The gray flies by first. Then a group of three led by
George Woolf. Then four more. Then a second or two
before Seabiscuit labors home, mopping up the rear.

_____

SHOT. SMITH.

He shakes his head in disgust. Smith glances at the usher next to him who shrugs and tears up a win ticket...

CUT TO:

207I EXT. "SADDLING PADDOCK." NIGHT ...

The crowds are gone and a few workers rake the earth of the saddling area.

>   SMITH
>   What the hell were you thinking?

ANGLE RED SMITH AND HOWARD.

They stand off to the side of the paddock at the top of the steps. A horse is being led back to the barns in the distance.

>   RED
>   He fouled me. What am I s'posed to do? Let
>   him get away with that?

>   SMITH
>   Yeah, if he's forty to one .

>   RED
>   He almost put me in the rail!

>   SMITH
>   Well, did he?

Red looks away seething. Howard kicks at the pavement.

>   SMITH
>   Look. We had a plan...

>   RED
>   He fouled me Tom! What am I supposed to do.
>   He cut me off!

They just look at him.

>   RED
>   HE FOULED ME!

Red is yelling. They all stand frozen for a beat.

>   HOWARD
>   (slowly)
>   Son...What are you so mad at?

CLOSE UP RED.

He almost opens his mouth to respond but the answer
stays inside him. The three men stand frozen for a
beat. Red whirls away.

                                              CUT TO:

207J NIGHTTIME.

THE BRIDGE over ARROYO SECO is lit up like a jewel.
In the distance, THE GREEN HOTEL sits upon a bluff
with its Victorian domes and turrets.

RAKED ANGLE. FROM THE BRIDGE.

Red stands at the very edge, looking over the side.
His breathing is heavy. He clutches the rail. The
whole thing seems like a suicidal cliche. It all
looks impossible but still...

UP ANGLE. RED. FROM THE ABYSS.

He stares down into the arroyo, looking into the
dark. Weighing his decision. A moment or two goes by
when Red suddenly reaches out of frame and hoists
something onto the rail.

CLOSER.

It's the pillow case. The sharp corners of his
father's books cut angles into the bag. Red balances
it there for a beat, not sure what to do. There is a
voice to his right.

                    MAN (O.S.)
          I'll take it.

ON THE BRIDGE.

Red turns to see a man (hobo, vagabond whatever)
standing further down the bridge. He looks out at Red
from a faint pool of light.

                    MAN
          What's that?

                    RED
          (pauses)
          Books.

                    MAN
          Well — if you're gonna toss 'em anyway.

ANGLE. RED.

> Red hesitates, not quite sure what to do. He
> stands there, silent for a beat, then...

                    RED
Fine.

DIFFERENT ANGLE

Red holds out the bag. (He's not going to walk.) The
man comes over and takes his booty. He opens the pillowcase and looks inside.

                    MAN
Wow. There's a lot of stuff in here.

>   (pulls out a book)

What's this?

                    RED
>   (glances at it/beat)

...Alexander Dumas.

                    MAN
What?

                    RED
Three Musketeers.

                    MAN
>   (staring at it impressed)

Oh. Sheesh.

>   (pulls out another)

What's this one?

                    RED
>   (looks at it — hesitates)

Leaves of Grass. Look do you read?

                    MAN
A little.

>   (stares at it)

So — it's about grass?

                    RED
No. It's about...

He stops. Remembers what it's about. Red looks down at the worn-out volume....

                              MAN
          What?

                              RED
                    (quieter)
          Well — It's about...

                                        CUT TO:

207K GRASS.

Lots of it. The lawns of SAN MARINO spread out before the camera blue-green in the moonlight. The mansions have all gone to bed for the night, even though their lawns are being sprinkled in the cool of the evening. After a beat or two, the image of a man carrying a pillow case walks into frame, lugging his burden away from the CAMERA. Red recedes down the sidewalk — almost Chaplinesque — as the weight of his library makes him list to the side.

                         RED (O.S.)
          I need to borrow some money.

207L EXT. HOWARD BARN. DAY.

Howard lowers the newspaper from his favorite perch outside of the barn.

REVERSE ANGLE.

Red stands in front of him with tweed cap and exercise jacket.

                         HOWARD
          Alright.

                         RED
          I haven't been to a dentist in...
                    (doesn't finish)
          I need to borrow some money.

                         HOWARD
          Fine.

                         RED
          And I'm not sure when I can pay it back.

                    HOWARD
          That's okay.

                    RED
          I mean — when we win. I can pay it back when
          we win...

                    HOWARD
          Sure.

                    RED
          That is — if you still want me to ride.

Howard lowers the paper completely — squints toward
the sun.

                    HOWARD
          Of course I still want you to ride.

Their eyes lock for a beat. He reaches into his pocket.

                    HOWARD
          How much do you need?

                    RED
          I don't know. Ten dollars?

                    HOWARD
          Here.

He extends the money.

                    RED
          Thanks.
               (takes it)
          I didn't know who to...

                    HOWARD
          It's fine.

Red nods — takes a breath then turns away from the
barn. He gets about fifteen feet away when he hesitates, looking down at the bills.

                    RED
               (head down/muffled)
          I appreciate it.

                                          CUT TO:

207M HORSE RACING (SOMEWHERE ON THE BACK STRETCH).

They thunder down the backside near a pack of horses
clumped together.

TIGHTER. ON RED.

He sits atop Seabiscuit, holding him steady with the reins.

Jostling goes on all around him but Red leans over Seabiscuit's withers talking only to the horse.

> RED
>
> That's it Pops. We're okay. Yeah we're okay. We got nothin' to worry about. We got all the time in the world.

The race moves on around them but the CAMERA stays with Red, tightening slightly as he guides Seabiscuit toward the far turn, talking the entire time.

> RED
>
> That's it Pops. Everything's fine, now. Nice and easy. Just like that.

A horse or two passes them gathering at the turn. Red switches the Biscuit to a left lead as the horse begins to gather.

TIGHTER STILL...

Seabiscuit begins to pull on the reins and Red can feel it.

Both of them begin to breathe a little harder as they pack approaches the stretch.

> RED
>
> Okay, Pops. You ready? What do you think? You ready to go?

He starts straining on the reins. Red sits a little higher in the irons. The turn spreads out before them. Red takes a deep breath...

> RED
>
> Okay, Pops...
>
> (clucks twice)
>
> ...Let's go.

Red flicks the reins and turns, Seabiscuit literally explodes. He lengthens his stride and drives with his haunches, devouring the field as he blows through the turn.

Red banks hard into the rail and holds on for the ride as Seabiscuit knocks off horses at a rate of one per second. By the time he clears the turn — he's going twice as fast as the rest of the field, scorching the race track in front of him. The track announcer goes up at least half an octave.

> ANNOUNCER
> And it's Seabiscuit by two, by three, by f...I mean five. Holy COW look at this horse fly...

SLOW MOTION. "THE BISCUIT."

Doing what he was born to do. Red and his horse soar toward the wire, flying through the air in twenty foot strides. As they hit the finish line, Red leaps up in the irons — embracing the victory — the first one in years.

SLOW MOTION. HOWARD.

He clutches his fists in pride and victory and God knows what else...Marcela throws her arms around him.

SHOT. SMITH.

He turns to the usher and gives a little nod. The man holds up his winning ticket.

EXTREME TELEPHOTO. RED.

He still stands in the irons as he gallops Seabiscuit out: his fist clenched in triumph...The whip high in the air...

> MATCH CUT TO:

207N WPA MURAL.

An American Worker in a foundry is wielding a hammer over his head (in the exact same position as Red). It's a classic image of 3'0s industrial might: molten steel, massive girders, the working man as superhero.

> MCCULLOUGH
> In the end, it wasn't the dams or the roads or the bridges or the parks or the tunnels or the thousands of other public projects that were built in those years. It was more invisible than that. Men who were broken only a year before suddenly felt restored. Men who had been shattered, suddenly found their voice.

208-221 OMITTED

222 CLOSE UP. CHARLES HOWARD.

He faces a bank of reporters, just outside the
entrance to the clubhouse.

>   HOWARD
>   ...Well, I just think this horse has a lot
>   of heart. You know he was down but he wasn't
>   out. He may have lost a few but he didn't
>   let it get to him...

>   (beat)

>   You know, we could all learn a lick or two
>   from this little guy.... Oh, and by the way
>   — he doesn't know he's little. He thinks
>   he's the biggest horse out there.

The reporters LAUGH. One throws a question:

>   REPORTER MAX
>   So you have big plans for this little horse?

>   HOWARD
>   Oh yeah...see sometimes when the little guy
>   doesn't know he's the little guy, he can do
>   great big things...

HIS POV.

Reporters SCRIBBLE. The WHIRRING SOUND of the news
reel cameras momentarily swallows the scene.

HOWARD gets the glimmer of a smile...

>   HOWARD (cont'd)
>   See, this isn't the finish line my
>   friends...

Puts his foot on the bumper of his Buick.

>   HOWARD (cont'd)
>   ...The future's the finish line. And
>   Seabiscuit is just the horse to get us
>   there.

There is a flurry of shutters...

>   CUT TO:

223 TICK-TOCK MCGLAUGHLIN.

In a darkened studio. He reads his nightly "column"
with a finger to his ear in the half-light.

> TICK-TOCK
> "...Just the horse to get us there." Well, you made a believer out of me Mr. Howard. It's time for this old tout to eat a little crow: four and twenty blackbirds to be exact...all baked up in some humble pie. And I'll take that a la mode!
>
> (beat)
>
> Oh. And one more thing Mr. Howard. I just want to say...

224 INT. TURF CLUB.

He stands face to face with Howard.

> TICK-TOCK
> Thanks for the champagne.

> HOWARD
> Don't mention it.

> TICK-TOCK
> You see the infield?

> HOWARD
> No. Not yet.

> TICK-TOCK
> Take a look. Your horse is sellin' out the cheap seats.

Howard turns and walks to the edge of the Turf Club, looking over the infield. The CAMERA travels with him.

> HOWARD
> Oh my gosh.

225 OMITTED

226-228 OMITTED

229 EXT. PADDOCK.

Red and Seabiscuit are led from the paddock toward the track by the lead pony. Red sits tall in the saddle. A crowd lines the sawdust path.

> REPORTER MAX
> Hey, Red. What do you think of all these folks in the infield?

> RED
> That's who we're running for. Folks with a quarter in their pocket.

                    REPORTER ROY
          Hey Red, isn't that a little horse for all
          this hoopla?

                         RED
                (turning in the saddle)

          "Though he be but little, he is fierce."

Seabiscuit throws his head.

                    2ND REPORTER
                (beat)

          What?

                         RED
          That's Shakespeare boys. That's Shakespeare.

Red turns and heads into the darkness of the tunnel.

229A OTHER SIDE OF THE TUNNEL...

He emerges into the light and glances toward the
infield. Red blinks a couple of times.

                    RED (cont'd)
          Holy cow.

Dozens of people clamor along the rail fighting for a
glimpse of Seabiscuit, most with nothing left to bet.
They reach toward him with a weird yearning: "There,
that's him. There he is..." In any other context it
might be a breadline or a soup kitchen.

ANGLE RED.

He seems a little stunned. Red turns the Biscuit's
head slightly, letting them get a look at their
horse. He takes a deep breath. Over this...

                    ANNOUNCER
          ...And it's Seabiscuit by three, by four, by
          five and half — look at this horse fly....

230 THE WINNER'S CIRCLE.

Red stands in the irons facing the infield.

                    ANNOUNCER
          ...to win the San Onofre

231 NEW SHOT. WINNER'S CIRCLE.

ANNOUNCER
...San Miguel

232 NEW SHOT. WINNER'S CIRCLE.

ANNOUNCER
...San Fellipe Handicap!

Red takes the blanket of flowers, and throws them up in the air, toward the crowd...

233-234 OMITTED

235 SLOW MOTION. MARIGOLDS.

The IMAGE turns to black and white as Red leaps out of the irons and shakes hands with Howard. It's quick and jerky, in vintage newsreel fashion. The flowers land in the infield, where dozens of kids scramble to pick them up.

TICK-TOCK
...That makes six consecutive victories for this little colt from nowhere, one shy of the record! Why he may just be the biggest sensation on four legs since Hope and Crosby!

236 REVERSE ANGLE. DARKENED MOVIE THEATER.

Charles, Marcela, Red, and Tom all sit together at the movies watching the newsreel of their horse — a lot more fun than church.

TICK-TOCK
Yes it's standing room only each time this pint-size pony slips on a saddle. And if you can't afford the quarter, a comfy tree limb can still get you a glimpse.

ANGLE OAK TREE.

It's dripping with spectators — almost like Christmas ornaments.

TICK-TOCK
So what's the secret of this rags to riches story?

237 BLACK AND WHITE. MOVIE SCREEN.

An on-camera interview with a horse racing tout.

                          TOUT
                   (into the lens)
          I have it on good authority they feed
          Seabiscuit two pints of ice cold beer before
          every race.

                          SMITH
          Oh my God..

                       TICK-TOCK
          Talking from trackside, in an equine exclu-
          sive, this is Tick-Tock McGlaugh for
          Movietone News!

                                              CUT TO:

238 EXT. BARN 38 SANTA ANITA. DAY.

Smith saunters toward Seabiscuit's stall whistling a
cowboy ditty. There are boxes stacked in front. Red
sits on one of them.

                          SMITH
          What's this?

                           RED
          Goldenrod beer.

             (beat)

          Good stuff, too. There's more inside.

Smith crosses over and looks inside the stall.

                          SMITH
                   (stunned)
          Where's the horse?

                           RED
          Signing autographs.

                          SMITH
          What?

                                              CUT TO:

239 A HORSE'S HOOF...

Being dipped in ink. It is guided over to a copy of
that day's racing program, where it makes a black
imprint on the cover. FLASHBULBS record the event.

WIDER.

Howard hands the program to one of the waiting
reporters.

>   HOWARD
>   Here ya go, Max. Let it dry for a minute
>   before you try to sell it.

A smattering of laughter.

>   REPORTER LEWIS
>   Hey, Charles. You think he's gonna break the
>   record?

>   HOWARD
>   Ask him.
>
>   (turns)
>
>   Hey Seabiscuit, you gonna win one more and
>   break the record?

Seabiscuit turns and glares at the reporter as if to
challenge the audacity of the question. More FLASH-
BULBS.

>   REPORTER MAX
>   Hey Charles, what do you think finally
>   turned this horse around?

>   HOWARD
>   Well, I think we just gave him a chance.
>   Sometimes all somebody needs is a second
>   chance.
>
>   (means it — and still...)
>
>   I think there's a lot of people out there
>   who know just what I'm talking about.

Sound bite! Dozens of flashbulbs go off at once.
Reporters start scribbling.

>   HOWARD
>   Here boys, take some horseshoes with you.
>   These are special — they never run out of
>   luck.

The reporters chuck their journalistic ethics and
clamor for a souvenir.

240 INT. TACK ROOM.

Smith is tearing the place apart...

                              SMITH
              Sam, where the hell are my horseshoes!

241 INT. TURF CLUB.

Lavish and ornate. There is tropical print wallpaper
and twelve foot brass palm trees. Smith stands face
to face with Howard just outside the entrance.
There's an invisible line.

                              HOWARD
              You quit?

                              SMITH
              I can't work like this. He's not a parade
              animal — he's a race horse.

                              HOWARD
              Look, a little bit of public...

                              SMITH
              I can't get him to be a great horse if I
              can't get the time to work with him. I sure
              as hell can't do it without any horseshoes.

                              HOWARD
                   (beat)
              What do you mean — he is a great horse.

                              SMITH
              We don't know that yet.

                              HOWARD
              He's won six stakes in a row.

                              SMITH
              Against who?

Howard hesitates.

                              SMITH
                   (quieter)
              This, is a great horse.

He hands the Racing Form to Howard who looks down at
it...

242 INSERT. DAILY RACING FORM.

A jet black animal fills the front page.

                                          CUT TO:

243 INT. MOVIE THEATER.

They are all back in their regular seats. This time they sit motionless.

> MOVIETONE ANNOUNCER
> First he smashed them in the Kentucky Derby...

244 SHOT. SCREEN. WINNER'S CIRCLE.

A massive black animal is draped with roses in the winner's circle. WAR ADMIRAL looks like the statue of a perfect horse: all muscle and power.

> MOVIETONE ANNOUNCER
> Then he crushed them in the Preakness...

245 ANOTHER WINNER'S CIRCLE.

He is surrounded by a huge entourage.

> MOVIETONE ANNOUNCER
> Then he destroyed all comers in the Belmont to snatch the triple crown!

246 RACING FOOTAGE.

Even in jerky black and white the display is awesome. He pulls eight lengths clear of the field asserting total superiority.

> MOVIETONE ANNOUNCER
> At almost eighteen hands, he's as big as he is fast. An undefeated behemoth, War Admiral has annihilated the competition in every race he's ever entered.

247 REVERSE ANGLE. THEATER SEATS.

> RED
> Eighteen hands!
>
> (whispers to Smith)
>
> He's an elephant!

> MOVIETONE ANNOUNCER
> Born of perfect breeding. Displaying perfect form. Boasting a perfect record — The millionaire Mr. Riddle may finally have created the perfect horse.
>
> (pause)

Until next time...This is Horace Halstedter for MOVIETONE NEWS!

Marcela leans over to Howard.

                    MARCELA
          Still want to see the movie?

                                        CUT TO:

248 EXT. HUNTINGTON HOTEL. NIGHT.

Their home away from home in Pasadena. It's an opulent 30's palace.

249 INT. HOWARD HOTEL SUITE.

The bedroom is dark. Marcela sleeps. Howard sits bolt
upright in bed staring out the window. After a beat.

                    HOWARD
          What the hell does that mean, anyway?

She wakes up startled and looks at him.

                    MARCELA
          ...What?

                    HOWARD
          Perfect. He's perfect. What the hell does
          "perfect" mean? You show me something that's
          perfect and I'll show you something that's not.

She stares at him groggy.

                                        CUT TO:

250 INT. TICK-TOCK'S "LAIR." DAY.

Howard sits side by side with Tick-Tock in the studio, giving an "exclusive" interview.

                    HOWARD
          ...Look, he's obviously the best horse in
          the East and we're obviously the best horse
          in the West. I just think the country
          deserves to see which horse is better.

                    TICK-TOCK
          Folks you can't see it but the gauntlet just
          landed on my desk.
               (THUDS the desk top)
          Are you talking about a match race, Mr. Howard?

                    HOWARD
          Whatever Mr. Riddle wants. Match race,
          stakes race...potato sack race. Just 'cause
          we're littler doesn't mean we're scared.

                    TICK-TOCK
          Right you are! And somewhere out there in
          the heartland of America, every little guy
          knows exactly what you mean. You hear that,
          Mr. Riddle? You have an appointment with
          destiny...You have a date with...with...

Goes blank.

                    HOWARD
          Destiny?

                    TICK-TOCK
          Destiny! Yes! Exactly! Destiny! And his name
          is SEABISCUIT!

             (flicks off the mic)

          Okay I got a little messed up there at the
          end, but I think they get the point.

                                        CUT TO:

251 FLASHBULBS - HUNDREDS OF THEM...

When the explosion clears we are sitting in
THE NATIONAL JOCKEY CLUB.
...which has nothing to do with jockeys. Opulent,
dripping with money, the place is festooned with crystal chandeliers and rich mahogany walls. Seated at a
central table is a breathing cadaver in an oversized
suit and pasty skin. Samuel Riddle is a cross between
Mr. Potter from *It's a Wonderful Life* and something
that melted in a wax museum. He puffs on a large green
cigar, which pollutes the general vicinity.

                    RIDDLE
          Well, I'm glad they finally have some racing
          in California...Do they use Western saddles
          out there?

A group of impeccably dressed minions laughs, oblig-
ingly.

                    RIDDLE
Look, comparing these two horses is ridicu-
lous. War Admiral is a real race horse who's
won every prestigious race in America. This
little colt of theirs is running out on some
cow track....
        (coughs)
If we responded to every fledgling challenger who wants to make a name for themselves, well...
        (smiles)
It wouldn't be fair to us but it wouldn't be
fair to them either...You wouldn't put Jack
Dempsey in the ring with a middleweight.

This draws nods from everyone around the table.
There's a flurry of FLASHBULBS.

                    RED (VO)
Middleweight!

252 EXT. HOWARD BARN. DAY.

They all huddle around a radio in the barn office.
Pumpkin and Seabiscuit listen from their stall.

                    RED
I'll kill him. I'll knock his goddamn block
off.

                    HOWARD
Easy...

                    RED
He's chicken.

                    HOWARD
I know.

                    RED
    (seething)
Middleweight...

                    MARCELA
You just gotta flush him out.

They turn and look at her.

> MARCELA (cont'd)
> Well — this is still America...

> HOWARD
> Yeah...

She shrugs...

> MARCELA
> Cash.

253 INT. "DOC" STRUBB'S OFFICE. SANTA ANITA. DAY.

Howard stands across the desk from his old Tijuana
buddy, Doc Strubb, now the Chairman of Santa Anita.

> STRUBB
> A hundred thousand dollars?

> HOWARD
> Biggest purse in American history.

> STRUBB
> I sure hope so.

> HOWARD
> You'd get every top Eastern thoroughbred.
> All of 'em. You'd put this place on the map.
> They may have all that blue blood crap, but
> our money's just as good as theirs....

> STRUBB
> Charlie...

> HOWARD
> This is our moment Doc. They're stuck in the
> past. This is the future.

>> (leans closer...)

> Don't you want to see it? Don't you want to see
> 'em piling off those train cars — coming out
> here to your track? That's victory in itself,
> Doc. That's the finish line right there.

> STRUBB
> ...You sell cars like this?

> HOWARD
> Hundreds of 'em.

254 CLOSE UP. TICK-TOCK MCGLAUGHLIN.

TICK-TOCK

Hold your horses folks. Just when you thought
you'd seen it all, Doc Strubb has gone and
raided the cookie jar. Yes, he has smashed the
piggy bank and sold the family silver.

(beat)

A HUNDRED THOUSAND DOLLARS FOR ONE HORSE
RACE. Makes me want to walk around on all
fours and throw a saddle on my back. Will
the Biscuit be the favorite? Not likely
folks. We're about to be invaded! Derby
Winners. Preakness winners. Belmont winners.
Oops. I guess, that's all one horse. At a
hundred thousand bucks, how could the
Admiral not want to dock his ship in this
friendly port?

(rapid fire sign off)

This is Tick-Tock McGlaugh...LIVE from
Clockers Corner.

255 EXT. NATIONAL JOCKEY CLUB.

Riddle hobbles down the front steps of the
limestone building toward a group of waiting
reporters. He pauses for effect...

RIDDLE
(beat)

No thanks.

He chortles to himself and hobbles off...

CUT TO:

256 INT. CHASENS. NIGHT.

Howard and Marcela sit in their favorite L.A. watering hole. Howard holds a telegram. A waiter prepares
crêpes suzette, tableside, in the foreground.

HOWARD
Shit.

MARCELA
Charles.

                         HOWARD
                    (beat)
         Shit!

                         MARCELA
              Yeah, I know what you mean.

                         HOWARD
                    (thinks for a beat...)
              Ah, the hell with it. We'll run him anyway.
              It's still gonna be great horses. If we win
              this thing he'll have to face us.

                    (eats an olive)
              And the worst that can happen is we win a
              hundred thousand bucks.

She raises an eyebrow. The crêpes flambé in a huge
burst of FLAME...

                                             CUT TO:

257-260 OMITTED

261 RAIN. (SANTA ANITA TRAIN DEPOT. DAY.)

Race horses from The East are loaded off special
train cars as they lumber down the ramp. Their blan-
kets display the crests of every major Eastern barn:
Claiborne, Meadow, Foxcatcher....

OVER THIS:

                         SMITH (VO)
              Okay, Special Agent is pure speed. He's
              gonna go to the lead but he can't handle the
              distance, so don't get sucked in.

                         RED (VO)
              I won't.

Special Agent is led by the CAMERA. The next horse is
a large roan gelding.

                         SMITH (VO)
              Indian Broom could be there too, but they
              probably won't burn him out. We'll know
              they're holding him back if they use a
              circle bit.

262 INT. RECEIVING BARN. DAY.

The SUN is spilling through the window now. Indian Broom is getting a special circle bit put in his mouth....

> SMITH (VO)
> The one to worry about is Rosemont. He closes like a freight train and he'll fight you for it at the end.

Indian Broom clears out to reveal ROSEMONT: a beautiful chestnut colt with a Foxcatcher Farms saddle blanket.

> SMITH (VO)
> You gotta have some momentum built up by the time he makes his move.

263 SANTA ANITA. RACE DAY.

A beautiful day out. Steam rises up from the flowers in the infield.

> SMITH (VO)
> Now it's still a little soggy from the other day so try to stay off the rail where it's deep.

> RED (VO)
> I figured I'd sit back about three wide.

> SMITH (VO)
> Fine.

264 INT. JOCK'S ROOM.

Red sits at his cubicle with Smith. He wears the Howard family silks.

> SMITH
> Other than that, just feel it. He'll tell you when he's ready.

They look at each other and nod. Deep breath...

> CUT TO:

265 OMITTED

266 TRACK.

The horses emerge from the tunnel into the light. When Red crosses onto the dirt, a cheer goes up from the crowd. Most of it is coming from his right. He turns...

267 DIFFERENT ANGLE.

From the grandstand it looks like another horse race, but from the INFIELD, it's a different story. Kids, families, loners, couples all crowd against the rail.

268 THE STARTING GATE.

The horses mill and circle like schooling fish. Even though the race is minutes away, a loud MURMUR starts to build. Red watches Special Agent load...Then Indian Broom...Then an assistant starter takes his bridle and loads Seabiscuit into the gate.

RED'S POV.

An empty track in front of him. A moment's still-ness...

269 SHOT. GRANDSTAND.

Howard raises his binoculars.

270 SHOT. THE RAIL.

Smith kicks at the dirt.

271 RED'S POV...

There's the BELL and the GATE BURSTS OPEN as ...

UP ANGLE.

Seventeen horses thunder TOWARD THE CAMERA like a cavalry charge.

BEHIND RED.

He settles in off the pace taking Seabiscuit away from the mud at the rail. Loose dirt flies every-where. He wipes at his goggles.

CLUBHOUSE TURN....

As predicted, Special Agent takes the lead, flying into the backstretch and thundering by the camera. There's a gap to the rest of the pack where Seabiscuit settles in at 9th.

INSIDE THE PACK.

It's a mess. Horses bump, jostle, pin each other at the rail. Jockeys grunt warnings to each other as the pounding goes on inside the pack:

"Easy Mac...Watch it...I'm here, I'm here...Nowhere to go Johnny...." From Red's POV he can see Special Agent through the mud seven lengths in front. He glances around.

FIVE LENGTHS FURTHER BACK. MOVING WITH ROSEMONT.

Up ahead, Seabiscuit is stalking Special Agent and THE CAMERA, along with Rosemont, is stalking Seabiscuit. As the end of the backstretch approaches the pack starts to stretch out a little. Some stragglers fall away. The stronger horses show their class.

ON SEABISCUIT.

He's pulling on the reins — begging Red to let him go. Seabiscuit has a bead on Special Agent and he literally chomps at the bit, driving with his neck and fighting to lengthen his stride.

> RED
> Okay Pops. Let's go.

Red clucks twice and the Biscuit takes off. He begins to weave between horses, picking his holes and darting through them. Seventh, then sixth, then fifth, then fourth....

FURTHER BACK...WITH ROSEMONT.

As soon as Seabiscuit moves, Rosemont begins to follow him.

Rosemont shoots through the holes Seabiscuit has opened up, stalking from four lengths back. When they come out of the turn Seabiscuit has overtaken Special Agent and has the lead, heading for home.

RED AND THE BISCUIT.

He flicks twice with the whip and the Biscuit begins to charge. There is nothing but wide open race track in front of them and the crowd literally starts to ROAR. Both of them are lifted by the sound of the CHEERS and they pick up the pace even more. Seabiscuit drives toward home on the lead. The place is going wild.

272 ANGLE. BOX SEATS.

Charles and Marcela leap to their feet along with everyone else.

273 ANGLE. RED.

He rides high in the irons — triumphant — exultant. Red rests the whip on Seabiscuit's neck and eases him toward the wire.

BUT SUDDENLY....

Without the urging Seabiscuit begins to slow. He starts to drift slightly — his stride slackens. All at once...

ROSEMONT EATS UP THE FRAME...

He explodes INTO VIEW FROM THE RIGHT SIDE, driving hard at Seabiscuit.

ANGLE. RED.

He still heads for home under a "hand ride" the whip idle on Seabiscuit's neck. Red hears a second surge from the crowd and turns his whole head to the right...

REVERSE ANGLE. BACKWARDS. PAST RED.

Rosemont is charging. Red goes to the whip and the Biscuit responds but it may well be too late. The two horses cross the finish line virtually together....

SHOT. AT THE WIRE.

There is A FLASH of light and...

274 A WHITE SCREEN...

Gradually the image of the PHOTOFINISH fades into view. You have to reach for it...Can't quite make it out. Finally it comes clear.......

ROSEMONT has nipped Seabiscuit by a nose...

275 ANGLE. GRANDSTAND.

A huge groan goes up from the crowd. It turns into...

276 A CHORTLE...THEN A COUGH FROM SAMUEL RIDDLE.

...who grins as best he can with a cigar in his mouth. He pauses somewhere on 5TH AVENUE, speaking to reporters.

                              RIDDLE
          Well I guess that little horse of theirs was
          just a glorified claimer after all.

                    (yellow smile)

          At least this puts an end to all this David
          and Goliath nonsense.

Riddle chortles to himself, then waddles off down the
block.

                                          CUT TO:

277 INT. JOCK'S ROOM...

Red wears a towel, headed for the showers. Smith follows him across the jockey's room.

                              RED
          It's not my fault. Not this time.

                              SMITH
          I told you look out for Rosemont!

                              RED
          I thought I had it.

                              SMITH
          You stopped riding.

                              RED
          I didn't see him!

                              SMITH
          What the hell are you talking about? He was
          flying up your tail!

                              RED
                    (whirling around)

          Yeah? Well, I can't...

He stops himself.

                              SMITH
          What?

                              RED
                    (long pause — a decision?)

          ...see out there.

Their eyes lock for a beat.

278 OMITTED

279 EXT. SADDLING STALLS. (JUST OUTSIDE JOCK'S ROOM)

The door to the Jock's room blows open as Smith bursts out. He's met by Howard coming the other way.

>   SMITH
>   He lied to us.

>   HOWARD
>   What?

>   SMITH
>   He lied to us. You want a jockey who lies to
>   us?

>   HOWARD
>   What are you talking about.

>   SMITH
>   He can't see. He's blind in one eye.

CLOSE UP. HOWARD.

Instead of anger, it's quieter than that. Hurt...hurt at the hurt....

>   HOWARD
>   (gently)
>   It's fine.

>   SMITH
>   It's fine?

>   HOWARD
>   Yeah, Tom.

>   (beat/softly)
>   "You don't throw a whole life away just
>   'cause it's banged up a little bit."

He pats Smith on the arm, then slowly moves on....

>   CUT TO:

280-281 OMITTED

282 HEADLINE.

With a huge picture of Red:

>   "THE HEADLESS HORSEMAN"
>   WHAT WAS HE THINKING?
>   Jockey Error Costs Biscuit The Big 'Cap!

The newspaper lowers revealing Howard, in his
favorite lawn chair outside the barn.

                    HOWARD
          (to himself)
     The hell with it.

                                        CUT TO:

283-284 OMITTED

285 EXT. UNION STATION. DOWNTOWN L.A. DAY.

Howard is positioned outside the huge train depot,
talking to assembled reporters.

                    HOWARD
          Alright, just a couple of announcements.
          (pauses)
     First: Red Pollard will remain as
     Seabiscuit's jockey, now and forever...

There is some murmuring. He continues

                    HOWARD
     Second: If they are too scared to come and
     race us, we will go and find them. We are
     going to enter every race where War Admiral
     is on the card and if he scratches, which he
     probably will, we will enter the next race
     where he is listed on the card. We won't
     come home until we've faced him: win, lose
     or draw.
          (pause)
     You know, I'd rather have one horse like
     this than a hundred War Admirals.

Scribbling. A few flashbulbs. Howard turns and heads
toward the door of the depot...

286 OMITTED

286A EXT. TRAIN. NIGHT.

It whizzes through the darkness at 60 miles an hour.
The CAMERA starts to track slowly along the side of
the car, coming to rest at the small platform on the
back. A familiar silhouette stands out there alone.

CLOSER. RED.

He tosses a cigarette and blows on his hands when the door opens behind him. Howard sticks his head out with a look that says everything: "Come on in. It's freezing out here." Red smiles slightly and relents crossing past Howard into the warmth of the car...

287 EXT. PAINTED DESERT. SUNRISE.

Pink, hot orange — purple and blue in the morning sky. The "Biscuit Special" streaks through the desert at first light.

288 INT. PRIVATE CLUB CAR.

Howard stares out the window at dawn: motionless...reflective...All at once the train starts to slow. There's a screech of brakes, a lurch, a clanging BELL. A conductor moves through the car.

> HOWARD
> Why are we stopping?

CUT TO:

289 EXT. ALBUQUERQUE NEW MEXICO. DAWN.

Two hundred people are at the train station. They spill out of the depot all over the train platform. Many are ragged. Howard stands on the back of the train a little surprised.

> HOWARD
> Well, look — I really don't know what to say. We appreciate it.
>
>   (motioning behind him toward the Biscuit)
>
> I'm sure he appreciates it too, he's just a little shy about speaking in public.

Laughter.

> HOWARD
> I guess all of you are here today because this is a horse who won't give up — even when life beats him by a nose.

CLOSE UP. HOWARD.

He pauses — his eyes flicker...He scans the crowd.

> HOWARD
> But heck — everybody loses a couple. And either you pack up and go home or you keep on fighting. Isn't that right?

The crowd APPLAUDS. Howard suddenly feels the power
of it...

                         HOWARD
          Now do you want to see a match race?

289A CLOSE UP. A TELEGRAPH KEY.

As it clacks out a press story.

                                    DISSOLVE TO:

289B A NEWSPAPER HEADLINE.

"MATCH RACE"

The CAMERA WIDENS OUT TO REVEAL a PAPER BOY, hawking
a late edition on a street corner.

                         PAPER BOY
          EXTRA. EXTRA. Biscuit on the warpath. Come
          and get it folks. It's all right here!

                                    DISSOLVES TO:

289C A TRAIN CAR.

Rolling over the headline. The headline DISSOLVES
into a new one:

          "LITTLE HORSE DRAWS HUGE CROWD"
          2000 in Denver

289D The train continues to roll. A new telegraph key
clacks. A new paper boy hawks another headline.

          "ADMIRAL BOMBARDED"
          Biscuit Presses for Match Race

Train car rolling over the headline...

          "CAVALRY CHARGE"
          5000 "See" Biscuit in St. Louis

290 EXT. ST. LOUIS MO. LATER...

The crowd has swelled even larger. Howard stands on
the railroad siding next to Seabiscuit and Pumpkin.

                         HOWARD
          Now I don't know what those other fellas are
          so scared of.

               (beat)

          I mean look at us. Our horse is too
          small...Our jockey's too big...Our trainer's

too old — sorry Tom — and I'm too stupid to
know the difference. You'd think they'd want
to race us instead o' running away.

HUGE CHEER FROM THE CROWD...The cheer continues right
into:

290A TICK-TOCK'S STUDIO.

Howard's voice and the crowd plays inside over the
radio.

>   TICK-TOCK
> Ladies and Gentlemen I'm staring out at a
> swarm of humanity.
>
> (turns up the cheering)
>
> A sea of hungry faces demanding the match of
> a lifetime. They're out here in the
> cold...in the wind...

He cues PAIGE who makes a "windy" noise into the mic.
He barely approves...

>   TICK-TOCK
> ...In the chill of a late October night.
> Here. Let me make my way over to one of them
> so you can hear for yourself...

He walks in a little circle.

>   TICK-TOCK
> Ma'am if I might...Why did you come out here
> tonight with your three young children clam-
> oring to get a glimpse of this little horse?
>
>   PAIGE
> Because we want to see a match race!
>
>   TICK-TOCK
> There you have it ladies and gentlemen. The
> voice of one, the voice of millions. And all
> around America they echo one simple cry:

291 OMITTED.

292   CROWD

> MATCH RACE! MATCH RACE! MATCH RACE!
>
> MATCH RACE...

SERIES OF HEADLINES SUPERED OVER THE CHEERING CROWD:

"RIDDLE MUTE"

"NO ANSWER FROM THIS RIDDLE"

"THE ADMIRAL SURRENDERS?"

MEANWHILE...The crowd is chanting...

> CROWD
> MATCH RACE! MATCH RACE! MATCH RACE!...

> CUT TO:

293 CLOSE UP. SAMUEL RIDDLE.

He looks dyspeptic and uncomfortable.

> RIDDLE
> Fine.

WIDER. INT. NATIONAL JOCKEY CLUB.

Howard sits across from him.

> RIDDLE
> But it's on my terms.

> HOWARD
> Any terms you want.

WIDER STILL.

He's surrounded by minions. Howard is alone. It looks like a board meeting at a bank.

> RIDDLE
> A mile and three sixteenths. I won't consid-
> er anything else.

> HOWARD
> Alright.

> RIDDLE
> I want a walk up start. With a bell. We
> won't be using any... "contraptions."

> HOWARD
> You mean a "starting gate"?

Riddle glares at him.

> HOWARD
> Fine.

                         RIDDLE
            And we run it here. At our home track.
            That's not negotiable

                         HOWARD
            Seems like a nice enough place.

                         RIDDLE
                (half a grunt)

            Oh, I think you'll find it quite comfortable
            Mr. Howard.

294 EXT. BARNS. PIMLICO RACE TRACK.

It's Xanadu. Mecca. The barns are as much a shrine to
aristocracy as anything to do with horse racing. Huge
spires rise from the top of the hundred year old
buildings. Brilliant white paint gleams in the sunshine.

                         RED (VO)
            Jesus Christ.

295 INT. BARN.

Unlike Santa Anita, all the stalls are housed pala-
tially inside the structure. Red, Tom, Marcela, and
Charles all gape at the cathedral ceilings and leaded
windows. Each stall has its own wood panelling.

                         RED
            I want to be a horse.

                         SMITH
            You're almost big enough.

                         RED
            That's very funny.

LONG SHOT. STALLS. (FROM BEHIND THEM)

A groom leads them down the long corridor toward
Seabiscuit's stall. Everyone whispers.

                         MARCELA
            Doesn't even smell like a barn.

                         HOWARD
            They probably deodorize it every morning.

                         SMITH
            They still crap.

Everyone looks over at him.

                         SMITH
         Well they do.

                                              CUT TO:

296 EXT. A GROUP OF BARNS.

Located around a central courtyard. The TITLE reads:
"WAR ADMIRAL'S COMPOUND"

It dwarfs the other barn both in size and grandeur. A
huge cupola reaches up to the sky. A perfectly
groomed walking ring lies under a hundred year old
willow tree. The place oozes aristocracy. There are
brass feed bins and a porcelain watering trough.

                      RED'S VOICE
They got us in the servant's quarters.

297 ANGLE. HILLSIDE.

The entire entourage "spies" on War Admiral's compound from an adjacent hill. Howard has borrowed
Smith's binoculars. It looks like a commando mission.

                         HOWARD
         Is that him?

He hands Smith the glasses.

298 REVERSE.

A black horse is being hot-walked in the paddock.

                         SMITH
         No. Too small.

The image begins to PAN to the right....

                         SMITH
         That's him.

SHOT. HOWARD.

He takes the binoculars and stares for a beat.

                         HOWARD
         Oh my God.

299 HIS POV. THROUGH BINOCULARS.

A HUGE jet black animal is being led back to his
stall. Every single muscle ripples in the sun. He
WHINNIES and jerks on the lead rope — a high-strung
prima donna.

_____

124

300 HOWARD.

Lowers the glasses, stunned.

> RED
> ...Maybe he's the kind of horse that just
> looks good in the paddock.

They turn and look at him.

THUNDERING HOOF BEATS:

301 EXT. TRAINING TRACK. DAY.

War Admiral flies down the stretch in a stunning display of power and speed. The SOUND of a single horse
is stirring.

302 ANGLE. HEDGE.

They watch the workout from way behind the backstretch...

> RED
> Wow.

CLOSER.

Smith stares straight ahead.

> SMITH
> We gotta get to the lead.

> HOWARD
> (turns/beat...)

Seabiscuit never goes to the lead.

> SMITH
> I know, but we gotta break first. If that
> monster shakes loose we'll never catch him.

> RED
> What? Retrain him?

> SMITH
> (shrugs)

We got two weeks.

CUT TO:

303 EXT. BALTIMORE STREET. DAY.

Red and Smith walk down a commercial block in their "street clothes." They turn a corner revealing a FIREHOUSE. Red stamps out a cigarette and approaches the firemen, washing their engine in front of the building.

> RED
>
> Excuse me.

The men look up.

> RED
>
> We'd like to buy your bell.

CUT TO:

304 EXT. SEABISCUIT'S BARN. PIMLICO.

The Biscuit and Pumpkin stand tied up outside the building. A huge CROWD OF PHOTOGRAPHERS and REPORTERS hangs over the fence, trying to get a shot...

305 INT. STALL.

Red and Tom Smith sit on stools in a far off corner. The firemen's bell has been rigged up to a large square battery, mounted on a board with a makeshift button. Smith hits it: there is a loud RING. They look at each other....

CUT TO:

306 EXT. MAIN TRACK. NIGHT.

Smith and Red lead Seabiscuit onto the track. It's almost pitch black and he's silhouetted by a single worklight. A nightwatchman unlocks the gate. Howard carries a flashlight.

> NIGHTWATCHMAN
>
> They didn't tell me you were comin'.

> HOWARD
>
> Probably just an oversight.

> NIGHTWATCHMAN
>
> You want me to turn on some lights or some-thin'?

> SEVERAL OF THEM
> (together)
>
> No!

CUT TO:

307 TOP OF THE STRETCH. DARKNESS.

Red sits atop Seabiscuit with Smith behind him. He holds a long thin buggy whip, almost six feet in length. They speak in half whispers.

> SMITH
> It's a predatory response. If I just brush it past his flank he'll bolt. We just want him to do it with the bell.

> RED
> How far do I take him?

> SMITH
> Hundred feet or so. Just enough to break first.

Red nods and settles in. Howard and Marcela watch by the rail. Smith positions himself behind Seabiscuit with the homemade bell in one hand and the buggy whip in the other.

> SMITH
> Ready?

> RED
> Yeah.

Smith RINGS the bell and brushes the whip across Seabiscuit's flank. The horse feels the "presence" behind him and bolts down the track. He disappears into the darkness. Howard and Marcela look at each other...

SERIES OF SHOTS:

With each successive RING...Seabiscuit bolts quicker and quicker from a standing start. The acceleration is incredible. Red clutches the mane as Seabiscuit loads his short back legs and explodes forward down the track. After several repetitions, Smith takes the buggy whip and tosses it aside. He holds the bell up in the air.

CLOSE UP. SEABISCUIT. SLOW MOTION.

Smith rings the BELL, and Seabiscuit bolts toward the lens, this time without any urging. It's a powerful display of will and determination. His mouth grips the bit. His body surges forward, out of the darkness devouring the track....

307B INT. BARN. DAY.

Smith sits outside the stall whittling on a feedbucket. A huge crowd of reporters jams the windows to the barn, hoping to catch a glimpse of the horse. Above Smith's head is a large handpainted sign: "QUIET! THIS HORSE IS SLEEPING!"

CLOSER.

Smith glances up at the reporters and starts WHISTLING even louder. It's out of key and intentionally irritating. After a while they can't take it anymore.

>   REPORTER ROY
>   Hey Tom, when are you gonna work that horse
>   out?
>
>   SMITH
>   When he wakes up I guess.

He whittles some more.

>   REPORTER SKIP
>   Yeah? When's that?
>
>   SMITH
>   Dunno. Day or two?

He continues to whittle as the reporters grumble. One gets disgusted and turns to leave. The CAMERA PUSHES in on Smith's face as he cracks a slight smile...OVER THIS:

>   RED'S VOICE (VO)
>   The whole track?

308-313 OMITTED

314 EXT. PIMLICO. MAIN TRACK. NIGHT.

Instead of the backstretch, Smith and Red stand in a small pool of light in the homestretch. Charles and Marcela stand off to the side.

>   SMITH
>   I just want him to do it once, with nothin'
>   in front of him.

Red glances into the darkness.

                              RED
          Yeah? But I can't see out there.

                             SMITH
          That's alright — he can.

Smith holds up the bell.

                              RED
          Oh, no. C'mon, Tom...Jesus!

Smith rings the bell and, all at once, the Biscuit
bolts. He lurches forward and disappears into the
darkness as an EXPLETIVE echoes out of the night.

RED'S POV. PITCH BLACK.

The HOOFBEATS POUND beneath him like a thunderclap or
a drumroll, but he (AND WE) can see absolutely nothing in front of us. Slowly, as Red's eyes begin to
adjust, the detail of the track starts to emerge.
First the white rail...then the hedge beyond
it...Then the dirt of the track.... All at a break-
neck speed.

                              RED
               (a whisper)
          Oh my God.

It's the ultimate act of trust between man and animal. Seabiscuit hurtles into the darkness and Red
lets him. The vague outline of the racetrack flies
toward us at forty miles an hour. All Red can do is
LAUGH...

                                         CUT TO:

315 EXT. BARN AREA. DAY.

He saunters in with his shoulders back and a resolute
look in his eye. He's ridden to the edge of the uni-
verse — what's another horse race. Red crosses over
to the Biscuit's stall where Pumpkin is sticking her
head out. He reaches into his pocket and pulls out a
carrot.

                             VOICE
          Red?

REVERSE

He turns to see an older trainer dressed in muck boots and a flannel shirt. He has a weathered face. Red stares at it for a beat.

316 FLASHBACK. SAME FACE.

It's talking to Red's father and mother.

> TRAINER
> Yeah. Your boy combed 'em out. Changed the tack...

Turns to a much younger Red.

> TRAINER
> Where'd a young fella like you learn so much about horses?

317 SHOT. RED. THE PRESENT.

> RED
> (still staring)

Oh my gosh.

> TRAINER
> Yeah, remember me. Guess I shoulda used you as a jockey, not a groom.

> RED
> No it was...That was great.

> TRAINER
> Well — I'm havin' a little trouble. (looks down at the ground) Got this one horse over at the Annex and I'm tryin' to sell a share in him — tough times and all.

> RED
> Oh. Well, I really don't have...

> TRAINER
> (laughs)

No, no. I don't want you to buy a share. I was just wondering if you'd breeze him for me. If folks saw Red Pollard workin' my horse...

He doesn't finish the sentence — doesn't need to. Red thinks for a beat.

> RED
> I'll breeze your horse for you.

318 THE GAP.

Red stands beside the trainer and a very skittish two
year old. The man cups his hands to give Red a boost
up, but when he does, the horse whinnies and bolts
yanking away from him. Red hops off....

CLOSER. HORSE.

He's whinnying and jerking with a wild look in his
eye. The trainer gets him under control. Looks over
at Red.

JUMP CUT TO:

319 RED ON HORSEBACK.

The trainer holds the bridle — giving him last minute
workout instructions.

>   TRAINER
>   Just take him for five furlongs at around a
>   minute one...

>   RED
>   Can he do that?

>   TRAINER
>   Should.

He lets go of the bridle and the two year old jerks
away, as Red struggles to keep him under control. He
takes him back toward the five furlong pole...

WIDE ANGLE. UP THE TRACK.

In the background is The Gap with its horses milling
around.

In the foreground a worker struggles to get a tractor
started.

He has the hood open and the engine exposed. The man
fiddles with the motor while a co-worker turns the
key.

>   WORKER
>   Try it now.

He turns the ignition but nothing happens. The engine
whines without turning over. The man stops.

SHOT. FIVE FURLONG POLE.

Red canters toward the pole erratically, then lets
the young horse loose. The colt takes off and flattens out into a pretty good gallop. Red settles in
over the withers.

SHOT. UP THE TRACK. LONG LENS.

The TRACTOR is out of focus in the FOREGROUND as Red
flies toward us. He grows larger and larger in the
FRAME as the man struggles to get the motor started.

> WORKER
> Okay. Try it again....

DIFFERENT ANGLE. TIGHTER. FOLLOWING RED.

He starts to ride past us, flying down the backstretch, when all at once there is a loud BACKFIRE
and the SOUND of an engine starting. Red's horse
props, rears and bolts sideways toward the far rail.
Red hangs onto the neck.

DIFFERENT ANGLE. THE RAIL.

The horse lunges with his front feet, actually trying
to vault it. He clears the first rail, but gets hung
up in the hedge beyond it, ripping out a section of
chain-link and heading toward the barn area. Red is
still in the saddle.

320 EXT. BARN AREA.

The horse is lacerated, dragging a section of chain
link around his back foot. He rips and tears wildly
around the stable area, trying desperately to shake
off the debris.

SHOT. RED.

He jerks back on the reins, trying to control the
horse and stay on at the same time. The colt tears
through the shed rows, slamming into a barn and
knocking over a feed trough. The grooms are scatter-
ing in every direction, screaming and running out of
the way.

WIDER.

Red's horse veers toward the hot-walking ring and
jerks into a large metal carousel where they tether
the horses for their cool down. Red gets clothes-
lined by the long metal bar and knocked clear out of
the saddle. His foot is still in the stirrup...

UP ANGLE. STABLE AREA.

The colt panics even more and drags Red behind him through the shed rows. He lurches around a corner, slamming Red, first into the corner of a building, and then into the bumper of a truck. Finally Red breaks loose.

EXTREME WIDE ANGLE. STABLE AREA. RED IN THE FORE-GROUND.

He lies motionless, his leg torn open and bleeding. Off in the distance, five grooms come running toward the CAMERA....

321 EXT. BARN AREA. LATER...

An ambulance screams AWAY disappearing in a cloud of dust.

322 INT. HOSPITAL CORRIDOR.

Charles, Marcela, Tom Smith, and Sam all sit together on a bench in the hallway. It looks just like church but with one person missing. Howard glances at his watch.

JUMP TO:

323 LATER.

He stands in the corridor talking to the doctor.

> DOCTOR
> Look, with a fall like that, he's lucky to be alive. The spleen was ruptured. He has a mild concussion, but most of the damage was restricted to his leg.

> HOWARD
> How bad is it?

> DOCTOR
> Oh, God, I don't know — shattered. Eleven, twelve breaks, something like that. We're gonna have to operate...

CUT TO:

324 EXTREME WIDE ANGLE. HALLWAY. MIDDLE OF THE NIGHT.

Howard sits in a chair at the end of the hallway, staring out the window into black. He's turned toward the wall partially obscured — a tiny figure swallowed by a hospital.

CLOSER.

He shifts slightly in his seat — leans on the arm of the chair. There's something in his hand.

INSERT. GAME.

He rolls the tiny ball back and forth, trying to land it on the moon. He can't quite do it. It hovers for a second, gets close, then rolls right back out again.

CLOSE UP. HOWARD.

He just stares at it. Frozen. Howard sits motionless for a beat, then the SOUND comes back all over again.

>   DOCTOR (OS)
>   Well, we did the best we could.

WIDER.

The doctor stands in front of them. Dawn is breaking through the window. He looks tired.

>   DOCTOR
>   He'll always limp but there's a good chance
>   he'll walk again.

>   HOWARD
>   Will he ride?

The doctor shoots him a look: "What, are you kidding me?" Howard nods. He turns and walks away.

325 INT. HOSPITAL ROOM. LATER.

Red's leg is up in traction. He's a mess. I.V. in his arm. Drugs in his eyes. The three of them stand at the side of the bed. Red rolls his head toward them.

>   RED
>   (faint)
>   You should see the other guy.

Marcela bites her lip. Howard forces a smile.

>   HOWARD
>   You're gonna be fine. Couple of months
>   you'll be up and around like new.

>   RED
>   (smiles slightly...)
>   I'm the one who makes up the stories, remember?

Howard takes a deep breath.

> HOWARD
> Well, yeah...Maybe a little longer than that.

Red nods. He shifts and winces. Howard hesitates.

> HOWARD
> Look — I think we're gonna have to scratch.

> RED
> No.

He turns. It hurts to turn. Red takes a deep breath.

> RED
> Don't scratch.

> HOWARD
> Son, he's a great horse, but he can't run by himself.

CLOSE UP. RED.

He shifts his gaze out the window. A tree branch is rustling.

There are lights in the distance....

> RED
> Don't scratch.
>
> (pause/quieter...)
>
> Call Woolf.

They all exchange a glance.

> HOWARD
> Nobody rides that horse but you.

> RED
> (faint smile)
>
> He's got a lot more than me on his back any-way.

326 EXT. HOSPITAL. DAY.

A cab pulls up to the front of the hospital. George Woolf steps out with his tack-bag and white buckskin jacket. He stares at the front of the building.

327 INT. CORRIDOR. LONG LENS.

Howard, Marcela, and Smith all stand together, speaking
quietly. They keep glancing toward the hospital room.

328 INT. RED'S ROOM. THROUGH THE DOOR.

Woolf sits beside Red, his chair pulled up to the
side of the bed. Red's leg is suspended in full traction, so the image is partially obscured, but Woolf
leans in close, hanging on the words.

>   RED
>   ...He's got a strong left lead
>   Georgie...banks like a fuckin' airplane. But
>   he might need help switching to it, so ease
>   him off the rail just before the turn.

>   WOOLF
>   Like you did in The Gold Cup.

>   RED
>   Exactly.

Woolf's been watching as usual.

>   RED
>   He needs a good warm up so take him out
>   slow. And when you do ask him, don't use the
>   whip. Just flick it twice and show him it's
>   there. He'll know it's time.

>   WOOLF
>   Right.

>   RED
>   And never on the left side.
>   (beat)
>   They hit him on the left side when he was a
>   baby.

Woolf nods. There's a pause.

>   WOOLF
>   I wish it was you, Johnny.

>   RED
>   Oh, don't worry, Georgie. I'll be right
>   there with you.

329 EXT. HOSPITAL.

Howard stands in the rain facing reporters.

> HOWARD
>
> No. We're not going to scratch. Red Pollard wants Seabiscuit to win this race more than anything in the world. He wouldn't let us scratch.

> REPORTER SAM
>
> So who's gonna ride him?

329A CLOSE UP. TICK-TOCK

> TICK-TOCK
>
> THE ICEMAN COMETH! Talk about a pinch hitter! It's like getting Babe Ruth off the bench! Nerves of steel. Ice water in his veins. Why George Woolf is...

330 EXT. WAR ADMIRAL'S COMPOUND. DAY.

Mr. Riddle talks to reporters in "casual" attire.

> RIDDLE
>
> Irrelevant. They can get the four horsemen of the apocalypse as far as I'm concerned, and it won't make a difference. War Admiral is the superior horse. It really doesn't matter who the "passenger" is....

He laughs at his own "wit" for a beat then walks away...

CUT TO:

331 NIGHTTIME.

Woolf and Seabiscuit thunder by the CAMERA at full gallop. Sure enough, Woolf sits "chilly" in the saddle.

332 INT. RED'S HOSPITAL ROOM. NIGHT.

> WOOLF
>
> Oh, yeah. He was flying. I tried to check him but he just fought me harder. Then I eased up and talked to him just like you said and he started to float.

> RED
>
> Exactly. Now show him the stick at the quarter pole and he'll give you a whole new gear...

333 EXT. MAIN TRACK. THE MIDDLE OF THE NIGHT AGAIN...

Woolf comes out of the turn tight to Seabiscuit's
withers. He flashes the whip in front of him like Red
said, and the horse gets the signal, flattening out
and accelerating down the stretch.

334 INT. HOSPITAL ROOM. NIGHT.

They are huddled in the dim light of the wall lamp.

> RED
>
> Good. Now force him to that left lead a lit-
> tle earlier, before the turn. He'll give you
> even more.

335 EXT. MAIN TRACK. AT THE TURN...

Seabiscuit banks at almost a 45 degree angle, pressing into the rail like a water skier....

336 INT. HOSPITAL ROOM.

> RED
>
> Great. Now shut the door.

DIFFERENT ANGLE.

It's two in the morning and the ward is asleep. Red
motions over to the door and Woolf shuts it even
though nobody could possibly be listening. He comes
back to the bed and pulls up a chair. Red motions him
even closer.

> RED
> (a whisper)
>
> Okay — you know how Smith wants you to fight
> for the lead by the first turn?

> GEORGE
>
> Well yeah. We were working with that bell. I
> was a little nervous about it...

> RED
>
> No, no. That's fine.
> (pause)
>
> But you gotta give it up on the backstretch.

> GEORGE
> (beat)
>
> Give it up?

                              RED
          Give him back the lead.

Woolf looks at him confused.

                              RED
               (beat)

          He fights for it Georgie. No one's ever
          fought harder. If you bring him head to head
          with that other horse and he looks him in
          the eye, there's no way he loses that race —
          no matter how tired he is. Just hold him
          like that through the turn — give him a good
          look at the Admiral, then let him go.

Woolf listens. Nods.

                              RED
          It's not in his feet Georgie. It's right
          here.

Red points to his own heart, like he's going to run
the race himself.

                                              CUT TO:

337 AERIAL SHOT. RACETRACK. DAWN.

It's empty now, in the early morning light....

                         MCCULLOUGH
          By ten AM the closest place to park was fif-
          teen blocks away.

338 SHOT. BALTIMORE STREET.

It is jammed with cars. Crowds of people start heading toward the CAMERA, provisioned for the day with
hats, parasols, paper fans....

                         MCCULLOUGH
          The volume of refreshments alone was stag-
          gering. Seventeen thousand gallons of lemon-
          ade. A hundred thousand hot dogs. Four thou-
          sand kegs of beer...

339 EXT. TRACK.

The grandstand is off in the distance. Workers unload
a phalanx of beer kegs from five or six trucks.

MCCULLOUGH
The race was broadcast on NBC and businesses
around America scheduled a half day of work
so their employees could hear the call...

    (beat)

...thanks in part to a missive fired by Mr.
Howard, only the day before.

340 EXT. SEABISCUIT'S BARN.

Howard carries one of Seabiscuit's saddles.

HOWARD
Look, I know this is a fancy track and all,
but I think they oughtta open up the infield
so normal folks can come see the race. You
shouldn't have to be rich to enjoy something
like this.

341 FULL SHOT. PIMLICO MAIN GATES.

They are thrown open and a flood of people hurry
toward the CAMERA, literally consuming it....

342 EXT. INFIELD RAIL.

They line the rail five deep. It's all walks of life,
but mainly the most walked. Parents, grandparents,
children. Dads hoist kids on their shoulders not
wanting them to miss the historic occasion.

343 INT. JOCK'S ROOM.

Smith is huddled with George Woolf.

SMITH
Okay, it's still kinda soggy at the rail, so
try to keep him out of there.

WOOLF
There's a dry tractor tread about five feet
out. I walked it last night.

SMITH
(nods...impressed...)

Good...Now he oughtta break just like we
worked on, but there's one more thing...

Smith leans in a little closer. He's about to share a
final confidence with Woolf...

                        WOOLF
          Let him catch me on the backstretch?

Smith looks at him surprised. Woolf twirls the stick
with confidence and winks at Smith.

                        WOOLF
          You're not the only one who knows this
          horse...

344 EXT. PADDOCK.

He is vaulted up into the irons. There are only two
horses in the paddock and there is a mob around each.
Howard stands at Seabiscuit's nose. Smith holds the
bridle.

                        HOWARD
          Safe trip, George.

                        GEORGE
                (grins/totally composed)

          And a short one.

Instead of waiting around, he gives Seabiscuit a little nudge and starts heading out of the ring. The
groom still guides him, but Woolf looks impatient. As
they do, they pass Riddle, War Admiral, and his jockey Charley Kurtsinger. Woolf nods at his rival.

                        WOOLF
          Charley.

                        KURTSINGER
          George.

                        RADIO ANNOUNCER
"The two jockeys have acknowledged each other. It's a
quick hello like boxers touching gloves..."

345 INT. RED'S HOSPITAL ROOM.

He lies in bed listening to the crackly sound of the
radio.

                        RED
          C'mon Georgie. This is no time for small
          talk.

                        ANNOUNCER
          Both horses are now on the main track and
          you can hear the ROAR FROM THE CROWD....

346 EXT. TRACK. POST PARADE.

It's almost DEAFENING. People are hanging off of every square inch of real estate and it does sound more like a boxing match than a horse race. Both jockeys acknowledge the ovation as they head onto the track. Woolf begins to jog the Biscuit slowly.

347 SHOT. GRANDSTAND.

Howard and Marcela settle into their box.

> RACK FOCUS TO:

MR. RIDDLE doing the same thing several boxes away. They nod curtly at each other...

348 TOP OF THE STRETCH.

The starter has positioned himself in a small tower by the side of the chute. As agreed upon, there is no starting gate — just the line, a flagman, and the starter himself. All at once, there is a flurry of activity.

> STARTER
> My bell! Where's my bell?
>
> (yells down)
>
> My bell is gone!

DIFFERENT ANGLE.

Tom Smith is standing by the side of the rail clutching his hand-made bell from the firehouse. As the assistants all scurry around, trying to find the bell, Smith ducks under the rail and walks calmly up to the tower.

> SMITH
> Here. Try this one.

The starter looks over at him quizzically, suspiciously. He takes the bell...Tests it.... Smith smiles, nods, and slips quietly past the rail.

349 SHOT. THE BACKSTRETCH.

Woolf has paused with Seabiscuit in the middle of the backstretch facing the grandstand — taking it in. The CROWD is more muffled back here and it actually feels like a moment alone. Suddenly and without any urging, Seabiscuit decides he's ready and jerks his head toward the start....

HIGH ANGLE. RACE TRACK.`

> ANNOUNCER
>
> ...And here come the two horses up to the
> line. They enter the chute. The flagman in
> his position. First it's War Admiral up to
> the line...Then he backs off...Now Seabiscuit
> walks up...

350 TIGHTER. THE CHUTE.

Palpable tension. First one horse walks up, then
backs off, then the other — each one jockeying for
position — trying to time the moment just right. All
the human commands are down to one word grunts:
"Okay...good.... Right, right..."

TIGHTER STILL.

Finally both horses walk up the line together. Woolf
leans over the top of the withers...So does
Kurtsinger...The crowd goes silent.... The world goes
still....

351 INSERT. SMITH'S BELL.

The starter's finger is poised over the makeshift
button. He presses down and...

352 SILENCE.

Actually the CRACKLY SOUND of the RADIO CALL. There
is thrill and tension in the ANNOUNCER'S VOICE but it
seems it comes from a million miles away — drifting
out over the airwaves of America.

> ANNOUNCER'S VOICE
>
> It's Seabiscuit who breaks first...Pounding
> down the homestretch...

353 SERIES OF STILLS. EMPTY STREETS.

No one on the sidewalks. No one in the restaurants.
No one waiting for subways or going to work. The
streets of the COUNTRY ARE LITERALLY EMPTY as everyone strains at their radio sets, to hear the staticky
call.

ANNOUNCER'S VOICE
They come by the grandstand for the first
time...It's Seabiscuit by a nose...Now by a
head.... War Admiral pressing him a neck
behind. They fly toward the clubhouse turn
both of them fighting for the rail and
it's...it's...SEABISCUIT — hitting the turn
first and driving for the backstretch.

CUT TO:

354 THUNDER. LIVE ACTION.

Both horses barrel out of the clubhouse turn and fly
into the backstretch. Seabiscuit is now a length and
a half in front, his body angled sharply through the
turn as he curves around it on a strong left lead...

SHOT. WOOLF.

He opens a two length lead settling over the front of
the horse. Past his shoulder we can see War Admiral
pressing on his right flank. Woolf drives with his
hands still holding a two length lead. It's a hard
thing to give up.

355 INT. HOSPITAL ROOM.

Red presses his ear to the radio...

ANNOUNCER
Seabiscuit now by two and a half...

RED
C'mon, Georgie. Don't fuck around.

356 SHOT. RAIL.

Smith clutches the binoculars to his head.

357 SHOT. WOOLF.

He's halfway through the stretch with the turn rapidly approaching. Woolf takes a deep breath, doubts the
wisdom of the whole strategy, but pulls back on the
reins anyway, grabbing a handful of horse. Gradually,
he begins to check.

358 ANGLE. GRANDSTAND.

ANNOUNCER
And here comes WAR ADMIRAL!

The crowd is going absolutely WILD. People stand on
chairs. Teeter on the railings. The NOISE is deafening and they haven't even hit the turn.

359 SHOT. SEABISCUIT.

He strains at the bit, fighting to stay out in front but
Woolf is pulling him hard, trying to hold him. After a
beat or two WAR ADMIRAL inches INTO THE SHOT, coming eye
to eye with the Biscuit. All at once, Seabiscuit starts
to drive harder, fighting wildly against the reins.
Woolf struggles to keep him in check.

> ANNOUNCER
> And they're...EVEN going into the turn!
> These two horses are neck and neck. It's
> Seabiscuit by a nose! Now War Admiral...Now
> Seabiscuit...Now War Admiral...And they're
> together as they hit the stretch!

UP ANGLE. THE TURN. FROM THE HOMESTRETCH.

The two horses fly INTO FOCUS, literally in a dead
heat. They blow through FRAME, their strides in
sync...

THE TWO HORSES TOGETHER.

Their heads bob in unison. The jockeys are shoulder
to shoulder. Seabiscuit strains to get free of
Woolf's hold.

Kurtsinger has gone to the whip in an attempt to urge
War Admiral. As they head down the stretch, the ROAR
of the crowd gets even LOUDER. Seabiscuit actually
turns his head and locks eyes with his rival:

SHOT. SLOW MOTION.

They bob heads together. Seabiscuit fixes a glance on
the larger horse, as if to say "How dare you. How
dare you even be next to me." Woolf continues to hold
him in check...

360 SHOT. SMITH.

He lowers the binoculars.

361 SHOT. HOWARD.

He clutches his program.

362. INT. HOSPITAL ROOM.

Red closes his eyes. He pauses for a beat...

> RED
> (quietly)
>
> Now, Georgie.

363 SHOT. WOOLF.

He CLUCKS twice and lets go. Seabiscuit suddenly EXPLODES.

His stride lengthens, his neck drives. War Admiral's eye rolls back in his head as the Biscuit pulls away.

> ANNOUNCER
> AND HERE COMES SEABISCUIT!

HEAD ON. THE BISCUIT.

He leaves War Admiral literally in his wake as he drives for the finish line. The big black horse recedes pathetically in the shot as Seabiscuit's stride lengthens more and more.

> ANNOUNCER
> It's Seabiscuit by three, by four, War Admiral is fading. He can't keep up. Seabiscuit by five. It's the Biscuit GOING AWAY!

SLOW MOTION. THE WIRE....

Seabiscuit and Woolf surge through the frame. It is total stillness for a beat — then War Admiral struggles home.

364 SHOT. HOWARD AND MARCELA.

They leap into the air — scream — embrace...

365 SHOT. RIDDLE.

He glances down, stunned...shocked...

366 SHOT. TOM SMITH.

He nods. Smiles slightly. Takes a deep breath of fresh air...

367 INT. HOSPITAL CORRIDOR.

A few patients sit in the hall, getting a slight change of scenery. The place is pretty still, and then...

                    RED'S VOICE (OS)
          GODDAMN SONOFABITCH! THAT IS SOME AMAZING
          HORSE!

An old lady in a wheelchair smiles to herself.

368 CRANE SHOT. OVER THE INFIELD.

They are most jubilant of all. The CAMERA CHASES
WOOLF down the track while he eases up Seabiscuit...

It passes over the heads of several thousand screaming fans who leap up and down with no sign of stop-
ping. It's a carnival.

                                        JUMP TO:

369 THE WINNER'S CIRCLE.

Woolf leaps down from the irons to an embrace from
Marcela and Howard. A radio mike is shoved in his
face.

                    REPORTER JOE
          Well you did it Ice Man! How does it feel?

                    WOOLF
             (he pauses)

          I just wish it was my friend Red up here
          instead of me.

The interview plays over the PA system and this
brings the loudest cheer of all. Woolf turns and
salutes the infield.

370 INT. RED'S HOSPITAL ROOM.

The CHEERING continues to play OVER as Red listens to
radio. Slowly, it begins to subside as his gaze
drifts out the window.

                                        CUT TO:

EXT. TRAIN PLATFORM. DAY.

A huge crowd is assembled to see the "Biscuit
Special" pull out of the station. It's quite an
entourage: Seabiscuit, Pumpkin, the Howards, Woolf,
Smith.... Seabiscuit is led up the long metal ramp to
a huge ovation from the crowd.

372 EXT. REAR OF TRAIN.

Howard watches nervously as Red's wheelchair is hoisted up and loaded in the back like a piece of cargo. Red looks out at the crowd that never saw him ride...

                                                                    CUT TO:

373 LATER...

The train streaks across the country at dusk.

374 INT. CLUB CAR. LONG LENS. GEORGE WOOLF.

From across the lounge, you can't hear what he's saying but the anecdote is clear. Woolf stands at the bar reenacting the race, his hands poised in front of him, grabbing imaginary reins. Marcela, Tick-Tock, and even a porter or two listen intently while Woolf describes holding Seabiscuit back, and then turning him loose at the quarter pole.

CLOSE UP. RED.

He watches from his wheelchair all the way across the car.

375 EXT. SANTA ANITA TRAIN PLATFORM. DAY.

The entourage disembarks. First Pumpkin, then the Biscuit, then the Howards...

                                                                    CUT TO:

376 EXT. RIDGEWOOD. DUSK.

Red arrives alone. An attendant moves around toward the rear passenger door and helps him into the wheelchair. Red lowers himself down with a wince. He pauses and looks out at the field...

                                                                    CUT TO:

377 NIGHT.

A light is burning in a downstairs window.

378 INT. LIVING ROOM.

Red sits in a large overstuffed chair in the massive living room of Ridgewood. Several books have been pulled down from the shelves and lie open on the table in front of him. Instead of reading, Red just stares...

                                                                    CUT TO:

379 THE SANTA ANITA BUGLER...

Playing "Call to the Post" as the horses walk onto the track.

> TICK-TOCK (OS)
> Well — hail the conquering hero. Yes he's back folks: The Little Engine that Could. No more match races for this little colt because frankly, they're all outta matches! Who's he gonna race — Pegasus? Oh I pity these other horses.

380 SHOT. TRACK ENTRANCE. (COMING OUT OF THE TUNNEL)

First there is a gray, then a jet black colt, then a huge OVATION as SEABISCUIT makes his way out onto the...

381 PORCH.

Red limps outside with the help of some crutches and pulls himself to a large wicker chair. He deposits himself and stares out at the mountains of Ridgewood....

382 THE STARTING GATE...

Woolf maneuvers Seabiscuit into the gate, stroking his neck. The bond is growing between horse and rider and he loads without incident. The other horses load in beside him. Woolf leans forward over the withers. The flag is up...

383 RED.

Closes his eyes. There's sunlight streaming in and it's an easy way to forget. He lies there, motionless.

384 THE RACE. (MOS)

Instead of the usual pounding, everything is QUIET — almost dreamlike. The horses fly down the backstretch with Seabiscuit five lengths off the pace. As they hit the turn Woolf eases him out and switches to the strong left lead. Seabiscuit finds a hole at the rail and starts picking off the horses in front of him with relentless precision. He's fourth, then third, then second, then...pop...just a pop. Quiet. Almost unnoticeable. "Pop."

385 RED.

Opens his eyes.... Another "pop"

386 HIS POV.

Off in the distance, a maid is beating the dust out
of a rug hung over a clothes line. Pop...pop....

387 THE RACE. (REPEAT FOOTAGE)

Seabiscuit rounds the turn: Third...Then Second...Then
"pop." WOOLF LOOKS DOWN. Seabiscuit pulls up. A horse
overtakes him.

388 SAME FOOTAGE. REPEATED.

Again and again like a loop.... He rounds the
turn...He picks off a horse...He drives for the lead.
"Pop..." "pop..." "pop..."

389 RED.

Bolts upright. He looks at the woman beating the rug.
Wrong sound. All at once he yanks himself out of the
chair and starts fighting his way toward the horse
along the railing.

390 RUNNING SHOT. BEHIND HOWARD AND MARCELA.

They fly down the stairs of Santa Anita, the CAMERA
CHASING BEHIND THEM.

391 SHOT. SEABISCUIT.

He limps past the line, LIFTING HIS FOOT IN PAIN.

392 SHOT. RED.

He fights his way inside. Hobbles toward a tele-
phone...

                                        CUT TO:

393 NIGHT.

The track is dark. Some lights burn on the backstretch.

394 INT. RIDGEWOOD. LIVING ROOM.

Red is dimly lit — speaks into the phone.

                    RED
          When will they know?

395 SHOT. STABLE OFFICE. THE BACKSTRETCH.

Marcela responds.

> MARCELA
> I don't know. Maybe an hour. I'm not sure.
> Charles is with the vet right now.

> RED (VO)
> Does it hurt when he bends it? 'Cause if it
> doesn't hurt when he bends it...

396 INT. RIDGEWOOD...

Red nods a couple of times and hangs up slowly. As he
does...

                                              CUT TO:

397 EXT. STALL 38.

Charles, Smith, Marcela, and Woolf all wait outside
the door.

IT's a mirror image of Red's hospital room, just not
as bright. After a beat or two, the veterinarian
emerges.

CLOSER.

They wait for him to speak — almost don't want him
to. He draws a long breath.

> VET
> (to Howard)
>
> Look, he ruptured the whole ligament. I put
> a splint on it, just to keep him immobilized
> but right now he's totally lame.

> VET
> (beat)
>
> He's not gonna race again.

Marcela cries. Howard flinches. Smith glances toward
the stall. After a beat, the vet leans closer to
Howard.

> VET
> (lowers his voice)
>
> Look, I know this is hard...
>
> (pause/lower)
>
> I'll put him down if you want me to.

SHOT. HOWARD.

He looks at the vet, then just like Red Pollard, hauls back his fist and PUNCHES him in the jaw.

CUT TO:

398 EXT. RIDGEWOOD. DAY.

A horse van pulls up the long gravel road that leads toward the house.

SHOT. PORCH.

Red is already balancing on his crutches, "standing" on the top step of the porch. As soon as he sees Seabiscuit, Red begins to hobble down the stairs that lead to the grass.

SHOT. VAN.

They lead the Biscuit out and he smells the spring air. Then he sees Red and tries to take a step. The weight won't hold him and he stumbles. Two grooms keep him steady.

SHOT. RED.

> RED
> (limping)

It's okay, Pops. I'll come to you.

FOLLOWING RED.

He hobbles across the gravel that leads down to the van. Seabiscuit SNORTS when he sees him, stumbling forward to get to Red.

DIFFERENT ANGLE.

Red comes up and puts his arm around the horse's neck. His crutch falls to the ground. They're quite a sight: these two cripples meeting each other in the middle of a driveway.

Seabiscuit leans in and nuzzles Red, who pulls a carrot from his pocket.

CUT TO:

399 RAIN.

Red sits on the PORCH with a book opened on his lap. He stares out at the spring shower.

400 INT. STALL.

Biscuit lies next to Pumpkin looking out at the paddock getting soaked.

401 INT. BARN LATER.

The sun is out. Red has pulled a stool next to The Biscuit and is working his foreleg back and forth. There is a long bandage up to the knee. Red's crutches sit beside the stool.

> RED
> See first you gotta get a little flexibility...then you can start to put some weight on it.
>
> (almost about himself)
>
> ...Then once you start to put weight on it, the whole leg starts to get stronger.

The Biscuit SNORTS.

> RED
> I know. I'm in a hurry too Pops. But you know what Hadrian said about Rome: "Brick by brick, my citizens. Brick by brick."

402 EXT. PASTURE. DAY.

It's SUMMER and the grass has grown leggy and wild — the tips of it turning brown. Red has a cane now, instead of crutches.

He limps next to Seabiscuit as they make their way waist deep through a high mountain meadow.

> RED
> See, they're Arabians so they don't need to drink. These horses can go five or six days without a drop of water. Like a camel.

SNORTS again...

> RED
> I'm not saying you should do it, I'm just saying that's what they do.

The Biscuit stops. Red stops too.

> RED
> Good idea. Take a little break.

403 EXT. LAKE.

They lie down together. Biscuit sleeps in the grass. Red lies against him, reading a book...

LATER...

Red still reads. He glances up to see the Biscuit standing down by the edge of the water. Seabiscuit bends down, and puts all his weight on his front hooves, taking a long drink.

CLOSER.

Biscuit sees a sudden ripple in the water and lurches backwards. It's a quick, jerky movement but he seems unbothered by it. After a beat, he leans down and takes another drink.

CLOSE UP. RED.

He takes the whole thing in...

                                        CUT TO:

404 CLOSE UP. AN EXERCISE SADDLE...

Two hands reach up and pull it down from the rafters...

405 EXT. PADDOCK.

The Biscuit is saddled by the edge of the fence. He points his face into the wind. Red stands next to him waiting for a boost up from Sam the stablehand.

                    SAM
          I don't know, Red.

                    RED
          We're just gonna walk in a circle.

                    SAM
          Can the leg hold you?

                    RED
          Horse weighs twelve hundred pounds, Sam. I'm
          an afterthought.

                    SAM
          No, I mean your leg.

Red looks at him for a beat then lifts up his pants leg. He has jammed a broomstick into his boot for support and lashed it to his knee. Sam looks at him — shakes his head...

CUT TO:

LONG SHOT. PADDOCK.

Red and the Biscuit hobble in a long slow circle. Red
has a huge smile on his face. It looks like a pony
ride.

CLOSER.

The reins are threaded through his fingers. Red's
shattered leg can't support the weight so he sits in
the saddle instead of balancing in the irons.
Still....

> RED
> "And here comes Seabiscuit, charging down
> the lane..."

Red throws his hands forward simulating a stretch
drive. The Biscuit continues to amble in a long slow
walk...

406 SHOT. KITCHEN WINDOW.

Howard watches it all through a screen.

CUT TO:

407 DINNER.

> Red has a huge plate of food. He loads on a
> second pork chop then glances up at the
> table where Howard and Marcela are both
> staring at him.
>> RED
>> (mouthful)
> What?

CUT TO:

408 FALL...

The colors have exploded and Red now walks through
the high country on Seabiscuit's back.

CLOSER. LONG LENS.

Red turns him gently as the path begins to curve. He
heads into some higher brush when all at once there is
a loud FLURRY of birds. A flock of quail erupts right
in front of Seabiscuit who bolts away. He canters for
five or six strides before Red can rein him in.

                            RED
            Whoa, Pops....

CLOSE UP. RED POLLARD.

His heart is racing. The reins are tight in his fingers. He has cantered. For five or six strides, he
cantered.

Red looks down at his horse who still seems strong
and right.

He takes a deep breath.

                                            CUT TO:

409 THE GARAGE.

Red wheels out a lawnmower with the help of Sam the
stablehand.

410 INSERT. LAWN MOWER.

As it cuts the grass.

411 FULL SHOT. THROUGH THE BARN DOORS. DAWN.

The CAMERA PUSHES behind them as Red leads Seabiscuit
through doors and out to the paddock. Facing the sun
it's hard to make out, but he has mowed the grass
into a long gentle oval.

                                            CUT TO:

412 SEABISCUIT.

He canters gently around the ring. Red's expression
is one of elation and pain as he supports himself on
the broomstick jammed into his boot top.

CLOSE UP. RED.

He eases up and throws his head back. Red has a huge
smile on his face — it's a different kind of finish
line...

413 INT. DINING ROOM. NIGHT.

Red sits at the table with Charles, Marcela, and Sam.
Marcela passes a large plate of ham to Red who takes
only a quarter of a piece and passes it on. The rest
of his plate is empty.

SHOT. MARCELA.

She takes a large bowl of sweet potatoes and hands it to Red.

He refuses that too, passing it across the table to Sam.

Howard glances over at Red's empty plate. It's quiet for a beat.

>   MARCELA
>   Okay, am I the only one who's gonna admit
>   what's going on here?

Everyone looks over at her...

                                                    CUT TO:

414 EXT. PADDOCK. DAY.

Smith approaches the paddock while Red talks a blue streak.

>   RED
>   ...You know, not a gallop but a full lope.
>   He changed gaits perfectly.

>   SMITH
>   Any tenderness around the tendon.

>   RED
>   No. And I rubbed him down afterward. Gave
>   him some more of that liniment you sent me.

They reach the fence. Seabiscuit comes over and nuzzles Smith.

>   SMITH
>   Hello old man.

He lets out a loud, strong WHINNY. It's defiant, competitive...Smith strokes his nose.

                                                    JUMP TO:

415 LATER...

Red is loping him in a circle around the ring. Smith, Howard, and Marcela all watch as Seabiscuit rounds the small oval with ease. Red clucks and he picks up the cadence slightly.

416 EXT. PORCH NIGHT.

They sit together on the porch of Ridgewood watching dusk happen over the hill. There's a pitcher of iced tea...

> MARCELA
> Is it really possible?

> SMITH
> Sure. Most folks don't give it a chance.
> Most folks just, you know...

He doesn't finish it. They know what most folks do.

> SMITH
> Best thing to do is get him down there and
> let him gallop a little. It's the only way
> we're really gonna know.

> HOWARD
> Can he handle that?

> SMITH
> Oh sure. I think so...

Smith stops short. He looks down the lawn.

REVERSE ANGLE.

Red is limping toward them in the fading light. He leans heavy on his cane, fighting his way up the gentle slope.

It's an agonizing, tortured image: a cripple, struggling to conquer the simplest task. Only one of them has really healed...

ANGLE. PORCH.

All three of them are hurting....

CUT TO:

417 EXT. "CLOCKERS CORNER." SANTA ANITA. DAWN.

It's blue light — barely daybreak. Smith stands at Clockers Corner next to Howard, while Seabiscuit breezes around the turn. It's not race speed by any means but it is a gallop.

Howard looks over at Smith, who looks at the horse...

CUT TO:

418 THE RAIL.

Smith and Howard stand by the edge of the track while the "exercise rider" lopes up to them. It's George Woolf.

>   WOOLF
>   He felt great. Ran smooth. Real relaxed. I
>   couldn't feel a thing.

>   SMITH
>   (nods)

>   Why don't we give him a full work on Friday
>   morning. Maybe six furlongs. See what we
>   got.

>   WOOLF
>   (surprised)

>   Sure. I'll be here.

Smith and Howard turn as Woolf heads Seabiscuit back toward the barn. They head up Clockers Corner toward the grandstand.

>   HOWARD
>   Could he be ready?

>   SMITH
>   For what?

>   HOWARD
>   C'mon. You know what.

Smith returns a look as they pass an old tout with his face buried in the Form. Howard hesitates, then looks down at him. The man slowly lowers the paper:

>   TICK-TOCK
>   Top of the mornin' to ya.

Howard nods.

>   TICK-TOCK
>   Nice Colt. Who is it?

>   HOWARD
>   Only a two year old. He's not ready yet.

>   TICK-TOCK
>   Oh. I thought maybe you were getting some
>   horse ready for the Hundred Grander.

>   HOWARD
>   No. Just a two year old.

He picks up Tick-Tock's coffee; smells it.

> TICK-TOCK
> Hair of the dog.

Howard nods.

> HOWARD
> Been here long?

> TICK-TOCK
> No, no. I just got here.
> (raises the Form)
> Catching up on my reading.

They nod. He nods....

CUT TO:

419 CLOSE UP. TICK-TOCK.

> TICK-TOCK
> STOP THE PRESSES! This isn't a scoop folks. It's
> three scoops, hot fudge and a cherry on top. And add
> some nuts 'cause this horse makes me CRAZY! GUESS
> WHO'S GONNA BE WORKING SIX FURLONGS ON FRIDAY MORN-
> ING? GUESS WHO MAY BE SHOOTING FOR THE "BIG 'CAP!" OH
> my Saints Alive! You guessed it. Man oh man — DID YOU
> EVER GUESS IT!

420 CLOSE UP. RED.

He shuts off his radio. Looks around Frankie's room.
His heart is pounding...

CUT TO:

421 EXT. SANTA ANITA TRAIN DEPOT. LONG LENS. MORNING.

In the TELEPHOTO SHOT all the travelers crush together. They hurry down the platform toward loved ones or
taxis. Off in the distance, being overtaken by everyone, is one lone figure hobbling on a cane....

422 EXT. THE GAP. MORNING.

There is a buzz of activity. Clockers Corner is full
of people all assembled for the morning workouts. The
Gap looks like the souk: jockeys, agents, touts,
horses...This isn't a normal morning.

423 EXT. STALL 38.

Smith and Howard walk Seabiscuit toward the track with Woolf up in the irons.

                    SMITH
          (looking up at Woolf)

     A minute twelve, a minute thirteen — some-
     thin' like that. If he starts to labor, slow
     it down.

                    WOOLF

     Gotcha...

                    SMITH
     Just try to see how he feels and....

All at once Seabiscuit WHINNIES and literally paws at the ground. He jerks his head over to the side and pulls on the reins.

REVERSE ANGLE.

Red is standing a few feet away, leaning on his cane and holding his riding boots. The horse WHINNIES again.

                    RED
     That's okay Pops. That's alright...

                    WOOLF
     Red.

                    RED
          (faint/quotes Julius Caesar)

     "And this the most unkindest cut of all."

Woolf says nothing. Red turns and starts to hobble away.

                    HOWARD
          (following him)

     Red, let me talk to you.

                    RED
     Talk to me.

He keeps walking. Howard moves in front of him.

                    HOWARD
     You can't do it Red. You could be crippled
     for the rest of your life.

Red looks at him and laughs.

                              RED
          I was crippled for the rest of my life. I
          got better. He made me better — Hell, you
          made me better...Jesus Christ....

There are tears in his eyes. Red shakes his head, and
starts away from him. He stops and turns back.

                              RED
          That's as much my horse as yours.

Howard makes a move toward him but Red waves him off.
He limps away, teetering on the cane....

                                             CUT TO:

424 THE TRACK.

Seabiscuit gallops by the finish line with Woolf in
the irons.

ANGLE. THE RAIL.

Several stopwatches click at once. Howard stands in
and amongst them.

                              MAN
                    (exuberant)
          One eleven and three! That's fantastic!

CLOSE UP. HOWARD.

Howard nods. It's a great time...

                              HOWARD
                    (beat)
          Goddammit.

425 INT. DOCTOR'S OFFICE. (WAITING ROOM) DAY.

Red sits next to Howard in the waiting room, his cane
laying across his lap.

                              HOWARD
                    (firmly)
          It's up to him, Red.

                              RED
          Yeah, but if he says...

                              HOWARD
          It's up to him.

426 INT. EXAMINING ROOM.

The doctor holds a homemade brace jury-rigged with
bent iron rods and leather thongs from an old bridle.

> DOCTOR
> You made this?

> RED
> Yeah. See it fastens around the boot and
> then up here at the top of the thigh. You
> barely feel anything when you're in the
> stirrup.

CLOSER.

The doctor nods. Holds brace up in front of him...

MATCH CUT TO:

427 AN X-RAY.

The "brace" is displaced with an image of Red's leg,
showing multiple breaks and pins. The doctor stares
at them for a long moment.

WIDER.

He is standing next to Howard. Red is outside. The
doctor points to all the carnage along the femur...

> DOCTOR
> Look, it could shatter at any moment. Even
> right now — forget about racing.
>
> (points)
>
> See that right there: that's barely healed.
> There's no way to know how much weight it
> could hold under stress.
>
> (turns)
>
> It's possible he could never walk again.

428 INT. CAR. LATER...

Howard drives. Red is beside him.

> RED
> Possible. He just said it was possible. Well
> hell — anything is "possible." We proved
> that already, didn't we?

> HOWARD
> This is different Red.

                              RED
               Yeah. This is really different.

They ride, silent for a beat.

                              RED
               It's not just a race. It's the Santa Anita.
               I had that race. I was there....

                         HOWARD
               I know.

He doesn't say anything else. They stare through the
windshield. Howard turns on the radio to fill the
void:

                                        CUT TO:

429 A HUGE CHALK BOARD.

It sits in the middle of a crowded paddock. There's
period script across the top: 1940 Santa Anita
Handicap. Below it are spaces for the entrants, half
of them filled in.

CLOSER.

A man writes carefully with a white piece of chalk —
it looks like a child's exercise: Wedding
Call...Whichcee...he pauses for effect: SEABISCUIT.
There's a ROAR from the CROWD.

                                        CUT TO:

430 INT. JOCK'S ROOM.

Howard sits with Woolf at his cubicle.

                         HOWARD
               Even with the brace it'll barely hold him.
               If he gets bumped — if he gets jostled...

                         WOOLF
               Want to know what I think?

                         HOWARD
               ...Sure.

                         WOOLF
               I think it's better to break a man's leg
               than his heart.

Howard looks at him for a beat...

                    HOWARD'S VOICE (V.O.)
               It's not just his leg...

430A EXT. BRIDLE PATH. SANTA ANITA. DUSK.

It's the long arcade of eucalyptus trees from the barn area to the track. Howard and Marcela are small amongst them.

> MARCELA
>
> Okay.

> HOWARD
>
> It's not, Marcela. He could fall. He could get trampled. If he gets thrown from that horse he could...

> MARCELA
>
> Die?

> HOWARD
>
> (beat)
>
> ...He could die.

She moves forward and reaches into the pocket of his coat. Marcela pulls out a small child's game.

> MARCELA
>
> You know, I try to do this all the time too. I can never quite get it to stay in there, no matter what I do. Every time I think I have it, it just rolls out again.

Their eyes lock. His suddenly have tears. Marcela wraps her hand around his arm and leans closer to him, like they're holding each other up.

> MARCELA
>
> (softly)
>
> Let him ride, Charles. Just let him do it.

He looks at her. Nods...

CUT TO:

431 SHOT. TICK-TOCK. AT CLOCKERS CORNER.

> TICK-TOCK (OS)
>
> JUMPIN' JEHOSOPHATZ! I could handle one comeback but this is ridiculous! What's next, Lazarus? Oh the heroism. The madness. The excitement. The...

CUT TO:

432 RACE DAY. INT. PRESS BOX.

...largest crowd ever to see a race here at Santa Anita. Fifty five thousand in the stands. Twenty thousand in the infield and it's only twelve o'clock.

                                        CUT TO:

433 RED'S LEG.

As the braces are being attached.

WIDER. INT. STALL 38.

It's a little bit solemn. Howard, Marcela, and Smith all watch as Red attaches the cumbersome apparatus to his leg. He stands and flexes with a wince. Marcela takes a small medal and jams it into Red's hand

                    RED
          What's this.

                    MARCELA
          St. Christopher. For luck.

                    RED
               (smiles)

          Little late for that, don't you think?

Howard can't help smiling too. Red looks over to the Biscuit.

                    RED
          C'mon, Pops. Let's go win us a race.

                                        CUT TO:

434 THE PADDOCK.

Red is hoisted gingerly up onto Seabiscuit's back.

                    SMITH
          Whichcee's the speed. He's gonna be off on
          the lead but I don't think he'll handle the
          distance. Just stalk him like always.

                    RED
               (testing the brace/winces)

          Right.

                    SMITH
          Wedding Call could make a late run and he's
          got some guts, so look out for him too.

                              RED
                           (winks)
          Won't make that mistake again.

Smith smiles at him.

                              RED
          Stop worrying, Tom. We're gonna be fine.

And he reins the Biscuit toward the track...

435 INT. TUNNEL...

It's pitch black with a blinding white light at the
end. Red rides toward it, Seabiscuit's head silhouetted
in front.

CONTINUING...RED'S POV

As they emerge onto the track all the familiar images
of Santa Anita start to come clear: the gleaming
white rail, the bright green turf, the ROAR from the
crowd: maybe for the last time. Red looks around and
the OVATION grows louder as the track announcer
declares their arrival:

                        TRACK ANNOUNCER
          And here's number four...SEABISCUIT.

You can't hear. They press against the rail. Lean out
of the boxes. The Biscuit gets a little spring in his
step and starts to jog down the track. Red winces,
grits his teeth and raises up in the irons.

436 SHOT. HOWARD.

He settles into his box. Bing is there. Giannini.
Strubb. Howard receives congratulations from all of
his old friends.

He's elated but nervous...

437 EXT. BARNS.

Marcela can't watch. She sits on a stablehand's stool
outside the barn staring down at the straw. She
glances up at the sound of a distant OVATION....

438 EXT. TRACK.

                          ANNOUNCER
          The horses are approaching the starting
          gate...

WITH RED...

He leads the Biscuit toward the gate, then pauses and
takes a hard look at it — soaking it up — making it
last. Red takes a deep breath and flicks the
reins....

                         RED
              Okay Pops. Let's go.

He loads into the gate. Red adjusts his brace slightly and hunches forward. A moment later he hears a
VOICE to his left.

                    WOOLF (OS)
              Hello old man.

DIFFERENT ANGLE.

Red turns to see Woolf, two horses away.

                         RED
              What are you doing here?

                       WOOLF
              Got another mount. Just 'cause I'm not rid-
              ing him doesn't mean I'm gonna sit the race
              out.

Woolf grins. Red smiles — shakes his head.

                       WOOLF
              See ya at the finish line.

And he yanks down his goggles.

439 HOWARD'S BOX.

He lifts up his glasses to see the start....

440 EXT. BARNS.

Marcela can't take it anymore. She bolts off the
stool and starts running toward the track.

FOLLOWING HER.

She approaches the grandstand just as the BELL goes
off. There's no time to make it to the box so Marcela
climbs up on a water truck parked just outside the
service entrance.

                                        CUT TO:

441 THE RACE.

Red sits off the lead about three or four lengths back, stalking Whichcee, just like Smith predicted. Seabiscuit banks well into the first turn, driving through it. When they come out the other side, they are five lengths back.

ON RED.

He's grimacing. Even through the dirt and the movement you can see the pain on his face. Red gets trapped in a pack with four of the trailers. Morning Star bumps him toward the rail, and Red cries out in pain. He eases back even further.

442 ON HOWARD.

He has a vice grip on the binoculars.

443 ON MARCELA.

She clutches the railing of the water truck.

444 THE RACE.

The field spreads out in the backstretch. Red finds a little room away from the rail and takes Seabiscuit wide of the pack.

As they head up the backstretch Whichcee is eight lengths in front of him. By the time they hit the five furlong pole, the lead has stretched to nine.

CLOSE UP. RED.

The time has come. He CLUCKS twice and eases off the reins.

Red asks the Biscuit to go, rolling his hands and flicking them forward.

Seabiscuit doesn't move.

> ANNOUNCER
> ...He's nine lengths back. Now ten...The Biscuit seems to be tiring. It's still Whichcee on the lead as they head toward the turn.

WITH RED...

The field is moving away from him. The lead gets larger and larger as he sees the front runners disappearing. Red tries to drive with his legs and even flashes the stick in front of him but it still doesn't do any good. It's a huge amount to make up.

445 SHOT. SMITH.

He knows just what's happening. Smith glances down...

446 WITH RED.

Another horse starts to fade as well. It tires and starts to drop away from the pack and coming toward Red: three lengths, then two, then one...After a moment, he looks over to see his old friend George Woolf beside him.

DIFFERENT ANGLE.

Without saying a word, Woolf pulls the two horses even, letting them run head to head. He lets Seabiscuit look his own mount right in the eye, then glances at Red and gives a little grin. All at once, Red feels a tug on the reins as Seabiscuit begins to gather under him.

CLOSE UP. RED.

He gets it. Red feels the straining. He holds Seabiscuit like that for a beat or two, letting him run head to head with the other horse then finally CLUCKS twice and lets him go.

> RED
> C'mon, Pops.

> WOOLF
> Have a nice trip, Johnny.

Seabiscuit surges forward devouring the racetrack in front of him. He makes up two lengths, then three, then four...

> ANNOUNCER
> HERE COMES SEABISCUIT!

SHOT. THE BISCUIT.

The horse is devouring the track with his old speed and hunger, almost like he remembers it again. Red hunches over the withers, driving with his hands as they make up ground on the pack — any pain in his leg a total afterthought. When they reach the turn, Seabiscuit has hit the back of the pack. Red hunches down further and begins picking off horses.

RUNNING WITH RED.

He begins to weave his way through the field, shooting through split-second gaps and forcing sudden holes at the rail. Red guides the Biscuit like a slalom skier, weaving in and out as the track announcer explodes.

> ANNOUNCER
> He's fourth, now third, now second. Oh my gosh — only Whichcee remains. They hit the stretch and it's...SEABISCUIT.

RED'S POV. SLOW MOTION.

Whichcee fades as he drives for the lead. The only image that remains is that of a wide open track: dirt, finish line, blue sky beyond...It looks infinite.

> RED'S VOICE (OVER)
> You know, everybody thinks we found this broken down horse and fixed him, but we didn't...

447 SHOT. SEABISCUIT. SLOW MOTION.

He drives down the lane, pushing toward the wire.

> RED'S VOICE (OVER)
> He fixed us. Every one of us. And, I guess in a way, we kind of fixed each other too.

448 SHOT. MARCELA.

She has tears of joy on top of the water truck.

449 SHOT. HOWARD.

The crowd goes wild. He lowers the binoculars to take it all in.

450 SHOT. SMITH.

He looks at the wire, then shakes his head.... Some horse.

451 SHOT. RED.

It hurts but who cares. Red crosses the wire and then, with his last ounce of strength, lifts himself up in the irons his whip high in the air.

{THE END}

SEABISCUIT

PRODUCTION NOTES

I N THE WINTER OF 1937, *America was in the seventh year of the most cat-astrophic decade in its history. The economy had come crashing down, and millions upon millions of people had been torn loose from their jobs, their savings, their homes. A nation that drew its audacity from the quintessentially American belief that success is open to anyone willing to work for it was disillusioned by seemingly intractable poverty. The most brash of peoples was seized by despair, fatalism, and fear.*

The sweeping devastation was giving rise to powerful new social forces. The first was a burgeoning industry of escapism. America was desperate to lose itself in anything that offered affirmation. The nation's corner theaters hosted 85 million people a week for 25-cent viewings of an endless array of cheery musicals and screwball comedies. On the radio, the idealized world of One Man's Family *and the just and reassuring tales of* The Lone Ranger *were runaway hits. Downtrodden Americans gravitated strongly toward the Horatio Alger protagonist, the lowly bred Everyman who rises from anonymity and hopelessness. They looked for him in spectator sports, which were enjoying explosive growth. With the relegalization of wagering, no sport was growing faster than Thoroughbred racing.*

Necessity spurred technological innovations that offered the public unprecedented access to its heroes. People accustomed to reading comparatively dry rehashes of events were now enthralled by vivid scenes rolling across the new Movietone newsreels. A public that had grown up with news illustrations and hazy photo layouts was now treated to breathtaking action shots facilitated by vastly improved photographic equipment. These images were now rapidly available thanks to wirephoto services, which had debuted in Life *in the month that Pollard, Howard, and Smith formed their partnership.*

But it was the radio that had the greatest impact. In the 1920s the cost of a radio had been prohibitive—$120 or more—and all that bought was a box of unassembled parts. In unelectrified rural areas, radios ran on pricey, short-lived batteries. But with the 1930s came the advent of factory-built console, tabletop, and automobile radio sets, available for as little as $5. Thanks to President Roosevelt's Rural Electrification Administration, begun in 1936, electricity came to the quarter of the population that lived on farmlands. Rural families typically made the radio their second electric pur-

chase, after the clothes iron. By 1935, when Seabiscuit began racing, two-thirds of the nation's homes had a radio. At the pinnacle of his career, that figure had jumped to 90 percent, plus eight million sets in cars. Enabling virtually all citizens to experience noteworthy events simultaneously and in entertaining form, radio created a vast common culture in America, arguably the first true mass culture the world had ever seen. Racing, a sport whose sustained dramatic action was ideally suited to narration, became a staple of the airwave. The Santa Anita Handicap, with its giant purse and world-class athletes, competing in what was rapidly becoming the nation's most heavily attended sport, became one of the premier radio events of the year.

In February 1937, all of these new social and technological forces were converging. The modern age of celebrity was dawning. The new machine of fame stood waiting. All it needed was the subject himself.

At that singular hour, Seabiscuit, the Cinderella horse, flew over the line in the Santa Anita Handicap. Something clicked: Here he was.

—LAURA HILLENBRAND
Seabiscuit: An American Legend

PRODUCTION INFORMATION

You don't throw a whole life away just 'cause it's banged up a little.

IT IS A STORY THAT INSPIRED A NATION . . . and one that almost didn't happen. It is the story of a country whose dreams had been shattered . . . and the people who found a hero in an average horse that could achieve the unthinkable.

It is the story of three lost men—Johnny "Red" Pollard (Tobey Maguire), a young man whose spirit had been broken; Charles Howard (four-time Oscar®-nominee Jeff Bridges), a millionaire who lost everything; and Tom Smith (Academy Award® winner Chris Cooper), a cowboy whose world was vanishing—who found each other and discovered hope in an unlikely place.

The odds were incredible.
The dream was impossible . . .
And somehow, it actually happened.

From Academy Award–nominated filmmaker Gary Ross *(Pleasantville, Dave)* comes the motion picture adaptation of the story that transfixed a nation from one of the most beloved and widely read nonfiction books of the past decade: *Seabiscuit.*

To film the tale of the down-and-out racehorse that took the entire nation on the ride of a lifetime, screenwriter/director/producer Ross has assembled an impressive list of seasoned and accomplished filmmaking talent, both in front of and behind the camera. Joining Maguire, Bridges, and Cooper in the cast are Elizabeth Banks *(Catch Me If You Can, Spider-Man)* as Marcela Howard, Charles Howard's wife; Hall of Fame jockey Gary Stevens (in his motion picture debut) as George "The Iceman" Woolf; and Academy Award nominee William H. Macy *(Fargo, Boogie Nights)* as reporter "Tick-Tock" McGlaughlin.

Producing, along with Gary Ross, are prolific and Oscar-nominated filmmakers Kathleen Kennedy *(A.I. Artificial Intelligence, The Sixth Sense)* and Frank Marshall *(Signs, The Bourne Identity),* and Jane Sindell. The film is based on the best-selling book by Laura Hillenbrand. Gary Barber *(Bruce*

Almighty, Shanghai Knights), Roger Birnbaum *(Bruce Almighty, The Recruit)*, Tobey Maguire, Allison Thomas *(Pleasantville)*, and Robin Bissell *(Pleasantville)* serve as executive producers.

Collaborating with Ross to re-create the world of the first decades of the twentieth century are director of photography John Schwartzman, A.S.C. *(The Rookie, Armageddon)*; two-time Oscar-nominated production designer Jeannine Oppewall *(L.A. Confidential, Pleasantville)*; Academy Award–nominated film editor William Goldenberg, A.C.E. *(Ali, The Insider)*; double Oscar-nominated costume designer Judianna Makovsky *(Harry Potter and the Sorcerer's Stone, Pleasantville)*; and Academy Award–winning composer Randy Newman *(Monsters, Inc., Toy Story)*.

ABOUT THE PRODUCTION

IN 1996, while working on an article on an unrelated subject, writer Laura Hillenbrand came across some material about the owner and the trainer of a Depression-era racehorse named Seabiscuit. Hillenbrand, who first got on a horse at the age of five, had brought together her love of horses and history by writing for *Equus* and a variety of other publications. She first read about Seabiscuit as a child and encountered him again and again in her work as a fan and chronicler of horse racing. While she knew the story of the knobby-kneed horse and his strange and inspiring career, she knew little about the people around him—the owner, the trainer, and the jockey. She had little idea that her discovery that day would lead to a publishing phenomenon.

Four years later, Hillenbrand submitted the book for publication. From the beginning, her expectations were modest. "I was thinking," remembers Hillenbrand, "'If I can sell five thousand copies out of the trunk of my car, I'll be happy.' I just wanted to tell the story."

So the author wasn't prepared for the call she received from her editor informing her that after only five days on sale, the book had already made it onto the best-seller list, debuting at number eight. The following week it rose to number two and, the week after that, *Seabiscuit, An American Legend* topped the list at number one.

The response to the book from critics and the public was overwhelming. Named one of the best books of the year by more than twenty publications—including the *New York Times*, the *Washington Post, Time, People, USA Today*, and *The Economist*—*Seabiscuit* was also honored as the BookSense Nonfiction Book of the Year and the William Hill Sports Book of the Year. The hardcover edition remained on the *New York Times* best-seller list for thirty weeks; the paperback edition debuted on the list the week of April 14, 2002, and hasn't left since (remaining there for more than sixty weeks).

In addition to being one of Hollywood's most gifted storytellers, director and screenwriter Gary Ross is also a longtime fan of horse racing. Ross's love for racing started early on. He and his wife, executive producer Allison Thomas, had spent a fair amount of time at the track before they came across the article "Four Good Legs Between Us," about three men and an unlikely racehorse named Seabiscuit in a little-known publication called *American Heritage*. The author was Laura Hillenbrand.

A heavy bidding war for the film rights to the proposed book ensued, at which point Ross decided to call Hillenbrand directly.

"I talked to her about horse racing," recalls Ross, who spent two hours on the phone with the author, "and specifically about Secretariat's Belmont, which to me is still the most amazing athletic achievement ever."

Hillenbrand sensed Ross's enthusiasm for horse racing. But more important, she believed that he loved the story for the same reasons she did.

Hillenbrand comments, "Gary recognized, as I do, that this is a story about people more than it is a 'horse story.' When I saw the movie, it was lyrical and beautiful and just wonderful—I was so happy with the way it came out. I had a lot of confidence in Gary Ross right from the start, from the first conversation I had with him, that we saw the story the same way. I was so pleased with the way he wove the story of these people together and created a much larger story. This movie is a very intricate patchwork, and I am very pleased."

She continues, "Lots of my readers say 'I've never been to a horse race' or 'I don't like horses,' but they say they liked the story. I think that's because of the people in it—and that was always my focus, these three men. That's why the cover of the book doesn't have the horse's head on it. I made a very deliberate decision to focus on the faces of the people so that you know this is a human story."

Behind the story of a famous racehorse was indeed a phenomenally human story, writ large across the dramatic landscape of a momentous period in American history, and it is told with all the thrill and excitement of Thoroughbred racing in its heyday.

IT WAS THE BEGINNING of the twentieth century. Charles Howard, the young owner of a bicycle shop in San Francisco, was startled by a loud rumbling. When he went to investigate the source of the noise, he saw the future—the strange contraption they called an automobile was barreling down the street toward him, leaving the hoofprints and wheel marks of horse-driven carriages in its dusty wake. Within a few years, Charles Howard owned the most successful Buick dealership in the West.

But the cars that had brought him success and fortune ended up stealing the thing he loved most. After his son was killed in an automobile accident, Howard's life spiraled downward, his marriage dissolved, and he was left empty and alone.

Hundreds of miles away, a cowboy named Tom Smith rode horses across a boundless and beautiful region that seemed to stretch out forever in every direction. But the boundlessness gave way to barbed wire and railroad tracks, covering the landscape like spiders' webs. The cowboy became obsolete and Tom Smith was a walking relic in the New World.

John Pollard was born into a lively and prosperous family of Irish immigrants, a home filled with books and songs. But the Pollards were hit by hard times; the family lost everything. At a makeshift racetrack Johnny Pollard, barely a young man, was left to make his way in the world doing the one thing he could—ride a horse. What he couldn't make racing he scraped together by boxing. Beaten down but determined, Johnny "Red" Pollard learned to look out for himself and to trust no one.

In 1932, newly elected President Franklin Delano Roosevelt inherited the leadership of a country with a jobless rate as high as 50 percent in some cities, where 2 million people wandered the country without homes or employment. Never before had America faced such great poverty and desperation. The hope of a young nation was slipping away behind bolted bank doors and at the end of ever-increasing breadlines.

A few years later, Charles Howard remarried a beautiful young woman named Marcela Zabala—the two had met at the track. Together the newlyweds decided to buy a horse. Howard had hired a peculiarly quiet and idiosyncratic trainer named Tom Smith, who spied a spark of promise in a difficult and awkward plain bay named Seabiscuit—the son of Hardtack, descendant of the great Man-O-War. Beaten up and beaten down, the horse had grown stubborn and reckless and was on his way to being discarded. But Smith saw something in the knobby-kneed bay, just as Charles Howard had seen something in Smith.

Tom saw the same inner spirit in a troubled jockey, and in 1936, on a beautiful fall day at the track in Saratoga, the Howards were introduced by their trainer to a young jockey named "Red" Pollard.

In the hands of Howard, his trainer, and his new jockey, the indomitable spirit sensed in Seabiscuit that first morning took hold of the horse. He transformed from an unruly, ungraceful animal to a head-turning record breaker. With an instinctual faith in Smith, Pollard, and Seabiscuit, Charles Howard, a consummate showman, challenged the (current) Triple Crown winner, a powerful, stunning black horse named War Admiral, to a match race. The resulting race became much more than a competition between two champion animals and their riders—it grew into a contest between two worlds: the East Coast establishment of bankers and their beautiful horses versus a nation of downtrodden but spirited have-nots who championed a ragtag team of three displaced men and their unlikely challenger.

Seabiscuit won the match race and went on to be named 1938 Horse of the Year. The victory, however, was bittersweet. Just before that race, Pollard had been seriously injured in an accident on another horse. When told that Red might never walk again, Howard was ready to cancel the race. But Pollard insisted that it go on and that his friend and fellow jockey George "The Iceman" Woolf ride Seabiscuit, which he did—to victory.

Months later, Seabiscuit was injured in a race. Howard brought both Red and Seabiscuit to his sprawling ranch in Northern California so the two friends could convalesce together. Red spent his days reading and taking the horse on walks under the California Oaks. Slowly, the impossible started to happen; walks turned into canters and canters into gallops, and soon Seabiscuit and Red were racing through the grass-covered hills of Howard's home.

In 1940, FDR. was reelected for an unprecedented third term. On a chalkboard at the Santa Anita Handicap, a man wrote "Seabiscuit" under the list of race entries and the crowd roared. The people's hero had returned, beating all the odds, to race once again—this time with an equally miraculous Red Pollard holding the reins. Together, horse and jockey crossed the finish line first, with retirement for both waiting on the other side.

Filmmaker Gary Ross was immediately attracted to the three-sided story as related by Hillenbrand. "I was knocked out by it," he says, "by these wonderfully heroic characters and this horse that became a folk hero."

HILLENBRAND LOVED the story of this horse and these three men. She loved horse racing and she worked very hard to bring that love to the page. But she knew there could be more. "There were things I couldn't do as a writer," says the author. "I can tell the story, but I can't show you the story. As soon as I spoke to Gary Ross I knew this was the man for it. I clicked with him immediately. I understood that he saw horse racing as I did, that he was somebody who was enthralled by the speed and the danger and the beauty of it, and that he would convey that on the screen, and I love the work he's done. I think my faith in him has been borne out, he wrote a brilliant screenplay and the movie is terrific."

The jockey, the owner, and the trainer were at the core of the story Hillenbrand wanted to tell. "My loyalties lie with my subjects, and in selling the film rights to my book, my priority was to find a director who would be true to who they were," says the author, "portraying them in a way that was consistent with their personalities and their circumstances. What sold me on Gary Ross was his dedication—bordering on obsession—to portraying these men, this horse, their era, and their story as they were. He went out of his way to adhere to events as they occurred, but when he reached a part of the story where he needed to fictionalize or compress events, he invariably called me and described each scene to ensure that he was being true to his subjects."

Adapting a book for the screen is always a challenge; it means facing the difficult choices of what to keep in and what to leave out. As Ross sat down to write the script, he faced the daunting task of distilling the author's exhaustive and detailed four-hundred-page account. One of his first steps was to outline the story. "When you are adapting a story for the screen," says Ross, "you extract the key elements of the story, the high points, what it is that attracted you to it in the first place."

What caught Ross's attention were these three men and their struggle to overcome incredible hardship and loss and their willingness to come together to find the courage to rebuild their lives. "Red lost his family, Howard lost a son, and Smith lost his way of life," explains Ross. "How do you transcend that kind of pain, overcome the grief?

"What I discovered in the story," continues Ross, "were three characters, all broken, who could have quit. Instead they reached out to one another and formed a unique nuclear family."

"In any good adaptation," Ross explains, "what you're really being faithful to is the spirit of the book; that was my compass, that's what I wanted to make sure I was honoring. Of course I would change details and fictionalize parts. That way I could capture the impact of the story, the meaning of the book. So every change I made I cleared with Laura, who was wonderfully open. It was like having a great collaborator. Every time I needed to fictionalize something I could just pick up the phone, call Laura, and say, 'How does this feel?'"

A book is like a child to an author, and handing it over to someone else is a difficult task. "I was always a little worried about what was going to happen with the screenplay," Hillenbrand confesses. "There's no way to tell the story exactly the way you do in a book. It's a four-hundred-page book and things have to be condensed and things have to be fictionalized and there's a lot that needs to happen to craft this into a movie that's a watchable length."

Then Ross sent Hillenbrand the script for her comments. "Right away, when I started reading it, I was just filled with rapture," says Hillenbrand. "It's so lyrical and beautiful. He has taken what is a wonderful story and infused it with his creativity and his visual sense. The final product is just fantastic."

For both Hillenbrand and Ross, the key to the story was the strange and unlikely relationship between the three men—Seabiscuit's jockey, Johnny "Red" Pollard; the trainer, Tom Smith; and the owner, Charles Howard. Each man had his own story that began before their paths converged because of one amazing animal.

"It's about three journeys," comments screenwriter/director Ross. "These were men who were broken, each for different reasons; they were like pieces and they needed one another to become whole again."

In many ways, the convergence of the main characters of the story mirrored the assembly of the filmmakers who were likewise drawn to the moving and memorable story.

Ross remembers, "I met with Kathleen Kennedy to talk about another project, and she asked me about *Seabiscuit.* I didn't really know her at the time, but she had a huge amount of enthusiasm and she'd produced some enormous projects."

Kennedy and Ross began a dialogue about the project and found that they were "kindred spirits" in the way they viewed the filmic telling of the story, especially with their agreement on the human relationships at the core.

"Tom Smith was down and out as a trainer and nobody really thought he was worth hiring anymore," explains producer Kennedy. "Charles Howard had gone through an extraordinarily sad experience in his life with the loss of a son and eventually the dissolution of his marriage. Red Pollard had suffered his losses, being left on his own at such a young age. And the fact that Pollard, Howard, and Smith and this funny-looking little racehorse came together and basically rebuilt their lives while creating a legend—those are the elements of a wonderful story."

Ross and the filmmakers then turned their attentions to bringing Ross's screenplay to life by putting actors' (and horses') faces to the historic names involved in *Seabiscuit.*

WHILE MANY OF THE ROLES in the film were open for casting, Ross had created the three top parts for three specific actors—starting with Tobey Maguire as the jockey Red Pollard. Ross and Maguire had known each other since the filmmaker had cast him in *Pleasantville* as a teenage boy nostalgic for a time that never was.

"I ran into Gary," Maguire recalls, "and he said, 'Why don't you pick up a copy of *Seabiscuit* and have a read?,' which is exactly what I did. I read the book and I thought it was fantastic. I just loved it."

Johnny "Red" Pollard had lived a hardscrabble life; abandoned at a track when he was still a boy, he struggled to make his way in a difficult world. Money he earned from amateur and often brutal boxing matches supplemented the meager income he made doing the one thing he loved— racing a horse.

Pollard was an anomaly, even among jockeys. In spite of his vagabond life, he always carried a bag of books, spun fantastic tales, and quoted Shakespeare in the jockeys' room. The too-tall jockey with a shock of crimson hair was a bundle of contradictions, a complex and enigmatic man.

Ross saw similarities in Maguire and Pollard and explains, "I knew Tobey. He has lived a difficult life and I knew he had a fire in him—a complexity and an innate toughness."

"I think Tobey is the De Niro of the new generation," notes Kennedy. "There is an edge to him as well as a vulnerability, and I think that's what Gary was looking for in casting the role of Pollard. There's a lot of rage and anger in Red, and at the same time, his connection with Seabiscuit was like no other jockey that came in contact with this horse. When the two of them came together, they kind of calmed each other down . . . enough for Red to discover who he was as a jockey and Seabiscuit to transform into a championship racehorse."

Maguire's list of roles in varied films like *Pleasantville, The Ice Storm, Wonder Boys,* and *The Cider House Rules* have earned him the respect and admiration of critics and the public alike. Coming off the tremendous success of *Spider-Man* and gearing up for the sequel, Maguire says *Seabiscuit* was a perfect opportunity for him.

"This is a great role for me," explains the young actor. "I want to challenge myself and find different things to play. I think this is a great next step for me. It's funny because Gary Ross knows me so well. He knew this would appeal to me."

"I think Tobey is immensely talented," adds Ross, "and I love working with him. He is street-smart and yet there is an incredible kind of compassion and wisdom in him. There is an understanding and a generosity of spirit that he has for his friends and loved ones that is very touching. And those were a lot of the contradictions that I saw in the character of Red Pollard."

"I think what's interesting," continues Maguire, "is that all three of the characters isolate themselves. They are lonely characters who have shut themselves off for various reasons. Tom Smith is in a new world in which he doesn't belong, Charles Howard loses his son, and my character loses his family home. Seabiscuit is the unlikely charm that brings the three of us together."

In addition to being a self-made man and a spirited entrepreneur, Charles Howard was an incredible showman. As producer Kennedy notes, "He exemplifies that kind of corporate P. T. Barnum, larger-than-life character. Howard went from bicycle repairman to changing the landscape of the West, opening the first Buick dealership, popularizing the automobile and becoming a wealthy man."

Four-time Academy Award–nominee Jeff Bridges was signed to play Charles Howard, a role he inhabits with charismatic authority. "Charles Howard is the linchpin in this group of people," notes Ross. "I was so lucky to have Jeff. He's such a great actor, with such a long career and so many unbelievable roles. He brings the solid legs of a patriarch."

Bridges, it turned out, had a personal connection to the story. The actor recalls, "I became aware of the book shortly after it came out. My cousin Kathy Simpson called me up and she said, 'I've just read a book, and you've got to play the part of Charles Howard.' And I said, 'You're kidding, who's Charles Howard?' She said, 'He owned Seabiscuit.' And part of the reason why my cousin was so excited was that our grandfather, Fred Simpson, used to go to the races three or four times a week. As a teenager, I remember driving him to the races at Santa Anita. Some time in his life, he probably bet on Seabiscuit. While we were shooting the picture, I could kind of feel his spirit smiling up there in heaven and looking down on us."

Producer Frank Marshall succinctly says, "Jeff Bridges is Charles Howard. He embodies that character."

"It's rare when you find a movie that is really the story of three people," Bridges observes, "and, in this case, this amazing horse, interwoven so beautifully, allowing the audience to care about each story. Laura certainly did that in the book and Gary Ross did a really terrific job carrying that right over into the script."

"Sometimes there are parts that fit like a glove," says actor Chris Cooper who plays Tom Smith, Seabiscuit's trainer. Smith was a man displaced by a rapidly changing world, a man who was more comfortable with horses than people. He was dubbed "Silent Tom" by a pesky and persistent racing press whom he took pleasure in dodging.

"Chris Cooper has had an extraordinary career," notes Kennedy. "He's managed to be very much a chameleon with the roles he has done. I think both Gary and I were really taken with the work that he had done in *American Beauty*. We had an early look at *Adaptation* and saw the character he played, which won him the Oscar. His extraordinary work in that film really convinced us that Chris was more than capable of getting inside Tom Smith."

Cooper raised cattle with his father for twenty years and came to the part with a good idea of what kind of man Smith was. Cooper offers, "The director has an enormous weight on his shoulders. I want to come in with something and take that burden off his shoulders. I came prepared, I came with this character in mind and Gary liked what I created."

"Chris brings a piece of the West with him," says Ross. "It's in his walk, his voice, his physicality. Even when we were shooting at a racetrack or a church or some fancy eastern barn, he made sure he never lost it. In every scene with Chris Cooper, you still feel the range—it's very much alive and you feel where he came from. That's just a great actor."

The woman who brings Charles Howard back from the brink of despair and helps him find a new life is a dark beauty named Marcela Zabala. "Marcela came into Charles Howard's life at a time when he wasn't really looking for anyone," explains Kennedy. "He was very much alone at that point because he was just getting over the death of his son. Marcela offered a little ray of hope."

Marcela Howard was half her husband's age and a graceful and fearless adventurer. While on safari, she took out a lion that had threatened their camp. At one point, she smuggled a blue monkey into the Waldorf-Astoria.

Recalls executive producer Robin Bissell, "We read a lot of people for Marcela. Elizabeth came in and we read the last scene in the movie between her and Jeff Bridges, which is with the child's game. She brought something so real to it, and it hammered us in the room."

"Elizabeth has the qualities of an old-time movie star," Bissell adds, "like Lauren Bacall—there's a beauty and a grace about her, but she can also be one of the boys, which is exactly what Marcela was. She was one of the guys, she fit right in."

For Banks, the role of Marcela posed challenges for a woman accustomed to the stronger role of women in the twenty-first century compared to her early twentieth-century counterparts.

The actress offers, "Some of my preparation consisted of becoming familiar with the physical world of Marcela—the clothes, her makeup and hair, her posture. It was really illuminating reading about the etiquette of male/female relationships back then. As a wife in the thirties, I don't actually speak as much as I am present. You let your husband take care of things. In one scene in the hospital, as a modern woman, I had the urge to walk up to the actor playing the doctor. But back then, a wife stood back, and waited for her husband to tell her about the situation. And so Marcela is a nice balance—a good combination of being this eccentric wild woman who had a way of pulling things out of men and getting her way . . . but in a very quiet, very behind-the-scenes way."

"The casting of Gary Stevens was probably the most spontaneously correct bit of casting I have ever experienced," comments Kennedy of Ross's decision to hire Hall of Fame jockey Stevens to play George Woolf. "I mean literally, Gary Ross walked through the jockeys' room, saw Gary, looked at him, and said, 'You know what? How would you like to play George Woolf?'"

Even though Ross had never spent any time with Stevens, he and the producers felt that the champion jockey, one of the finest riding today, was capable of acting.

"Sometimes you just get hit with an instinct," Ross explains. "He looks like a movie star, and there was a cocky bravado, a kind of confidence."

With a lot to be confident about, Stevens is arguably one of the sport's greatest living riders. A Hall of Fame jockey with more than 4,700 wins in his career, he has 8 Triple Crown victories (3 Kentucky Derbys, 2 Preakness and 3 Belmonts). In addition, he's won 8 Breeders' Cup Classics and his horses have earned more than $200 million in combined earnings.

Stevens wasn't sure Ross was serious when he offered him the part. "I thought it was a joke at first, but after the Kentucky Derby, I went ahead and agreed to play the part. At that time I had no idea how big it was going to be."

The filmmakers sent Stevens for a few days of training with respected acting coach Larry Moss. But Moss sent Stevens home after a day.

Despite his filmmakers' opinions, Stevens downplays his skills as an actor. "Fortunately for me, I don't have to do a lot of acting," he quips. "George Woolf is very similar to me—I mean, he was a top-class rider and he liked to have a good time. His nickname was 'The Iceman.' They said he had ice water running through his veins. Nothing bothered him, he thrived on the big races and it's just a character that I feel very, very comfortable playing."

But Ross, who studied acting with famed teacher Stella Adler, knows there's a little more to acting than simply being yourself. "Every scene Gary has done he has been prepared, he has totally understood what to do," says the director. "I don't know where this came from, he just has a natural ability. It was one of the biggest surprises for me, how good an actor he turned out to be."

Of the parts written specifically for a particular actor, the role of Tick-Tock McGlaughlin was the second for Ross. And for him, only William H. Macy, another *Pleasantville* alum, would do.

Ross created the role of the fast-talking radio announcer. He recalls, "Tick-Tock McGlaughlin just hit me while I was in the middle of the script. I knew I was going to need a track reporter once the story shifted to Santa Anita. I'd seen those kinds of touts. But the character, his sense of humor, his rapid-fire delivery and play on words, his boozing and carousing, all just came to me in real time while I was writing. I think I'd written one monologue of it when I realized, 'Oh, this is Macy.' I normally don't have such happy accidents."

Macy was thrilled to play the part he describes as a cross between radio legend Walter Winchell and a carnival barker. "Gary is a great writer," says the actor. "In order to tell the story, he needed a bit of a Greek chorus, someone to move it along and to tell us what we were seeing. And second, I think he just landed on the idea of spicing up this story with this insane character. So he created this great character for me, who has all of these hysterical speeches, which I deliver as fast as I can humanly speak."

Lastly, the screenwriter/director/producer created a third role for a very different kind of voice: noted historian David McCullough. Ross states that one of the draws of Hillenbrand's book was her ability to bring the history of the period alive. To replicate that, he chose to incorporate a narrator. The Depression was a story in itself, dramatic and complex, and Ross believed it needed to be told.

He observes, "It was a time when people from all different walks of life were thrown together. So one of the first decisions I made was to have McCullough narrate the film. I wrote the lead for Tobey, I created Tick-Tock for Bill Macy, and I wanted David McCullough as the narrator."

"We wanted to be able to tell the story of these three men and the horse," adds executive producer Allison Thomas, "but in order to get the full impact of their lives you really had to have a broader understanding of the Depression."

"There were two ways I could think of to do that," continues Ross. "I could try to establish the historical context dramatically or force it into the movie in a way that the movie may not be able to hold. But I thought the better way would be just to tell it. Why do I have to be a slave to the dramatic devices of creating a bunch of characters to reveal something when it could be so exciting to shatter the fourth wall, using something unique like documentary filmmaking techniques, use somebody as iconic vocally as David McCullough and give the audience a sense of realism that would be much more compelling than anything I could possibly dramatize? I felt that that was a much more interesting way to go."

"When I read the screenplay," recalls historian McCullough,"I just thought, 'This is wonderful, this is really a great story. And if I can help tell it, I would be delighted to do so.'"

"Anything David McCullough says you tend to believe," observes Frank Marshall. "There's just something about the credibility behind that voice that works on so many levels, whether it's a PBS documentary or, as in this case, narrating a film."

Behind the voice is one of the country's most respected historical writers. With two Pulitzers and two National Book Awards, the former president of the American Society of Historians has been called a master of the art of narrative history. In addition to his best-sellers, *Truman* and *John Adams*, McCullough has authored books on the Brooklyn Bridge, the Panama Canal, and Teddy Roosevelt. He has been an editor, essayist, and lecturer and has appeared on *Smithsonian World* and *The American Experience.* He has narrated numerous documentaries, but *Seabiscuit* is the first feature film to which he has lent his voice.

"Feature films very rarely use a narrator," McCullough explains, "but in this case, it's so important to understand the background, understand what was happening in the country at that time. And that is hard to do if you're just doing it through dialogue. It's a very significant and important passage in our story as a country and as a people. That's why it's so wonderful when a film like this comes along, which not only captures the spirit of the time, and the setting and the context of what was happening, but does so with a great story, a real story."

McCullough's success lies in part in his understanding of an essential human impulse. "We want to go back in time," says the historian, "and I think it's part of human nature. Almost every fairy tale begins with 'Once upon a time, long, long ago.' And very often 'once upon a time, long, long ago' was not an easy time."

Even while filmmakers were hard at work filling the roles of *Seabiscuit*'s two-legged actors, they were highly concerned with making sure that the best horses available would be slotted for the equine rolls—for all of the scenes involving the illustrious racehorse and his competitors scripted to take place in locations that varied from racetrack to horse farm to open countryside.

Rusty Hendrickson, a renowned motion picture horse wrangler responsible for spectacular horse sequences in dozens of films like *Dances with Wolves* and *The Patriot,* was brought on board by the filmmakers to secure and train the horses that would be used in the filming.

The Montana native had previously worked with all three of the leading actors—with Tobey Maguire on *Ride with the Devil,* Chris Cooper in *The Horse Whisperer,* and Jeff Bridges on Hendrickson's first film, *Heaven's Gate.* *Seabiscuit* proved to be a different kind of project for the motion picture veteran who was used to working on Westerns and he welcomed the challenge of working with racehorses.

"We knew that we were going to be putting real jockeys on these horses," explains Kathleen Kennedy. "We knew that we had to make sure that the horses were sound and we knew that they would have to be running many, many different races in order to tell the story, so we came to the conclusion pretty early that we would buy these horses and we would create our own racing stable."

Hendrickson worked with the company to purchase more than fifty horses from around the country to participate in the film's numerous racing scenes. For the safety of the horses, any set of horses grouped for a particular race could only run a few takes and the animals were limited to racing only every other day. To make this rotating schedule possible, the production needed Thoroughbreds in a variety of colors. For the sake of not only the animals but the jockeys riding them, it was imperative that the horses were able-bodied and sound. Each horse was brought on only after it passed a thorough examination by the production's veterinarian.

"Rusty did a marvelous job securing all the horses," says Hall of Fame jockey and *Seabiscuit* race designer Chris McCarron, who worked closely with Hendrickson throughout the production. "These horses have played an immeasurable role in our success."

There was, of course, one particular horse role that required particular attention. Director Ross observes, "A Seabiscuit comes along once in a century. Here was a horse that had amazing character and intelligence and a very idiosyncratic personality. He used to sleep much of the day—but he was also very fierce, very competitive. And he could be playful or lazy."

Seabiscuit was a one-of-a-kind horse and the filmmakers never imagined they could find his twin. Instead, they sought several horses that could embody a variety of traits that, when subjected to the magic of moviemaking, would emerge on the screen as a single horse.

"When you pick a horse," explains Hendrickson, "you don't know what his capabilities are. So we have several horses to cover the different personality traits of Seabiscuit."

Hendrickson went looking for horses that resembled Seabiscuit, a thankfully unremarkable bay horse. "He was not particularly attractive," Hendrickson continues. "He was a small horse, about 15 hands, weighing about 1,150 pounds. He was a bright blood bay with dark points and no white markings. It was lucky for us that he was a very ordinary-looking horse."

Seabiscuit's looks, however, were the only ordinary thing about him. In order to portray this strange and special horse over the course of seven years of his life, the production needed a wide variety of horses: they needed a horse that would stand still; a horse that could angrily rear; a horse that would bite; a horse that would lie down (alongside another horse and a dog at the same time); a horse that could be ridden with multiple cameras close by; a horse that actors, trained to ride but novices nevertheless, could ride without risk of being thrown. On top of all of that, they needed a horse that could win and they needed a horse that could lose.

Ultimately, five horses raced regularly as Seabiscuit (with two more filling in on occasion), plus another three "trick" horses, making it a grand total of ten "Biscuits." While there was never any intention of creating a star, as the production progressed, one horse emerged as the "hero" horse. Fighting Furrari was the animal used primarily with the cast, in such important scenes as Red Pollard in the winner's circle, George Woolf in front of the cheering crowds at Pimlico, and Pollard and horse recuperating at Ridgewood.

No matter how outstanding the animal, it takes an equally outstanding jockey to guide the animal around the track—they don't ride themselves.

"These guys are truly professional athletes," says Tobey Maguire, who underwent rigorous training to prepare for his role as jockey Red Pollard (see below). "It's a team sport—the horse is definitely doing the running, but without the pilot, it's not going to happen."

The production was doubly blessed with the participation of arguably two of the greatest jockeys in the sport today. In addition to Hall of Famer Stevens as George Woolf, Hall of Famer Chris McCarron was brought on board to work as the film's race designer (a title that encompassed a wide range of responsibilities), working side by side with Gary Ross on all of the horse sequences.

"From the beginning," recalls executive producer Thomas, "we wanted to have Chris involved in the film." Lucky for the production, McCarron had just decided to retire from racing in June of 2002.

"What was interesting," she continues, "is he had just retired and then started working with us and was immediately comfortable in this other environment. He had no learning curve at all. He just jumped right in. Later on, he even rode in the film as War Admiral's jockey Charley Kurtsinger."

"We realized that the horse racing component of the movie was probably going to be our biggest technical challenge," says producer Kathleen Kennedy. "Chris was instrumental in helping us find what our approach to the movie would be regarding the horses."

One of McCarron's first tasks was to find the professional jockeys who would ride the Thoroughbred racehorses in the film. "One of my jobs," explains McCarron, "was to find and secure some of the jockeys that were going to be participating in the film, and fortunately I found a number of riders who were very capable and who also happened to be available. We were able to get a good group of riders. And quite frankly, they've done an absolutely marvelous job—all of which has been considerably more difficult than just going out there and riding a typical race."

McCarron recruited twelve jockeys from all over the United States. The jockeys were eager to participate in a film that would capture so much of the sport they loved.

"I was very pleased that Gary wrote so many races into the script," says McCarron. "I also knew that for all those races to be authentic and realistic, it was going to be a serious challenge for the jockeys, especially since we were using real racehorses."

Without overstating the obvious, Thoroughbred racing is an incredibly dangerous sport. As Laura Hillenbrand writes in her book: "Serious insults to the body, the kind of shattering or crushing injury seen in high-speed auto wrecks, are an absolute certainty for every single jockey. Today, the Jockey's Guild, which covers riders in the United States, receives an average of twenty-five hundred injury notifications per year, with two deaths and two and a half cases of paralysis. According to a study by the Rehabilitation Institute of Chicago, each year the average jockey is injured three times and spends a total of almost eight weeks sidelined by injuries incurred on the track."

Mindful of these sobering statistics, the production took many steps to curtail those dangers while reenacting the numerous racing scenes. That the production was successful, not only in achieving its goals of capturing the sheer power of Thoroughbreds racing down the track, but in doing it without incident or injury to horse or human, is a testament to the filmmakers, the crew, the jockeys, the actors, and the horses themselves.

MAGUIRE HAD GONE TO THE RACETRACK as a kid and had done some riding on Ang Lee's Civil War drama, *Ride with the Devil,* but the actor would need intense preparation before he could realistically portray a jockey.

"There was a lot of transformation that had to happen," explains Ross. "Tobey is five foot eight" and Red was five seven. Any jockey who is that tall is obviously going to really fight with weight. So Tobey went on a huge reduction program in order to get to the place where he could play the part. He weighed about 160 when it started. I thought if he got to 150 he would look gaunt enough to sell it. He ended up getting down to 137."

Maguire underwent extensive physical training with L.A. Kings strength trainer Joe Horrigan. "From the beginning we treated him like an athlete," says Horrigan. "He had sixteen workouts a week, six strength, six cardio, three equicizer, and one boxing."

The actor, who had bulked up to play *Spider-Man,* now had to become lean while increasing his muscle mass. The actor went on a supervised 1,650-calories-per-day diet while maintaining his rigorous workout schedule. Horrigan trained Maguire utilizing many of the same methods used by Olympic weight lifters and he said that Maguire was a natural athlete.

"I've had Hall of Fame athletes who would have struggled through this," continues the impressed strength trainer. "He has good genes. Tobey acquired new motor skills quickly, which is a sign of a good athlete."

Director Gary Ross was equally impressed with Maguire's commitment and hard work. "He was really, really in amazing shape," says Ross. "His body fat got down to something like six percent, which is borderline unnatural."

In addition to his workouts with Horrigan, Maguire trained with the film's race designer McCarron, who secured an "equicizer" for the jockey-in-training. (Used by professional jockeys to train, the mechanical racehorse would also come in handy for Ross and the filmmakers—more below.)

"We brought the equicizer over to Tobey's house," explains McCarron, "and I would go there about three times a week and work with him for about an hour and a half per session. He caught on very quickly. He's a good study . . . he's a great study, for that matter."

McCarron admits to a little satisfaction watching the young actor sweat while training to do something that many people think is no more difficult than riding a horse. "It was fun for me," he confesses, "to see the pain and discomfort in his face when he was first getting down in the crouched position that a jockey has to maintain."

Maguire worked hard learning how to keep the thigh-burning balance necessary for rider and horse to race as one. Riding a Thoroughbred horse is more than a skill; it is an art, a concert of two very different bodies, the immense and powerful horse thundering down the track and the slight, near-weightless jockey expertly guiding him to the finish line.

"You need to know where to place your hands," McCarron continues, "how to push on a horse's neck and get the most out of your upper body strength. You need to know how to stay perched on a horse's back so you are in perfect unison with the horse."

Maguire's training paid off. "He just took to it immediately," says his director. "He has incredible balance, incredible form. I mean, the first tape that we saw we realized he was absolutely going to look like a jockey."

As a dozen professional jockeys would be on set through much of the filming, judging the young actor's racing prowess, McCarron decided to show some video footage of a racing Maguire to some of the other jockeys. "When I first showed a few jockeys, they couldn't believe that after only five weeks' time he had such incredibly good form. He looks like a great jockey."

Although the majority of the actors recruited by Ross and the filmmakers were not called upon to portray jockeys themselves (although most did ride in several scenes) almost all of the cast had some form of preparation and training prior to filming, which also included riding.

Though not required to ride any of the Seabiscuits, Bridges had his own set of challenges in bringing to life an almost larger-than-life character. Early on, he contacted author Laura Hillenbrand while he was preparing for the role.

"It was really terrific to have Laura available to answer some questions that I had in the beginning of my preparation process," says Bridges. "She was so gracious and open and went far beyond any of my questions, and really filled me in on a lot of the details about Howard and Seabiscuit. She gave me a lot of photographs and lent me a few personal items of Howard's that she happened to have. It was great to have those in my pocket, kind of feel his spirit there, too."

In addition to culling his own past for clues to building Tom Smith's character, Chris Cooper worked on changing the way he spoke. He succinctly says, "The one big choice I made was to find a completely different voice for Tom."

From becoming accustomed to the social norms of the period to simply practicing talking quickly, each actor had his special preparation to help him bring his character from the page to life before Ross's cameras.

Well before shooting began, trainer Rusty Hendrikson spent weeks working with the horses, prepping them for their big-screen debuts.

"First thing Rusty did after he acquired the horses was to unwind them a little bit," says McCarron. "They came from a racetrack setting and they were pretty geared up. Rusty had to just get them settled so they would be cooperative."

Hendrickson conditioned the horses so they would be comfortable not only with the cameras but with a Hummer and a truck loaded with cameras, cranes, and people riding alongside them—no small feat with these tightly wound, easily spooked horses. As Chris explains, "Horses are really afraid of things way up above their heads, and we had to be very careful with these cameras on the crane arms, making sure they were all moving slowly enough to where they didn't spook the horses."

Once the horses had eased into life before the cameras, Hendrickson teamed up with McCarron for a week, running what they called "jockey school," working with the jockeys to get them accustomed to the horses.

During the school, Hendrickson, McCarron, and the jockeys spent a week working with the horses, getting to know them and finding the best fit between horse and jockey. "We spent five days at the Pomona Fairplex taking the horses through their training regimen, getting them accustomed to the insert car, to the positions that we needed them to be in. We also worked them in the starting gate, getting them accustomed to standing in the gate for longer periods than they're used to," McCarron explains.

In addition to preparing the horses for unusual work, the time also allowed the jockeys to get used to the horses. "It was Gary Ross's idea to have the rehearsals," McCarron continues. "I hadn't thought of that, but I'm certainly glad that he did. It gave everybody a good chance to get familiar with the horses and their habits, their likes and dislikes."

Ross took the bold step of starting principal photography with one of the most difficult scenes in the film—the bug boy race. True to life and meant to illustrate the extreme circumstances that jockeys like Red Pollard endured, the race was shot with the film's jockeys fighting atop the horses . . . all at thirty-five miles per hour.

"If you fight in a race today," explains jockey Joe Rocco, "you get ruled off for life."

Today's racehorses were not used to flying crops and fisticuffs, even though the production's crops were made of foam. "They had to tolerate riders swinging away at each other," says McCarron. "The horses can hear that noise and see all that commotion on their backs and can easily get spooked." But all of the pretraining inured the racehorses to the fighting, noise, and distraction.

The jockeys, most of whom have been racing for many years, were amazed at how the horses learned to be unafraid of this less than orthodox racing practice.

"Horses are pretty much unpredictable," says jockey William Hollick. "They spook very easily from sudden movement. We had to pretty much jump all over each other in practice just to get them used to things—like our hands flashing past their faces."

Jockey Joe Rocco recalls, "When we first got on them they were ducking and weaving all over the track. But Rusty did a tremendous job getting these horses relaxed and calmed down enough to shoot the scene."

Jockey Luis Jauregui, who grew up at the track and whose father trained racehorses, came to have a great deal of respect for Hendrickson and the film's wranglers. "I've been around horses my whole life and I've learned so many things from Rusty and these guys, in the way they respect horses and work with them. Everything has revolved around the horses. Rusty is a great horseman."

"**ONE OF THE FIRST THINGS I REALIZED**," the director recalls, "is that the camera had to be moving with the horse—it had to be in the middle of the race. I had to get close enough to the real horses so we could feel what it's like." Ross was determined to capture the intense physicality of the sport. This, like many of the challenges the production team faced, was met with a combination of innovation and extraordinary planning.

Ross needed a cinematographer who was willing to take risks, to try new things, someone who was willing to go on what was guaranteed to be a wild ride. And through an unusual recommendation, he found one.

As Ross recalls, "My son Jack, who was six at the time, came to me and said, 'Dad, you have got to see this movie, this is the man who should photograph your movie.' And I said, 'Well, Jack, okay, I'll go see the movie.' He was convinced I would love it and he was absolutely right. I was knocked out."

The movie was *The Rookie* and the cinematographer was John Schwartzman.

Ross recalls, "I got there late so I didn't see the credit. I watched the film without knowing who shot it. I appreciated the lyricism in the way he shot a lot of the film. There was so much beautiful storytelling, lit so beautifully and in a gutsy way. My son said, 'Dad, you know the best shot in this movie?' and I expected him to say 'The home run.' But he said, 'When Jimmy Morris is throwing that ball against the fence and all you can see is the fence in focus and Jimmy Morris is all fuzzy behind it.' And he was right, it was an amazing shot."

"The irony," says Schwartzman (whose credits read like a box-office report of high-earning action films like *Pearl Harbor, Armageddon,* and *The Rock*), "is you think you get more work off a big film with a huge budget that is very widely promoted, but in fact, it was *The Rookie* that landed me in Gary's office."

Unlike a day at the track, the outcome of the races being reenacted for the cameras was a foregone conclusion. The production needed the horses to not only run around the track alongside a camera car, but to also run in order.

"Every race that we run is a race that is in the history books," reminds jockey/actor Gary Stevens. "The details of each one of those races is written down and it's very important that we have the scenes choreographed as close as we can to the original."

"Thoroughbreds are unique animals," executive producer Allison Thomas explains, "and they are notoriously high-strung and unpredictable. In addition to millions of dollars of equipment, we had to ensure the safety of the jockeys, the actors, and the crew. For that, we relied on Rusty and Chris and their knowledge of these horses."

Every morning at eleven for two months prior to shooting, Ross held a race meeting; in addition to John Schwartzman, the meeting included McCarron, Hendrickson, Julie Lynn (production manager for the horse unit, coordinating any activity involving horses and/or jockeys), stunt coordinator Dan Bradley, script supervisor Julie Pitkanen, and first assistant director Adam Somner.

"We would talk through every single race and every single setup," recalls Ross. There was an outline of the track on a huge board in the conference room of Ross's production company on which the filmmaker would describe the action, chart out the camera movement, and explain where each of the horses were in relation to one another every step of the race.

"They would see what their horse resources had to be," says Ross, "how the horses had to match up, what the turnaround times would be, and then take all this information to first A.D. Adam Somner."

"Some horses are very, very quick and have early speed," offers McCarron, who organized the specifics and his observations of each of the horses onto an Excel spreadsheet, grading every horse on the basis of its strengths and weaknesses. "Each one had singular traits. Some horses have more stamina, some horses don't like to be on the inside, some don't like to be behind horses and get dirt kicked in their faces."

"Some horses were hard to pull back, others would be harder to use to pass," adds Hendrickson. "We just got together every morning and worked it all out. By matching abilities and kind of handicapping the horses, knowing what we needed, we figured out which horses would race on that day."

Re-creating the races was challenging because, as everyone found out, Thoroughbred horses are bred to win . . . not to place, or show, and particularly not to lose. While the horses acquired by the production were not Triple Crown hopefuls, they were also only running in spurts across distances much shorter than the traditional mile or so. And, as Ross points out, "Even the slowest horse can win over three lengths."

"The riders couldn't hold their horses back because it would look obvious," says Hendrickson. (Therefore, one of the key attributes looked for during horse casting was patience.)

McCarron counters, "They are racehorses and they are very competitive. It's difficult to keep them at a certain speed; they want to go faster."

And because each race was choreographed, the jockeys needed to adhere to the race plan without making it look staged. "When we ride in a typical race, we receive instruction from the trainer and basically just have to worry about ourselves," explains Chris. "But for filming, we had to position the horses exactly where Gary Ross wanted them to be and keep everybody on their marks, whatever the proximity was—whether it was two lanes, three lanes, half a lane, or just a length between the two. That's been a real challenge and the riders have done very well."

This choreographic balancing was facilitated by the use of wireless receivers. Each jockey was fitted with an earpiece, through which they would hear McCarron's instructions.

"My job has been to understand exactly what Gary wanted and to translate that vision into jockey jargon," McCarron explains. "I might say to them, 'Make believe that you are going to work this horse five-eighths of a mile, and you're going to start off nice and easy. Then, you're going to let another horse hook in with you and you're going to stay in company . . . then, all of a sudden, you're going to be chasing this pack that is up there eight, ten lengths in front of you and you're just going to explode through the pack.' And that's what they have to do."

While conceptualizing his screenplay, screenwriter and director Ross found a dramatic organization in Hillenbrand's account of Seabiscuit's races.

He recalls, "Each race had a three-act structure. The premise was established in the clubhouse turn, the complications in the back stretch, and the conclusion of the third act happened coming out of the far turn and into the homestretch."

The discovery allowed Ross to find the unique character of each race.

It also meant that he would have to find a way to bring that character—different in every race—to the screen.

Hillenbrand's detailed descriptions of the races allowed Ross to see racing in a way he never had before. While no stranger to the track, Ross hadn't fully appreciated how visceral horse racing could be.

"I wasn't really aware of how concussive, how violent, how fast, how exciting a horse race really is," says Ross, "until I read her book and it was brought alive for me." And so Ross was determined to capture Hillenbrand's vivid descriptions of racing on film.

"The challenge," he continues, "is to show these horse races in a way that is faithful to Laura's descriptions. Because in the book, she made people understand—this isn't the race you're used to seeing from up in the grandstand, with all the little horses running around the track. You're *in* it."

"It's an extraordinary thing to see this creature moving at forty miles an hour with the grace that it does," says Hillenbrand. "Gary's shown that in a big way. That excites me because this is why I go to the horse races. I'd like to see more people going and I'd like them to see it with my eyes. And I think Gary's done that."

In order to successfully bring the story of each race to life and show the audience the drama and fierce power of Thoroughbred horse racing, Ross would need to shoot from *inside* the race. "I have to have the jockey's point of view. I have to be able to frame those moments when jockeys talk to one another while they're racing. I need to track all the subtleties that occur during the race."

The director would need close-ups and medium shots, like any film, to give the scenes dimension and depth . . . except these scenes were happening on the backs of 1,200-pound, highly sensitive animals thundering down an uneven surface at forty miles an hour with real people balanced precariously on their backs.

"During our race meetings over the summer," Schwartzman recalls, "we immediately began brainstorming ways of getting the camera close to the action. Part of it was meeting with the horse trainers and asking, 'If we put a camera on a crane that will allow us to extend an arm out thirty feet, can we run alongside the racehorses at forty miles an hour? Will they freak or will they just run?' That was sort of step one."

Even before the film went into preproduction, while adapting Hillenbrand's book, Ross wrote out a shooting plan for every scene. "I would say things like, 'We'll start with a crane move here, and we'll pop in these characters here, and we barely see them because they're silhouetted.'"

These shooting plans evolved into detailed accounts of how each scene would look and feel, how it would be lit, and how it would be shot. Out of this came another innovation that was crucial to the production's success: a race book. Like an NFL playbook, it was a computer-drawn, two-dimensional representation of where the cameras, horses, and jockeys were for each shot during every race. The multicolor race books were distributed to every crew member involved in shooting the races, including camera operators, stuntmen, jockeys, and assistant directors.

The extensive planning was helped (as was much more that would come later on) by the fact that Ross had spent months writing the material he was now directing. Observes Kathleen Kennedy, "I love working with a screenwriter/director because every single scene you are discussing, whether it's in preproduction or during principal photography, is informed by the person who wrote the material. We were faced with a very, very complicated movie, with a lot of technical challenges, and Gary was so clear about what his intent was in each of those scenes that it made the job of delivering what he needed much, much easier."

Extensive planning was a necessity. As Ross points out, "everything had to be choreographed and scheduled within an inch of its life."

Including the daily race meetings, which carried into production. At Santa Anita, where the crew shot for nearly six weeks, Ross created a makeshift track on the linoleum floor inside the betting hall in the grandstands. Using electrical tape on the floor with plastic horses and toy trucks standing in for the full-sized versions, he would review the day's work with the crew, always bearing their race books in hand.

ROSS AND THE FILMMAKERS were acutely aware of period authenticity—which usually translated into finding appropriate locations rather than coming to rely heavily on construction. In their trek to find locations that could stand in for some of the historic meccas of the horse racing world during the Depression, Ross, Kennedy, Marshall, and executive producer Robin Bissell toured the country's racetracks searching for suitable places in which they could re-create Seabiscuit's story.

First assistant director Adam Somner relates, "There were three elements that were crucial while we were scouting: first, we wanted, as much as possible, to use the real places from the story; second, we looked for racetracks that hadn't been too modernized; and third, we needed to be able to have access to the tracks."

The group ended up crisscrossing the country, beginning with a one-hundred-year-old stock farm in Hemet, California (used for the bug boy racing sequence). The company also utilized the track, grandstands, and back area at the Pomona Fairplex in California (after some modification), which doubled for Tijuana's Agua Caliente racetrack.

Following filming of scenes in Hemet and Pomona, California, location shooting moved to Saratoga to shoot scenes taking place in the New York City Jockey Club. From Saratoga, they went on to horse country, Lexington, Kentucky, home of Keeneland racetrack, to shoot the match race between Seabiscuit and War Admiral; for fourteen days they worked to re-create the historic race, filling the grandstands and the infield with more than 3,500 extras.

The filmmakers were lucky to have one of racing's greatest gems right in their backyard. Santa Anita Racetrack, which opened Christmas Day of 1934, nestled at the foot of the San Gabriel Mountains, fourteen miles northeast of Los Angeles, is a beautifully maintained track. The art deco creation of architect George Kaufmann, the picturesquely situated track still beautifully evokes the heyday of early twentieth century Thoroughbred racing. The scene of several milestones in Seabiscuit's career still stands as one of the world's most renowned sporting landmarks.

The large and nearly empty racetrack was an ideal place to shoot a film in many respects. The company was allowed to use much of the vast space inside the grandstands for holding, dressing, and making-up the thousands of extras on the big racing days; they were able to build a handful of small sets in which to shoot several scenes as well. This arrangement allowed Ross to shoot William H. Macy in Tick-Tock's lair simultaneously with the horse racing.

THE PRODUCTION had a set number of days they could shoot at the historic Santa Anita track. The company had to be out several days before the track opened for the season—there would be no exceptions. This meant that Ross had to find a way to double up the work, shooting the racing and the dramatic scenes at the same time.

"I would be off shooting a dramatic scene," recalls Ross. "The horse unit was on the track and I would be directing that via a wireless communication device, seeing the images transmitted to me on a separate set of monitors. It was a bit of a touring circus in that respect, a lot going on at once. Frank Marshall and I would talk throughout the day. Fortunately, I could see the images, and since I had rehearsed all the work in the morning with everyone, it made it a manageable touring circus . . . but a touring circus nonetheless."

"John worked very closely with Gary to literally outline every single shot of the horse racing prior to shooting," says producer and former camera operator Kathleen Kennedy. "They chose equipment through a long series of tests to determine what would be the best suited for use with the horses, what would be the best way to achieve the feeling of being inside these races."

Says Schwartzman, "If there's a piece of equipment that can move a camera, we have used it on this movie. From sticks where we are locked off to the Strato crane, with its hundred-foot arm, and everything in between. The only thing we haven't done is put the camera underwater."

The need for innovative thinking with regard to shooting was necessitated in large part out of concern for the safety of the horses.

"A racehorse can do limited takes every other day. So suddenly we were faced with this problem," Schwartzman explains. "We need to do twelve different shots a day, let's say three takes per shot. How are we going to be able to do this? We had to run multiple cameras because we didn't have an unlimited budget for horses."

"We needed a huge amount of flexibility in how we could move and maneuver the camera around the horses," says Ross, "and we did that by utilizing a technocrane on the camera car using a mount for the camera called an XR head—it's made by Westcam, the people who make the helicopter mounts. It's a phenomenally stable piece of technology. It compensates for any jiggle or rattle and can hold a rock-solid image on an eight-hundred-millimeter lens. I mean, it's a truly remarkable piece of engineering."

Schwartzman adds, "The horses run on dirt tracks that are very rough to drive on. We contacted a company that makes gyro stabilization camera platforms, and they had just invented a new one. We decided to test it out, and it turned out to be an extremely important piece of equipment for us. It really allowed us to get right in there."

The camera car, a Hummer, rigged with two cameras (one for wide shots, another for tight shots), would then follow the horses, sometimes tracking as close as four or five feet from the animals' heads as they raced around the course.

Cameras, cars, crew, horses, jockeys—with so many variables, synchronization of effort was crucial. A walking rehearsal at the track followed the morning meetings.

"You can't visualize sports, I know this from tennis," Ross explains. "You can't imagine it. People needed to understand the rehearsal in their muscle memory. They needed to feel it. So one of the things we discovered was that the walking rehearsal was essential. We would do it without the horses. The guys on the camera car, the grips, the camera operators, and the driver would all pretend to do what they were doing, and the jockeys would run along the ground as if they were on horseback. It looked like a Jacques Tati movie—the camera operator pretending to operate and the boom operator pretending to use the boom and all of us jogging down the track."

Even with all of the advanced technology at his disposal, Ross still wanted to bring the viewers even closer to the racing action. Several of the scenes involved jockeys holding discussions while in midrace; one race in Agua Caliente, Tijuana, called for a half-page of dialogue between jockeys. Also, the director needed to capture the jockeys' expressions, like when Red rides Seabiscuit for the first time. Even the use of the most accomplished rider would not enable Ross and his cinematographer to get the camera in for a close-up—not in a predictable enough way to be able to bank on getting the shot.

The answer to the problem came unexpectedly.

While he was still writing the script, Ross came upon something called an equicizer while touring around the track with Chris McCarron.

"It was a funny-looking contraption that resembled a hobby horse," Ross recalls. "It was a mechanical horse that had springs, a weird wooden head and a carpet body."

McCarron explained that this was a device that simulated the experience of riding a racehorse, something he and other jockeys used during their morning workouts and for rehab. Ross started thinking. He then asked special effects supervisor Michael Lantieri and key grip Les Tomita to commission a vehicle for him. Lantieri and Tomita enlisted the services of NASCAR racer and insert car owner Allan Padelford, who actualized Ross's concept and built what came to be known affectionately as the S.S. Seabiscuit.

"It's a twelve-foot by twenty-foot rolling platform with steering in the rear and in the front," Lantieri explains. "It's built to a sixteen-and-one-half hands high spec, so it would be level running alongside the horses. It's got a 454 Chevy engine built under the hood and it can travel around the track at forty to fifty miles an hour."

In order to be able to closely capture two jockeys in action, Ross had two equicizers modified with realistic horse heads placed atop his newly created vehicle. The equicizers themselves were mounted onto tracks, enabling them to shift positions (one in the lead, now the other) while the entire platform was being powered around the racetrack. All the while, the entire moving vehicle could be surrounded by the other horses in the race and Ross, through the ingenious combination of several cutting-edge filming techniques with specially designed hardware and camera equipment, was able to capture the smaller moments between two jockeys amid the larger, frenetic world of Thoroughbreds and their riders in midrace.

The ingenious S.S. Seabiscuit became an invaluable tool that enabled the crew to execute a variety of shots, getting in as close as needed and in virtually any position required. Adam Somner offers, "One of the reasons we were able to accomplish what we did was because Gary was committed to maximizing his shots, which is why the S.S. Seabiscuit was such a creative way to problem solve while actually improving what we were able to get. That's pure Gary."

INGENUITY also played a vital role for both costume designer Judianna Makovsky and production designer Jeannine Oppewall. Both were struck by the scale of the panoramic tale Ross was bringing to the motion picture screen and realized that a variety of operational modes would be required to get the job done.

"It's a very large film," observes Makovsky, "and it's not just about three men and a horse. It's about the Depression and America. The first thing that struck me is how every walk of life has to be represented. It's a bit daunting to know that you're going to have to be filming everything that existed within a given time frame."

Seabiscuit presented a challenge to the designer who, during particularly large shooting days, had to dress upwards of 650 extras. To secure enough costumes for the crowd scenes, the production pulled from more than thirty-five rental houses in the United States, England, and Italy. Of course, the specialty clothing in the film—for the lead actors and particularly all of the custom silks adorning the jockeys—were painstakingly created.

While some existing authentic pieces from the period were utilized (particularly women's hats, either onscreen or as models from which to create reproductions), their age kept their use to a minimum. "Although we tried to use as much period clothing in the background as we could," Judianna notes.

Having worked on several period films before, including Gary Ross's *Pleasantville*, Makovsky was no stranger to research. In addition to her own extensive library, the designer relied on the resources available in the Library of Congress and became a self-confessed Internet surfer.

Much of Makovsky's design came through in the contrasts between the established, moneyed East Coast society and the freer, upstart West Coast society, represented by the challenge match race between Seabiscuit and War Admiral.

She explains, "I tried to give the East Coast of America a completely different look from the West, because a lot of the film is about this little horse from California infringing on their world." She and Ross decided on a darker, more severe look for War Admiral's backers, versus the freer, looser, more colorful people in Seabiscuit's world.

For the leading roles, the designer worked with Ross within specific areas to outfit the characters in their appropriate attire, often basing some of the core designs on photos of the actual people. She clothed Charles and Marcela Howard in "casual wealth," with Charles in variations on a single-breasted, three-piece suit switching to period Western-themed attire (worn around the paddocks and his estate) and Marcela evolving from a somewhat arty, actressy-type into a stylish woman appropriately outfitted for every occasion. Tom Smith remained the "old cowboy" that he was, with low-key functional clothing that included cardigans, as well as somber suits, which the trainer began to wear "when he realized he was with a famous horse."

Makovsky admired the transformation Tobey Maguire underwent to play Red, a down-on-his-luck fighter who becomes the champion jockey. Most of Red's earlier clothing is nondescript and worn repeatedly, in keeping with a man living through the Depression with little more than a pillowcase of books slung over his shoulder. His transition mostly occurs in the authentically reproduced crimson and white Howard silks.

Judianna says, "The original jockeys' silks were much more tailored garments. Our Howard silks, as well as George Woolf's and the silks on War Admiral's jockey, are accurate. We actually had Woolf's original britches and we copied his boots. The Howard red is copied from the originals—although Gary [Ross] and John [Schwartzman] were so great, sitting with me while we tested several pieces of red fabric to get exactly the right one on camera."

The director lauds Makovsky's work and says, "I don't think there's a better costume designer in the world. There is an obsession to detail in what she does that's almost amazing."

Actor Cooper comments, "The look of the clothes is important—it helps the actor get to the place he needs to be to be believable."

"It's pretty straightforward. I just started asking questions," explains production designer Oppewall on how she began to confront the large canvas of *Seabiscuit*. "I didn't know much about horses. I'd been to the racetrack once in my life before. So I had to start learning the language."

She acquired a book on Thoroughbred racing, Xeroxed the glossary out of the back, and kept the page with her until it sank in.

Like her colleague, the production designer had previously worked on a number of period pictures and could rely on her own completed research, which she augmented with classic images from federal historical records. And, like Makovsky, she found the contrasts among the societal delineations very telling.

"Most of the movie takes place in the rarefied world of Thoroughbred racing, where, by and large, a lot of the people were not that affected by the Depression," observes Oppewall. "However, Seabiscuit became a symbol and this whole other world entered the picture, as the infield is filled with ordinary people, paying twenty-five cents to see their hero."

Oppewall classifies *Seabiscuit* as a "find and fix movie," where period appropriate structures, furnishings, and props are secured and groomed for the screen with cameras shooting around (or postproduction eliminating) anachronistic elements. Building commences if such "finds" aren't available.

Each of the locations had its own shortcomings that required "fixing." Santa Anita had added a modern Clockers Corner, which had to be ignored; production added awnings and some architectural details that had been original to the structure but had been removed over time, in addition to modifying the tote boards and removing modern signage. Saratoga required comparatively little work to bring its vintage look to the fore. Keeneland had modern additions that also needed to remain off camera. Hemet, although surrounded by condos and restaurants, proved to be somewhat of a time capsule once inside. The Los Angeles County Fairgrounds' track and grandstand were modified to look like Tijuana's Agua Caliente racetrack.

A ranch in Hidden Valley, California, became the site of the Howards' country estate, Ridgewood, with some existing lesser structures augmented by new buildings to give the full range of exteriors and interiors required. The impressive and sprawling ranch house was entirely created and so splendidly rendered that when the daughters of actor Jeff Bridges visited the set, they had to be convinced that it was not a "real" house, which they believed until they mounted the stairs to discover the nonexistent second story.

In addition to the magnificence of Ridgewood, several interiors were completely constructed for the film to Ross's specifications, including three different jockeys' rooms (Keeneland, Agua Caliente, and Santa Anita). Perhaps one of the designer's favorite creations was Tick-Tock's lair, which the director and Oppewall dubbed "kinky and stinky."

While *Seabiscuit* proved a challenging but rewarding project for the entire production team, the shoot had to overcome a particular unfortunate situation, what businesses refer to as force majeure, while at Keeneland.

Jeannine Oppewall remembers, "We set up the track for shooting in Kentucky—infield beer tents, food vendors, awnings for the horse paddock—by Saturday night, so that the greensmen could finish on Sunday and we could shoot on Monday. Then we had a charming tornado, which blew through half of the set. So early Sunday morning, we were out there examining the shredded dressing with flashlights, salvaging what we could. It had blown half of the set down and left the other half just mysteriously standing on top. Overnight, we reset some of them and pieced together from the torn pieces what we could."

The tireless efforts of all paid off. Jeff Bridges sums up, "When you come into a place where the character that you're portraying actually lived and walked, something about that adds to the experience—and, ultimately, to the film."

"This was a story I really wanted to tell," concludes screenwriter/director/producer Ross, "and to do it, we had to honor the history while translating it to film. It was a huge task—a story that spans years and comes to embody a nation during a particular time. But I'm proud of this film, and I think we've managed to convey it all on the screen."

Universal Pictures / DreamWorks Pictures / Spyglass Entertainment Present a Larger Than Life / Kennedy/Marshall Production of a Film by Gary Ross: Tobey Maguire, Jeff Bridges, and Chris Cooper in *Seabiscuit*, starring Elizabeth Banks, Gary Stevens, and William H. Macy. The casting is by Debra Zane, C.S.A. The music is by Randy Newman. The costume designer is Judianna Makovsky. The film editor is William Goldenberg, A.C.E. The production designer is Jeannine Oppewall. The director of photography is John Schwartzman, A.S.C. The executive producers are Gary Barber, Roger Birnbaum, Tobey Maguire, Allison Thomas, and Robin Bissell. *Seabiscuit* is based on the book by Laura Hillenbrand. The film is produced by Kathleen Kennedy, Frank Marshall, Gary Ross, and Jane Sindell. *Seabiscuit* is written for the screen and directed by Gary Ross. The film is distributed worldwide by Universal Pictures. © 2003 Universal Studios. www.seabiscuitmovie.com

ABOUT THE CAST

A young actor whose work exhibits seasoned ability and versatility, **TOBEY MAGUIRE (JOHNNY "RED" POLLARD / EXECUTIVE PRODUCER)** has attained considerable industry notice with his breakout performances in several feature films.

This past year Maguire starred in the live-action action-adventure blockbuster *Spider-Man,* which earned a record-shattering $114 million in its weekend debut. Maguire plays the iconic web-spinning hero for director Sam Raimi with a screenplay by David Koepp. Willem Dafoe appears as the Green Goblin.

Maguire is currently filming *Spider-Man 2,* the highly anticipated sequel in the Marvel Franchise.

Maguire also has an exclusive, two-year, first-look film production deal with Sony Pictures. He made his first outing as producer last year by teaming with producer Julia Chasman and Industry Entertainment's Nick Wechsler on a big-screen adaptation of David Benioff's novel *25th Hour.* The film is directed by Spike Lee and stars Edward Norton.

In 2001, Maguire lent his voice to the comedy blockbuster *Cats and Dogs.* The story chronicles the ongoing turf war between cats and dogs occurring undetected right in their owners' backyards. Directed by Larry Gutterman, *Cats and Dogs* combines live action, CGI animation, and animatronic action, along with the voices of Alec Baldwin and Michael Clark Duncan, among others; it stars Jeff Goldblum and Elizabeth Perkins.

In 2000, Maguire starred opposite Michael Douglas in Curtis Hanson's *Wonder Boys.* Adapted by Steve Kloves from Michael Chabon's best-selling novel, the drama follows a middle-aged professor and formerly successful novelist who suffers through a midlife crisis during a writers' retreat. Maguire plays James Leer, one of Douglas's students, a promising novelist with a tendency to fictionalize his own background. The film also stars Robert Downey Jr. and Frances McDormand.

In Lasse Hallstrom's critically acclaimed *The Cider House Rules,* Maguire stars as Homer Wells, the apprentice and surrogate son of Dr. Wilbur Larch (Oscar winner Michael Caine), a physician and abortionist who runs an orphanage in rural Maine. The film received seven Academy Award nominations and won two awards. Based on John Irving's novel, the film follows Homer as he leaves the orphanage, falls in love, and then connects his unusual past with his prospects for the future.

Maguire played Jake Roedel, a bushwhacker, in Ang Lee's Civil War epic *Ride with the Devil* for Good Machine and Universal Pictures. The film costars Skeet Ulrich, Jeffrey Wright, Jewel, Simon Baker, and Jonathan Rhys-Meyers as young Americans striving to define themselves and the country they had always called home amid national turmoil. *Ride with the Devil* was adapted by Lee's longtime collaborator, James Schamus, from Daniel Woodrell's novel *Woe to Live On.*

Maguire also starred in Gary Ross's comedy-fantasy *Pleasantville.* Maguire and costar Reese Witherspoon play a bickering nineties brother and sister who are magically transported into the world of a wholesome fifties sitcom. The film also stars Joan Allen, Jeff Daniels, and William H. Macy.

In 1997, Maguire received critical notice for his role in Ang Lee's *The Ice Storm,* opposite Joan Allen, Kevin Kline, Sigourney Weaver, and Christina Ricci. James Schamus adapted Rick Moody's novel about familial dysfunction in Watergate-era Connecticut and received the Best Screenplay Award at the Cannes Film Festival.

Maguire first gained attention with his performance in Griffin Dunne's Academy Award–nominated short film *Duke of Groove,* with Kate Capshaw, Uma Thurman, and Kiefer Sutherland.

Maguire's additional credits include Woody Allen's literary satire *Deconstructing Harry,* alongside an all-star cast that includes Allen, Kirstie Alley, Demi Moore, Judy Davis, Billy Crystal, and Robin Williams. He also appeared in Terry Gilliam's gonzo-comedy *Fear and Loathing in Las Vegas,* based on the novel by Hunter S. Thompson, opposite Johnny Depp and Benicio Del Toro; the film version of Andrew Wellman's prize-winning novel, Jeffrey Levy's *S.F.W.,* opposite Stephen Dorff, Reese Witherspoon, Jake Busey, and Joey Lauren Adams; and *This Boy's Life,* opposite Robert De Niro, Ellen Barkin, and Leonardo DiCaprio.

J EFF BRIDGES (CHARLES HOWARD) is one of Hollywood's most successful actors and is a four-time Academy Award nominee. He earned his first Oscar nod in 1971 for Best Supporting Actor in Peter Bogdanovich's *The Last Picture Show,* costarring Cybill Shepard. Three years later, he received his second Best Supporting Actor nomination for his role in Michael Cimino's *Thunderbolt and Lightfoot.* By 1984 he landed top kudos with a Best Actor nomination for *Starman;* that performance also earned him a Golden Globe nomination. In 2001 he was honored with another Golden Globe nomination and his fourth Oscar nomination for his role in *The Contender.*

Bridges's most recent film was Universal's *K-PAX,* a drama costarring Kevin Spacey. He has also completed the independent thriller *Scenes of the*

Crime, as well as the ensemble piece *Masked and Anonymous,* directed by Larry Charles and featuring an all-star cast, including Bob Dylan, Penelope Cruz, Jessica Lange, and John Goodman.

The actor's multifaceted career has cut a wide swathe across all genres. He has starred in numerous box-office hits, including Terry Gilliam's off-beat comedic drama *The Fisher King* (costarring Robin Williams), the multi-award nominated *The Fabulous Baker Boys* (costarring his brother Beau Bridges and Michelle Pfeiffer), *The Jagged Edge* (opposite Glenn Close), Francis Ford Coppola's *Tucker: The Man and His Dream, Blown Away* (costarring his late father Lloyd Bridges and Tommy Lee Jones), Peter Weir's *Fearless* (with Isabella Rosselini and Rosie Perez), and Martin Bell's *American Heart* (with Edward Furlong, produced by Bridges's company AsIs Productions). *American Heart* earned Bridges an IFP/Spirit Award in 1993 for Best Actor.

In the spring of 1999 he appeared in the suspense thriller *Arlington Road* (costarring Tim Robbins and Joan Cusack, directed by Mark Pellington). He recently played a major featured role in *The Muse* (an Albert Brooks comedy starring Brooks, Sharon Stone, and Andie McDowell) and he starred in *Simpatico,* the screen version of Sam Shepard's play (with Nick Nolte, Sharon Stone, and Albert Finney). In 1998 he starred in the Coen Brothers' cult comedy *The Big Lebowski.* Before that, he starred in Ridley Scott's *White Squall,* Walter Hill's *Wild Bill,* John Huston's *Fat City,* and Barbra Streisand's romantic comedy *The Mirror Has Two Faces.*

In the fall of 2000, Bridges received excellent reviews for his role as the president of the United States in Rod Lurie's political thriller *The Contender,* costarring Gary Oldman and Joan Allen.

Bridges's other acting credits include *Stay Hungry, Fat City, Bad Company, Against All Odds, Cutter's Way, The Vanishing, Texasville, The Morning After, Nadine, Rancho Deluxe, See You in the Morning, Eight Million Ways to Die, The Last American Hero,* and *Heart of the West.*

In 1983, Jeff founded the End Hunger Network, a nonprofit organization dedicated to feeding children around the world. Jeff produced the End Hunger televent, a three-hour live television broadcast focusing on world hunger. The televent featured Gregory Peck, Jack Lemmon, Burt Lancaster, Bob Newhart, Kenny Loggins, and other leading film, television, and music stars in an innovative production to educate and inspire action.

Through his company, AsIs Productions, he produced *Hidden in America,* which starred his brother Beau. That television movie, produced for Showtime, received a Golden Globe nomination in 1996 for Best TV/Cable Film and garnered a Screen Actors Guild nod for Best Actor for

Beau Bridges; the film was also nominated for two Emmy Awards. Current AsIs projects in development include *The Giver,* based on Lois Lowry's Newbery Award–winning novel.

One of Jeff's true passions is photography. While on the set of his movies, Jeff takes behind-the-scenes pictures of the actors, crew, and locations. After completion of each motion picture, he edits the images into a book and gives copies to everyone involved. Jeff's photos have been featured in several magazines including *Premiere* and *Aperture,* as well as in publications worldwide. He has also had gallery exhibits of his work in Los Angeles and London.

The books, which have become valued by collectors, were never intended for public sale, but in the fall of 2003, powerHouse Books will release a major hardcover book containing a compilation of Jeff Bridges photos taken on numerous film locations over the years.

Not long ago, Jeff fulfilled a lifelong dream by releasing his first album, *Be Here Soon,* on Ramp Records, the Santa Barbara, California, label he co-founded with Michael McDonald and producer/singer/songwriter Chris Pelonis. The CD features guest appearances by vocalist/keyboardist Michael McDonald, Grammy-nominated Amy Holland, and country-rock legend David Crosby. Ramp Records also released Michael McDonald's album *Blue Obsession.*

In his spare time, Jeff is also an accomplished painter. Jeff, his wife, and their three children divide their time between their home in Santa Barbara, California, and their ranch in Montana.

Academy Award–winner **CHRIS COOPER (TOM SMITH)** has established himself as an actor at the top of his form with an impressive string of honest and striking performances. Most recently, Cooper played the pivotal role of Laroche in *Adaptation,* written by Charlie Kaufman *(Being John Malkovich)* directed by Spike Jonze. The film is loosely based on Susan Orlean's novel, *The Orchid Thief,* which follows a sexually frustrated screenwriter's attempts to adapt Orlean's anecdotal novel for the screen. The film also stars Nicolas Cage and Meryl Streep. Cooper's performance garnered him the Best Supporting Actor Oscar.

Cooper was recently seen in *The Bourne Identity* for Universal Pictures in the strong supporting role as the mastermind of the CIA's controversial clandestine operation, Treadstone. Directed by Doug Liman *(Go), The Bourne Identity* was based on Robert Ludlum's 1980 novel of the same name, about an amnesiac who is rescued from near death by the crew of an Italian fishing boat and finds himself being pursued by hired killers.

In 2000, Cooper portrayed Colonel Burwell opposite Mel Gibson in *The Patriot,* a Revolutionary War epic directed by Roland Emmerich. In the same year, Cooper appeared with Jim Carrey in the comedy *Me, Myself, and Irene* for directors Peter and Bobby Farrelly.

Nominated for a 1999 Screen Actor's Guild Award for his performance, Chris Cooper received outstanding acclaim for his supporting role alongside Kevin Spacey and Annette Bening in the Academy Award–winning film *American Beauty.* In a stunning and dramatic display, Cooper portrayed a stern ex-marine colonel who persistently monitored his son's every move.

In 1999, Cooper starred as the father of an amateur rocket enthusiast in the acclaimed coming-of-age drama *October Sky,* which was screened at the 1999 Venice and Deauville Film Festivals with great notice. He had previously earned a Best Actor nomination in 1997 from the Independent Spirit Awards for his work in John Sayles's *Lone Star.* Nearly a decade earlier, Cooper made his feature film debut in Sayles's *Matewan.*

Among his previous film credits are Robert Redford's *The Horse Whisperer, Great Expectations, A Time to Kill, Money Train, This Boy's Life, Guilty by Suspicion,* and *City of Hope.*

On the small screen, he has had roles in a number of long form projects, including the miniseries *Lonesome Dove* and *Return to Lonesome Dove.* He most recently starred in HBO's *Breast Men,* and includes among his other credits *Alone, One More Mountain, Ned Blessing, Bed of Lies, Darrow, In Broad Daylight, A Little Piece of Sunshine, Law and Order,* and *Journey to Genius.*

Born in Kansas City, Missouri, Cooper attended the University of Missouri School of Drama and started his professional career on the New York stage. His theater credits include *Of the Fields Lately* on Broadway, *The Ballad of Soapy Smith,* and *A Different Moon.*

Cooper resides in Massachusetts with his wife and son.

ELIZABETH BANKS'S (MARCELA HOWARD) natural talent, striking presence, and undeniable energy are quickly earning her a reputation as one of the most promising young actresses in Hollywood.

Banks most recently appeared in Steven Spielberg's critically acclaimed *Catch Me If You Can.* The film, based on the true story of young con artist Frank Abagnale, starred Leonardo DiCaprio and Tom Hanks. Banks plays a bank teller who is unwittingly instrumental in teaching Frank some tricks of the con-artistry trade.

Banks appeared in two other major motion pictures in 2002: She co-starred with Madonna, Jeanne Tripplehorn, and Bruce Greenwood in Guy Ritchie's *Swept Away,* the story of a group of socialites whose boating trip goes awry, and she also appeared as Betty Brant (a role director Sam Raimi created for her) in the box-office hit *Spider-Man*. The film about the iconic web-spinning hero starred Tobey Maguire, Willem Dafoe, and Kirsten Dunst.

Banks's additional feature credits include roles in John Singleton's *Shaft*, with Samuel L. Jackson, and *Wet Hot American Summer*, starring Janeane Garofalo and David Hyde Pierce. She has also appeared in several independent features, including *The Trade* and *Ordinary Sinner*, which won the Best Film Award at the 2002 Slamdunk Film Festival in Sundance.

On the small screen, Banks has appeared in several guest-starring roles, including a highly acclaimed performance in *Law & Order: SVU*, HBO's *Sex and the City*, and NBC's *Third Watch*.

Her extensive theater credits include roles in American Conservatory Theater's productions of *Hurly Burly*, *Bethlehem*, *A Midsummer Night's Dream*, *A Woman of No Importance*, and *Uncle Vanya*, as well as the Guthrie Theater's production of *Summer and Smoke*, directed by David Esbjornson.

Originally hailing from Massachusetts, Banks received her Bachelor's degree from the University of Pennsylvania and her graduate degree at the American Conservatory Theater. Banks currently resides in Los Angeles.

Hall of Fame jockey **GARY STEVENS (GEORGE "THE ICEMAN" WOOLF)** has won more than 4,700 races in his career. He has had the distinction of his mounts earning more than $200 million, with 8 victories in Triple Crown races, including 3 Kentucky Derby titles. He has won 8 Breeders' Cup races with a combined $13 million purse, making it the single richest day in horse racing. He has raced in every racetrack in North America, as well as in Hong Kong, Japan, Dubai, Ireland, and France.

Born on an Idaho farm, Stevens was always a lover of horses. His father trained horses, first as a hobby and then as a profession. At six, a degenerative hip ailment forced his leg into a brace. Although doctors predicted he would wear the brace for years, he was able to walk without it a mere eighteen months later. The determination and willpower that have carried Stevens through many hardships and injuries throughout his career was present even at that early age.

Gary followed in his brother Scott's footsteps, riding his first race at fourteen. At sixteen, he left home to pursue racing professionally. Stevens briefly retired in 1999, but not being able to stay away from the sport he loves, he returned eleven months later to once again compete at the top of his game.

Stevens recently released his autobiography, *The Perfect Ride*

(Kensington Publishing). The book chronicles the extreme highs and devastating lows of his life, which have taken him around the world on the backs of some of the most famous horses in racing history.

Stevens has four children and makes his home in the Southern California hills overlooking the Santa Anita racetrack. When not racing, you can find him on the golf course.

Seabiscuit serves as Stevens's acting debut.

Oscar- and Emmy-nominee and SAG Award–winner **WILLIAM H. MACY (TICK-TOCK MCGLAUGHLIN)** is one of the most distinguished talents of his generation. In the upcoming months, Macy continues to demonstrate his versatility in several diverse roles, adding to his already impressive credits.

Macy most recently received outstanding critical acclaim and won the SAG Award for his role as Bill Porter in TNT's *Door to Door* opposite Kyra Sedgwick, Helen Mirren, Kathy Baker, and Felicity Huffman. The movie, which Macy cowrote, tells the true story of the life of Porter, an award-winning door-to-door salesman with cerebral palsy. The movie aired to unprecedented ratings for a TNT original movie premiere and to date has received a Peabody Award, an AFI Award, a Critic's Choice Award, a Golden Satellite Award, a Writer's Guild nomination, and an American Cinema Editors nomination. Macy won the SAG award for Best Actor in a Television Movie, the Best Actor Award from the Golden Satellite Awards, and was nominated for a Golden Globe.

Macy will next be seen in the romantic drama *The Cooler,* which also stars Alec Baldwin, Maria Bello, Shawn Hatosy, and Ron Livingston. The movie is currently slated for a fall 2003 release. The actor is currently in production on *Spartan* for director David Mamet; the film also stars Val Kilmer, Derek Luke, and Johnny Messner. Macy also recently wrapped production on the independent film *U-Boat* for director Tony Giglio; the period action film follows the crew of the U.S.S. *Swordfish* during the height of Hitler's infamous U-boat campaign.

Macy can currently be seen guest-starring in the Showtime original series *Out of Order,* which explores what it's like to be married and work in Hollywood. The series also stars Eric Stoltz, Felicity Huffman, Kim Dickens, Justine Bateman, and Dyllan Christopher.

Macy will next rejoin writing partner Steven Schachter for the TNT remake of the 1962 comedy *Gigot,* with Macy and Schachter penning the script and Schachter directing. He will also be seen in the Showtime Original Picture *Stealing Sinatra,* which depicts the 1963 botched kidnapping of Frank Sinatra Jr. Directed by Ron Underwood, Macy stars as John Irwin, one of three kidnappers who eventually turned himself in.

Macy is best known for his portrayal of Jerry Lundergaard in *Fargo*, for which he received an Oscar nomination and won an Independent Spirit Award as Best Supporting Actor. He also garnered nominations for Funniest Supporting Actor in a Motion Picture (American Comedy Awards), Best Actor (Chicago Film Critics), Best Supporting Actor (Dallas/Fort Worth Film Critics), and Best Actor in a Drama (International Press Academy).

Macy's distinguished film credits include *Magnolia, Pleasantville, Happy Texas, State and Main, Jurassic Park III, Focus, Welcome to Collinwood, Psycho, A Civil Action, Boogie Nights, Wag the Dog, Air Force One, Ghosts of Mississippi, Mr. Holland's Opus, The Client, Shadows and Fog, Murder in the First, Searching for Bobby Fischer, Radio Days,* and *Panic.*

In the realm of television, Macy has been no less prolific. He received an Emmy nomination as Best Guest Actor in a Drama Series for his recurring role as Dr. David Morgenstern on *ER*. His episodic credits include *L.A. Law, Bakersfield P.D., Civil Wars,* as well as the pilot and several episodes of *Law and Order*. Macy also had a recurring role on Aaron Sorkin's *Sports Night,* receiving an Emmy nomination for his performance. His telefilm credits include *A Murderous Affair, Heart of Justice, Standoff at Marion,* and *Andersonville,* as well as the miniseries *The Murder of Mary Phagan* and *The Awakening Land.*

In addition to the politically charged BBC telefilm *The Writing on the Wall,* Macy has also appeared in two Mamet vehicles, *The Water Engine* and Showtime's *Texan*. In 1999 he starred opposite his wife, Felicity Huffman, on the TNT film *A Slight Case of Murder* (written by Macy and Schachter and directed by Schachter), receiving another Emmy nomination for his work. Macy has also written several television scripts (with Schachter), including an episode of *thirtysomething,* the HBO movie *Above Suspicion,* and the USA Networks movie *The Con,* starring Macy and Rebecca DeMornay.

Born in Miami, Macy lived in Georgia until age ten before moving to Cumberland, Maryland, where his love for acting began while playing Mordred in *Camelot*. Elected junior and senior high school class president, he set out to become a veterinarian at Bethany College in West Virginia, but after performing in "play after play," Macy transferred to Goddard College in Vermont, where he came under the tutelage of theater professor David Mamet.

In 1972, Mamet, Macy, and Steven Schachter moved to Chicago, where they collectively built the St. Nicholas Theater. Macy originated roles for several of Mamet's classic original productions, including Bobby in *American Buffalo* and Lang in *The Water Engine,* and soon established his feature film presence with writer/director Mamet. He earned critical praise for his performances in other Mamet vehicles, including *Oleanna, Homicide, Things Change, House of Games,* and *Wag the Dog.*

Moving to New York in 1980, he continued to build his reputation in the theater as an originator of new roles in such off-Broadway productions as *Baby with the Bathwater; The Dining Room* (later filmed for PBS's *Great Performances*); *Life During Wartime; Mr. Gogol and Mr. Preen; Bodies, Rest and Motion;* and Mamet's *Prarie du Chen, Oh Hell,* and *Oleanna.* His stage credits, approaching fifty during his ten years in New York, also include the Broadway production of *Our Town,* Tony Award winner for Best Ensemble.

Macy was also seen on the London stage in the spring of 2000, where he costarred in the revival of Mamet's *American Buffalo* at the Donmar Warehouse. Following the run in London, the play moved to the Atlantic Theater Company in New York for a record-breaking run.

Along with his acting career, Macy has also earned respect as a teacher and director. Having led theater classes in Chicago and at New York University, today he serves as director in residence at the Atlantic Theater Company in New York. His extensive directing résumé includes *Boy's Life* at Lincoln Center, the Los Angeles production of *Oleanna* at the Tiffany Theater, as well as *Lip Service,* an HBO film that won an ACE Award for Best Theatrical Production. Most recently, Macy directed the play *The Joy of Going Somewhere Definite* at the Atlantic.

In 1998, Macy was honored by ShoWest when he was named Best Supporting Actor of the Year for his body of work.

Macy is married to Emmy-nominated actress Felicity Huffman, who starred on the critically acclaimed series *Sports Night.* They live in Los Angeles with their two daughters.

ABOUT THE FILMMAKERS

Two-time Academy Award–nominee **GARY ROSS (DIRECTOR / SCREENWRITER / PRODUCER)** is a filmmaker who delves into America's favorite pastimes and lauded institutions to create some of the most beloved films in recent history. A true Renaissance man, Ross's career includes directing and producing, in addition to his first calling as a gifted screenwriter.

Ross exploded onto the film scene with his first produced screenplay, *Big.* The 1988 blockbuster comedy, starring Tom Hanks as a child whose wish to be a grown-up is granted, grossed more than $100 million in domestic box office receipts and garnered two Oscar nominations (for Gary Ross's and Anne Spielberg's original screenplay and Tom Hanks's performance). Ross also coproduced the motion picture, which was directed by Penny Marshall.

Ross drew on his knowledge and love of the American political process for his screenplay of the Capra-esque comedy hit *Dave*. Starring Kevin Kline as an ordinary guy recruited to stand in for the president of the United States, the film also starred Sigourney Weaver and was directed by Ivan Reitman. Ross received his second Academy Award nomination for his original screenplay for *Dave*. He also won the Writer's Guild Paul Selvin Award for a screenplay that "embodies the spirit of the constitutional and civil rights and liberties which are indispensable to the survival of free writers everywhere."

In 1998, Ross decided it was time to direct one of his scripts. The result was the Oscar-nominated *Pleasantville*. A social comedy with equal parts heart and mind, *Pleasantville* tells the story of two teens (played by Tobey Maquire and Reese Witherspoon) who are inexplicably transported to the black-and-white world of a fictional 1950s television town. Their presence there ripples through the fairy-tale community, whose residents are consequently granted the chance to experience the wonders, comedies, and dangers of "real" life. Later that year, Ross's production company, Larger Than Life, found a new home at Universal.

Throughout Ross's career, he has remained active in local and national politics. During his college years, Ross spent his summers working on Capitol Hill as an intern. In addition to exploring the fictional political world in *Dave*, he keeps his feet firmly planted in real politics, having written numerous speeches for such political luminaries as President Bill Clinton and attending the Democratic National Convention as a delegate.

Ross also remains active in civic and charitable work. During his tenure as president of the Los Angeles Library, Ross established mentoring programs for inner-city youth and expanded teenage and youth-at-risk services throughout the Los Angeles library system. For his service he was awarded the 1999 Light of Learning Award by the Los Angeles Public Library. In 2000, Ross gave the keynote address for the American Library Association in Chicago. He also received the ACLU's Bill of Rights Award for 2000.

KATHLEEN KENNEDY'S (PRODUCER) record of achievement has made her one of the most successful executives in the film industry today. Among her credits are three of the highest grossing films in motion picture history—*E.T. The Extra-Terrestrial, Jurassic Park,* and *The Sixth Sense,* which she produced with Steven Spielberg, Gerald R. Molen, and Frank Marshall, respectively.

She currently heads The Kennedy/Marshall Company, which she founded alongside director/producer Frank Marshall in 1992. In 1999 and 2000 three films produced by The Kennedy/Marshall Company were released. The first, Universal's *Snow Falling on Cedars*, was directed by Scott Hicks, award-winning director of *Shine*. It was followed by *The Sixth Sense*, which starred Bruce Willis and received six Academy Award nominations, including Best Picture. The next release was *A Map of the World*, starring Sigourney Weaver and Julianne Moore. The Kennedy/Marshall Company also recently produced the IMAX film *Olympic Glory*, which was released in May 2000.

In the summer of 1995 the Kennedy/Marshall Company released the Marshall-directed *Congo*, which Kennedy produced with Sam Mercer, and *The Indian in the Cupboard*, directed by Frank Oz and produced by Kennedy, Marshall, and Jane Startz.

That same year Kennedy produced the Amblin Entertainment/ Malpaso Production *The Bridges of Madison County*, directed by Clint Eastwood. It was followed by Amblin Entertainment's Jan DeBont–directed action thriller *Twister*, which Kennedy produced with Ian Bryce in 1996. Kennedy also served as executive producer on the Spielberg-directed *Jurassic Park* sequel *The Lost World*.

Kennedy began a successful association with Steven Spielberg when she served as his production assistant on *1941*. She went on to become his associate on *Raiders of the Lost Ark*, associate producer of *Poltergeist*, and producer of *E.T.* While *E.T.* was becoming an international phenomenon, Spielberg, Kennedy, and Marshall were already in production on *Indiana Jones and the Temple of Doom*, which she and Marshall produced with George Lucas.

In 1982, Kennedy cofounded Amblin Entertainment with Spielberg and Marshall, for which she produced or executive produced such films as *The Flintstones*, *Hook*, *Always*, *Gremlins*, *Gremlins II—The New Batch*, *An American Tail*, *The Land Before Time*, *Young Sherlock Holmes*, *The Goonies*, *Innerspace*, *The Money Pit*, **batteries not included*, *Dad*, *Joe Versus the Volcano*, *Noises Off*, *An American Tail: Fievel Goes West*, *Cape Fear*, and *We're Back*.

Kennedy also teamed with Spielberg, Marshall, and Quincy Jones to produce *The Color Purple*, which earned eleven Academy Award nominations in 1985, including Best Picture. Later that same year, Kennedy, Spielberg, and Marshall produced 1985's highest grossing film, *Back to the Future*, and later produced its two highly successful sequels—*Back to the Future, Part II* and *Back to the Future, Part III*.

In 1988, Kennedy again earned the distinction of top-grossing film of the year for *Who Framed Roger Rabbit?*, which she produced with Marshall and Robert Watts. She then went on to produce *Empire of the Sun* with Spielberg and Marshall, which the National Board of Review named Best Picture of the Year.

Kennedy served as executive producer on the critically acclaimed Spielberg-directed Holocaust drama *Schindler's List*, which garnered seven Academy Awards in 1993, including Best Director and Best Picture.

Kennedy also produced Marshall's 1990 directorial debut *Arachnophobia*, with Richard Vane, and reteamed with Robert Watts to produce Marshall's second film, *Alive*, in 1993.

Raised in the small Northern California towns of Weaverville and Redding, Kennedy graduated from San Diego State University with a degree in telecommunications and film. While still a student, she began working at a local San Diego television station. Following jobs as a camera operator, video editor, floor director, and news production coordinator, Kennedy produced the station's talk show, *You're On*. She then relocated to Los Angeles and worked with director John Milius prior to beginning her association with Spielberg.

More recently, in 2001, Kennedy produced the Spielberg-directed *A.I. Artificial Intelligence* with Bonnie Curtis. That same year, she produced *Jurassic Park III* with Spielberg and Gerald Molen. At the end of 2001, she served as executive producer on M. Night Shyamalan's *Signs*, starring Mel Gibson, released in August 2002.

With an impressive number of landmark films to his credit as a producer, **FRANK MARSHALL (PRODUCER)** has also excelled as a director, and found the time to devote himself to numerous endeavors in public service and sports.

Marshall has more than fifty films under his belt as producer, including *Raiders of the Lost Ark*, *Indiana Jones and the Temple of Doom*, *Indiana Jones and the Last Crusade*, *Poltergeist*, *Gremlins*, *The Goonies*, *The Color Purple*, *An American Tail*, *Empire of the Sun*, *Who Framed Roger Rabbit?*, *The Land Before Time*, the *Back to the Future* trilogy, *Cape Fear*, and *The Sixth Sense*.

His most recent film producing credits include two international blockbusters: Marshall served as producer on M. Night Shyamalan's *Signs*, starring Mel Gibson, and as executive producer on *The Bourne Identity*, starring

Matt Damon. He is slated as executive producer on the upcoming Bernie Mac comedy *Mr. 3000.*

The filmmaker has already made several trips to the Academy Awards, having been nominated in the Best Picture category in 1982 for *Raiders of the Lost Ark* and again in the same category for *The Color Purple* with fellow producers Steven Spielberg, Quincy Jones, and Kathleen Kennedy. One of his most recent projects, M. Night Shyamalan's 1999 box-office smash *The Sixth Sense,* was nominated for six Academy Awards, including Best Picture.

As a director, Marshall's credits include the summer 1995 hit adventure *Congo,* based on Michael Crichton's best-selling novel; the sensitive true-life drama *Alive,* from Piers Paul Read's nonfiction book; the thriller *Arachnophobia;* and an episode of the Emmy Award–winning HBO miniseries *From the Earth to the Moon.*

Marshall began his motion picture career as assistant to Peter Bogdanovich on the director's cult classic *Target.* He was then asked by Bogdanovich to serve as location manager for *The Last Picture Show* and *What's Up, Doc?* before graduating to associate producer on the filmmaker's next five movies, including *Paper Moon* and *Nickelodeon.*

Marshall was line producer on Martin Scorsese's *The Last Waltz,* the heralded musical documentary on The Band. He then began a two-film association with director Walter Hill, first as associate producer on *The Driver,* then as executive producer of *The Warriors,* both of which have also attained a certain cult status among cineastes. Marshall was also line producer of Orson Welles's legendary unfinished film, *The Other Side of the Wind,* to which he periodically returned from 1971 through 1976.

Raiders of the Lost Ark marked the beginning of Marshall's epochal collaboration with Steven Spielberg, George Lucas, and Kathleen Kennedy. Following the productions of *E.T. The Extra-Terrestrial* and *Poltergeist* (which he produced), in 1981 he formed industry powerhouse Amblin Entertainment with Spielberg and Kennedy. During his tenure at Amblin, Marshall also produced such films as *Fandango, Young Sherlock Holmes, Innerspace, *batteries not included, Dad, The Money Pit, Noises Off, Always,* and *Hook,* as well as his directorial debut, *Arachnophobia.*

Marshall left Amblin in the fall of 1991 to pursue his directing career. Together with Kathleen Kennedy, he formed The Kennedy/Marshall Company, under which *Alive* was the company's first release. In 1995 he directed *Congo* and produced the highly acclaimed film *The Indian in the Cupboard* with Kennedy and Jane Startz. In 1997 he directed his episode of *From the Earth to the Moon,* which centered around the Apollo 11 moon landing.

The Kennedy/Marshall Company's most recent productions include *Snow Falling on Cedars, A Map of the World, The Sixth Sense,* and *Olympic Glory,* the first official large format film of the Olympic Games. Upcoming projects include another large format film, *The Young Black Stallion,* directed by Simon Wincer.

Marshall continues to find time for his love of music, sports, and magic. He has produced several record albums over the years and continues to run in distance races worldwide. Combining his passions for music and running, he, along with America's premiere miler Steve Scott, founded the Rock 'N' Roll Marathon, which debuted in 1998 in San Diego as the largest first-time marathon in history.

Marshall is a vice president of the United States Olympic Committee, a board member of the Los Angeles Sports Council, cochairman of The L. A. Mentoring Partnership, and a member of the UCLA Foundation Board of Governors. He is a recipient of the acclaimed American Academy of Achievement Award, the UCLA Alumni Professional Achievement Award, and the California Mentor Initiative's Leadership Award.

Prior to her involvement with *Seabiscuit,* **JANE SINDELL (PRODUCER)** ran the motion picture literary department at Creative Artists Agency, where she spent eleven of her twenty-two years in the agency business. During her tenure at CAA she managed all aspects of the careers of her clients, including Paul Newman, Billy Crystal, Kevin Costner, Lowell Ganz & Babaloo Mandel, Eric Roth, Barry Levinson, Sydney Pollack, and Gary Ross. Some of the many films with which she has been intrinsically involved are *Forrest Gump, Nobody's Fool, Big, Dave, Dirty Dancing, Stand By Me, City Slickers, The Insider,* and *Pleasantville.*

In 1998, Sindell left CAA to partner with longtime client Gary Ross in forming Larger Than Life Productions. After one of her former colleagues at CAA told her about a recently published excerpt of *Seabiscuit,* Larger Than Life and Universal won the rights for the article that was the basis for Laura Hillenbrand's best-selling book. *Seabiscuit* is Sindell's first film as a producer.

After graduating Phi Beta Kappa from Stanford University, Sindell got her start in the business at the William Morris Agency. Although the agency was not at that time accepting women into their agent training program, she became one of only two women to have been promoted to agent from within the company. She was an agent in WMA's television department before moving to International Creative Management, where after several years, she was asked to head its motion picture literary department. Sindell was subsequently recruited by CAA, where she managed all day-to-day operations of the agency's screenwriting business.

Sindell is currently an independent producer.

LAURA HILLENBRAND (NOVELIST) has been writing about history and Thoroughbred racing since 1988 and has been a contributing writer/editor for *Equus* magazine since 1989. Her work has also appeared in the *New York Times, Washington Post, USA Today, Talk, American Heritage, Reader's Digest, ABC Sports Online,* the *New York Post,* and many other publications. She is a two-time winner of the Eclipse Award, the highest journalistic honor in Thoroughbred racing. In addition to her work on the film *Seabiscuit,* she served as a consultant on the PBS *American Experience* documentary on Seabiscuit's life. An alumna of Kenyon College, Hillenbrand lives in Washington, D.C.

GARY BARBER (EXECUTIVE PRODUCER) founded Spyglass Entertainment with partner Roger Birnbaum, where they share the title of cochairman and chief executive officer.

Most recently, Spyglass cofinanced the record-shattering Memorial Day box-office hit *Bruce Almighty,* starring Jim Carrey and directed by Tom Shadyac; the film earned $85.7 million over the holiday, establishing it as the biggest nonsequel opening for a comedy ever. Barber served as executive producer on the film.

Spyglass released the blockbuster film *The Sixth Sense,* starring Bruce Willis and Haley Joel Osment (cumulative $661 million worldwide) in August 1999. This was followed by the international release of the highly acclaimed film *The Insider,* starring Al Pacino and Russell Crowe, and directed by Michael Mann. Both films received numerous Academy Award nominations.

In 2000, Barber produced *Keeping the Faith,* a romantic comedy starring Ben Stiller and Edward Norton, and *Shanghai Noon,* an action comedy starring Jackie Chan and Owen Wilson. Barber also served as an executive producer on the hit film *Unbreakable,* written and directed by M. Night Shyamalan and starring Bruce Willis.

Recently, Barber produced *The Count of Monte Cristo,* a remake of the classic, directed by Kevin Reynolds (*Robin Hood: Prince of Thieves*) and starring Jim Caviezel, Guy Pearce, and Richard Harris; and *Reign of Fire,* a science fiction adventure directed by Rob Bowman (*The X-Files*). Recent Spyglass productions, all of which Barber and Birnbaum produced, include *Abandon,* written and directed by Academy Award winner Stephen Gaghan

(*Traffic*); *The Recruit,* starring Al Pacino and Colin Farrell and directed by Roger Donaldson; and *Shanghai Knights,* the hit sequel to *Shanghai Noon.*

Barber has produced or executive produced more than thirty-five feature films, including *Ace Ventura: Pet Detective* and its highly successful sequel, *Ace Ventura: When Nature Calls;* the 1991 blockbuster *Robin Hood: Prince of Thieves* starring Kevin Costner; *Young Guns II;* and *Pacific Heights.*

R OGER BIRNBAUM (EXECUTIVE PRODUCER) founded Spyglass Entertainment with partner Gary Barber; they share the titles of co-chairman and chief executive officer. The company develops and finances all of its projects independently.

Most recently, Spyglass cofinanced the record-shattering Memorial Day box-office hit *Bruce Almighty,* starring Jim Carrey and directed by Tom Shadyac; the film earned $85.7 million over the holiday, establishing it as the biggest nonsequel opening for a comedy ever. Birnbaum served as executive producer on the film.

Instinct, starring Anthony Hopkins and Cuba Gooding Jr., was the first Spyglass Entertainment film, released in 1999, followed by *The Sixth Sense,* the record-breaking hit starring Bruce Willis. Other significant Spyglass hits include *Rush Hour 2,* which reteamed Jackie Chan and Chris Tucker; *Shanghai Noon,* starring Chan and Owen Wilson; *Unbreakable,* the hit follow-up from *The Sixth Sense* director M. Night Shyamalan; and *Keeping the Faith,* the directing debut of actor Edward Norton.

Spyglass also produced *The Count of Monte Cristo,* directed by Kevin Reynolds and starring Jim Caviezel, Guy Pearce, and Richard Harris; it was filmed on location in Ireland and Malta. Spyglass previously teamed with Tom Shadyac on the director's supernatural drama *Dragonfly,* starring Kevin Costner.

In addition, the company produced *Reign of Fire* with Richard Zanuck (*Driving Miss Daisy, Jaws, The Sting*), which Rob Bowman (*The X-Files*) directed; *The Recruit,* starring Al Pacino and Colin Farrell and directed by Roger Donaldson; and *Shanghai Knights,* the hit sequel to *Shanghai Noon.* Spyglass is also cofinancier and international rights holder on *Abandon,* a film directed and written by Stephen Gaghan (*Traffic*) and starring Benjamin Bratt and Katie Holmes.

Prior to founding Spyglass, Birnbaum, through Caravan Pictures (the production company he helped build with partner Joe Roth), was responsible for such box-office hits as the original *Rush Hour, Six Days/Seven Nights, Inspector Gadget, Grosse Pointe Blank, The Three Musketeers, Angels in the Outfield,* and *While You Were Sleeping.* Before joining Caravan, Birnbaum held the title of president of worldwide production and executive vice president of Twentieth Century-Fox, where he developed such films as *Home Alone, Sleeping with the Enemy, Edward Scissorhands, Hot Shots, My Cousin Vinny, The Last of the Mohicans, Die Hard 2,* and *Mrs. Doubtfire,* among others.

Earlier in his career, he produced the popular *The Sure Thing,* directed by Rob Reiner, and *Young Sherlock Holmes,* in association with Steven Spielberg's Amblin Entertainment. For television, he executive produced the telefilms *Scandal Sheet, Happily Ever After, When Your Lover Leaves,* and the award-winning *All the Kids Do It.*

Born in Teaneck, New Jersey, and educated at the University of Denver, Birnbaum was vice president of A&M Records and Arista Records, and a senior executive with the Robert Stigwood Organization before entering the film business.

ALLISON THOMAS (EXECUTIVE PRODUCER) is a film and television producer with Larger Than Life at Universal Studios. In addition to executive producing *Seabiscuit,* she served as a coproducer of *Pleasantville.*

Thomas is also a social and political activist. She served on the boards of the California Women's Law Center (1996–2002, copresident, 1999–2001) and Para Los Ninos (1998–2002 and 1993–1995). During her career, Thomas has worked with President Jimmy Carter, Governor Edmund G. Brown Jr., the Los Angeles Unified School District, and U.S. Senator Alan Cranston. She currently serves as a commissioner on the board of the Los Angeles Public Library.

Thomas also founded two companies that offered public relations services to companies in the high-tech and interactive-entertainment arena. Clients represented included the American Film Institute, Steve Jobs's NeXT Computer, Pixar, and RealNetworks. Thomas sold her share of the companies in 1997 in order to spend more time with her then preschool-age twins.

Thomas graduated cum laude in 1978 from Princeton University with a BA in American Politics. She received her MBA from USC in 1987.

ROBIN BISSELL'S (EXECUTIVE PRODUCER) longtime association with Gary Ross, Allison Thomas, and Larger Than Life Productions began when he was hired as Ross's assistant just prior to beginning production on *Pleasantville,* eventually becoming an associate producer on the film. In 2001, Bissell signed a three-year contract as a producer with Larger Than

Life. He produced the In Memorium segment for the 2002 Academy Awards.

Prior to coming to Los Angeles, Bissell studied at both the University of Maryland and Oxford University, and later formed the band Everything, signing a deal with A&M Records. Everything released its first LP, *oops*, and toured with such acts as the Steve Miller Band, the Doobie Brothers, and Jellyfish. Just prior to working with Ross, Everything was disbanded. Bissell briefly continued his musical career by composing two songs for the *Pleasantville* soundtrack, as well as a track for the Coen Brothers' *The Big Lebowski*.

JOHN SCHWARTZMAN, A.S.C. (DIRECTOR OF PHOTOGRAPHY) recently shot *The Rookie*, starring Dennis Quaid and Rachel Griffiths. Prior to that he served as cinematographer for producer Jerry Bruckheimer and producer/director Michael Bay on *Pearl Harbor, Armageddon,* and *The Rock.* He has also worked with director Ron Howard on Imagine Films' *Ed TV.* His other feature film credits include *Mr. Wrong, Pyromaniacs, A Love Story, Airheads, Benny & Joon,* and *You Can't Hurry Love.*

Born and raised in Los Angeles, Schwartzman completed graduate studies at the University of Southern California Film School and then spent a year as Vittorio Storaro's apprentice on *Tucker: The Man and His Dream.* After photographing a few smaller features, he began working on television commercials through Propaganda Films.

In addition to shooting feature films, Schwartzman directs television commercials through Ridley Scott's production company RSA-USA. He has also filmed numerous music videos, working with such stars as Madonna and Paula Abdul.

JEANNINE OPPEWALL (PRODUCTION DESIGNER) is a two-time Academy Award nominee, earning her most recent nod for her work on Gary Ross's *Pleasantville.* Her design of the too-perfect world in that film also brought her a Los Angeles Film Critics Award for Best Production Design. Oppewall had earned her first Oscar nomination, as well as a British Academy Award nomination, for her evocation of the gritty milieu of 1950s Los Angeles in Curtis Hanson's *L.A. Confidential.*

Oppewall more recently served as production designer on the films *Catch Me If You Can, The Sum of All Fears, Wonder Boys,* and *Snow Falling on Cedars.*

A graduate of Bryn Mawr College, Oppewall began her career as a curator and researcher for famed designer Charles Eames. Segueing to films, she worked with production designer Paul Sylbert on such films as *Hardcore, Blow Out,* and *Resurrection.* Her first film as a production designer was Bruce Beresford's *Tender Mercies.*

Her subsequent film credits include *Maria's Lovers; The Big Easy; Ironweed; Music Box; White Palace; Sibling Rivalry; School Ties; The Vanishing; Corrina, Corrina; Losing Isaiah; The Bridges of Madison County;* and *Primal Fear.*

WILLIAM GOLDENBERG, A.C.E. (EDITOR) was nominated, along with Paul Rubell and David Rosenbloom, for an Academy Award for editing Michael Mann's controversial film *The Insider,* starring Al Pacino and Russell Crowe. Goldenberg was also part of the editing team on Mann's action thriller *Heat* and, more recently, edited Mann's acclaimed biographical motion picture *Ali.*

Goldenberg's other motion picture editing credits include Gary Ross's *Pleasantville, The Long Kiss Goodnight, The Puppet Masters, Alive* (coeditor), and the IMAX feature *The Journey Inside.* He most recently served as editor of the hit family comedy *Kangaroo Jack.*

He collaborated with editor Michael Kahn (as additional editor or assistant) on *Hook, Toy Soldiers, Arachnophobia,* and *Always.* In addition, he edited the short *Kangaroo Court,* directed by Sean Astin, which was nominated for an Academy Award for Best Live Action Short.

Goldenberg worked on the HBO films *Body Language* and *Citizen X,* for which he received an Emmy nomination for Outstanding Editing for a Miniseries or Special.

As an assistant editor, Goldenberg worked on *Punchline, Something in Common,* and *Jo Jo Dancer, Your Life Is Calling.* He served as associate editor on *Welcome Home, Roxy Carmichael* and as apprentice on *The Breakfast Club* and *Jagged Edge.*

Two-time Academy Award–nominee JUDIANA MAKOVSKY (COSTUME DESIGNER) has seventeen years of experience in the industry, where her talents as a costume designer are highly regarded.

She has created inspirational costumes for nearly every period and for almost every genre of feature films, from 1950s American suburbia, Westerns, and sports epics to a storybook Victorian setting and a contemporary version of Charles Dickens. Her talents were recently recognized with her second Oscar nomination for her imaginative work in the blockbuster *Harry Potter and the Sorcerer's Stone.* In 1998, she received her first Academy Award nomination for her costuming of Gary Ross's *Pleasantville,* for which she was also honored by her peers with a Costume Designers Guild Award.

She also designed the costumes for *The Legend of Bagger Vance,* starring Matt Damon; *For Love of the Game,* starring Kevin Costner; *Gloria,* designing the costumes for Sharon Stone; *Practical Magic,* starring Sandra Bullock and Nicole Kidman; and *Great Expectations,* starring Ethan Hawke and Gwyneth Paltrow.

Makovsky's additional feature film credits include *The Devil's Advocate, Lolita, White Squall, A Little Princess, The Quick and the Dead, The Ref, The Specialist* (again, costuming Sharon Stone), *Six Degrees of Separation, Reversal of Fortune, Big,* and *Gardens of Stone.*

Her telefilm costuming credits include *Wild Palms, Miss Rose White, Margaret Bourke-White;* she also designed the costumes for the pilot of Robert De Niro's series *Tribeca.*

Prolific, Oscar-winning composer **RANDY NEWMAN (COMPOSER)** recently took home the statuette for his original song "If I Didn't Have You" from the smash animated hit *Monsters, Inc.,* for which he also received an additional nomination for Best Original Score, bringing his superlative career total to sixteen Academy Award nominations (with one win).

Newman has chronicled life in America in the late twentieth century perhaps more than any other contemporary songwriter, yet he has proven to be more than merely the consummate musical storyteller of the rock era. In addition to his Oscar, Grammy, and Emmy award–winning work, he also composed the critically acclaimed theatrical musical *Faust.*

Born into a prestigious musical family in Los Angeles, Newman became an accomplished pianist and began writing and recording songs as a teenager, eventually becoming a staff songwriter for Metric Music and penning a number of chart hits for such acts as The Fleetwoods, Cilla Black, Judy Collins, Manfred Mann, and Jackie DeShannon. He was signed by Reprise Records in 1967, and his self-titled debut album was released the following year. His first Grammy nomination came in 1969, and hit albums and awards continued to follow (including the number two *Billboard* hit "Short People" in 1977 and the anthemic "I Love L.A." in 1983).

Newman's scoring breakthrough was 1982's soundtrack to the feature *Ragtime,* securing the composer both a Grammy and two Oscar nominations (for score and song, "One More Hour"). His score for 1984's *The Natural* garnered him a Grammy and another Academy Award nod. In addition to composing songs for *Three Amigos,* he also earned a screenplay credit alongside Steve Martin and Lorne Michaels.

More award-winning scores and songs followed: *Parenthood* (score and Oscar-nominated song "I Love to See You Smile"); *Awakenings* (score); *Avalon* (Oscar-nominated score); NBC's *Cop Rock* (Emmy-winning song, "He's Guilty"); *The Paper* (Oscar-nominated song "Make Up Your Mind"); *Maverick* (Oscar-nominated score); *Michael* (score); *Toy Story* (Oscar nods for both score and the song "You've Got a Friend in Me"); *James and the Giant Peach* (Oscar-nominated score); and *Cats Don't Dance* (songs).

In 1999, Newman made Oscar history by receiving three nominations for his work on three different films: Gary Ross's *Pleasantville* (Best Original Dramatic Score); *A Bug's Life* (Best Original Comedy Score); and *Babe: Pig in the City* (Best Original Song, "That'll Do"). The same year, a four-CD boxed set spanning his prodigious career, *Guilty: 30 Years of Randy Newman,* was issued to critical and popular acclaim. Two more Academy Award nominations followed: for "When She Loved Me," from *Toy Story 2,* and for "A Fool in Love," from *Meet the Parents.*

In 1995, Newman's long-awaited musical based on *Faust* premiered at the La Jolla Playhouse in San Diego and the soundtrack album, *Randy Newman's Faust,* was released; the album features performances by James Taylor, Don Henley, Elton John, Linda Ronstadt, Bonnie Raitt, and Newman himself. The musical's opening at Chicago's Goodman Theatre in 1996 prompted *Time* magazine to name *Faust* one of the top ten theatrical events of the year.

Newman is also the recipient of the first Henry Mancini Award for Lifetime Achievement in film composing from the American Society of Composers, Authors and Publishers (ASCAP).

Hall of Fame jockey **CHRIS MCCARRON (RACE DESIGNER)** won 7,141 races and earned more than $264 million in winnings in his 28-year riding career. McCarron has won virtually every major race in North America: 6 Triple Crowns (2 Kentucky Derbys, 2 Preakness Stakes, 2 Belmont Stakes) and 9 Breeders' Cup Classics. Three times he has led the nation in both races and money won.

When McCarron won the 1996 Breeders' Cup Classic aboard Alphabet Soup, he became the first rider to surpass $200 million in career earnings.

McCarron is only one of three jockeys to win racing's prestigious Eclipse Award for outstanding achievement as both the nation's leading apprentice in 1974 and as the nation's leading journeyman in 1980. He has received the George Woolf Memorial Award for service and conduct and the Turf Publicists of America Big Sport of Turfdom Award. He was inducted into the National Racing Hall of Fame in 1989, in his first year of eligibility.

McCarron represented the United States in All-Star jockey competitions seven times, twice in Great Britain, twice in Japan, twice in Dubai (victorious in 1994) and at Santa Anita (victorious in 1999). He won the National Thoroughbred Racing Association Jockey Challenge at Lone Star Park at Grand Prairie, Texas, on June 21, 2002.

In 1987, McCarron teamed up with his wife, Judy, and actor Tim Conway to establish the Don MacBeth Memorial Jockey Fund for disabled riders.

McCarron retired from riding on June 23, 2002, and was named vice president and general manager of Santa Anita Park in March of 2003.

As one of the film industry's preeminent casting directors, **DEBRA ZANE, C.S.A. (CASTING)** has helped create the movies that reflect our era. Her unerring instincts and professional savvy have helped to bring to life many of the last decade's most honored films: *Catch Me If You Can, American Beauty, Traffic, Pleasantville, Wag the Dog,* and *Men in Black* are only some of the outstanding movies marked with her imprint.

After graduating from Sarah Lawrence College, where she concentrated on theater, Zane moved to Manhattan to study acting for four years. But her true niche was behind the camera. Relocating to California in the late 1980s, she worked on a Jon Avnet film and met the casting director—an encounter that changed everything. She had found her calling, the job she describes as "solving the ultimate puzzle" in a film. For the next seven years, she worked with casting master David Rubin, eventually becoming his partner before she founded her own firm in the mid-1990s. In 2000 she was recognized by her peers, who awarded her the Casting Society of America's Artios Award for Outstanding Achievement in Feature Film Casting for a Drama for *American Beauty.* In 2001 she received the same award for *Traffic.*

Her other feature film casting credits include *Road to Perdition, Ocean's Eleven, K-PAX, The Legend of Bagger Vance, Galaxy Quest, The Limey, Get Shorty,* and *Matchstick Men.*

PHOTO BY JEFF BRIDGES